HER LOST SISTER

A totally gripping psychological crime thriller

GRETTA MULROONEY

Tyrone Swift Book 7

JOFFE BOOKS

First published 2020
Joffe Books, London
www.joffebooks.com

ISBN 978-1-78931-373-4

In memory of Aunt Nora
'Keep on keeping on'

PROLOGUE

Woman Drowned at Sea

The body of Ms Kelly Dwyer has been found on a beach in Anglesey, North Wales. Ms Dwyer, 26, originally from Rossdown, County Galway, disappeared from the Dublin to Liverpool ferry a month ago. Her sister Faith Black, 23, who was travelling with her, was found on deck with head injuries just after the ship docked and can remember little about what happened on board. She was admitted to hospital in Liverpool and treated for injuries.

There was a force ten gale in the Irish Sea on the night of 2 October when Ms Dwyer and her sister were travelling back to London. The ship was navigating strong winds and waves up to twelve feet high. After Ms Dwyer and her sister went on deck for some air, Ms Dwyer would have fallen from a height of more than twenty metres into the water.

A spokesperson for the ferry company gave this statement: 'We would like to offer our sincere condolences to Ms Dwyer's family. Conditions were stormy and very rough on 2 October. Passengers had been strongly advised not to go on deck as the sea was heavy that night, with sudden squalls and high waves. It is almost impossible for a passenger to fall from one of our ferries. Luckily, this type of incident is rare.'

Ms Dwyer and her sister had been to visit family in Rossdown and were going back to their home when the dreadful tragedy occurred.

Ms Dwyer's eldest sister Orla Black told us that she did not wish to comment on these events.

Police have been unable to determine how Ms Dwyer fell from the ferry, and how Ms Black acquired her head trauma, which seems to be connected to her memory loss. The police have appealed for any passengers who were travelling that night and might have seen anyone acting suspiciously to contact them.

A requiem mass will be held for Ms Dwyer on 4 December, 11 a.m. at St Bridget's church in Rossdown.

CHAPTER 1

'She's not the Faith who left here for that ferry, that's for sure. They've been doing their best for her at the hospital, but she's in a bad way and she won't admit it,' Orla Black said. 'She seems so troubled. She was here again this April for a week and I could see she was fretting. When I asked her what was wrong, she muttered something, so I asked again and she got defensive and angry. She was never like that before, just snapping at me. She's not the same person since that journey. People think I lost one sister, but I lost two, and that's the truth of it.'

Tyrone Swift kept a level gaze on her. Orla seemed nervous and upset as she talked about her youngest sister. She kept moving her teacup around on its saucer. Drips trickled over the edge of the cup, and now and then, she caught them with a fingertip. She began talking again before he could speak.

'There's always been looks and comments about us here because of what happened in the past, and now we're the focus of the gossips again. Old memories refreshed, old grievances aired. I have to take a deep breath before I leave the house. Sometimes I feel the weight of the past sitting on my shoulders as I walk down the street. Now Ty, will you have another cup of tea?'

She'd already picked up the pot, ready to pour. He could see she was trying to calm herself with the task, so said yes, even though he didn't want it. Swift had been in Connemara for four days and was awash with tea the colour of dark tan leather. If he had a blood test now, it would reveal pure tannin. He'd arrived at Orla Black's house an hour ago to discuss what had happened to her sisters, but so far, Orla had been asking all the questions. With a sharp and relentless curiosity, she'd been getting Swift to talk about some of his recent cases as a private investigator and his time as a detective in the Met and with Interpol. Every time he tried to get the visit back on track, Orla leaned forward and ambushed him again. She did so now.

'And your aunty Maura tells me you've been beaten up a fair few times. Knifed and such, drugged and half drowned even. Are you sure they pay you enough?' She had a high-pitched, grating voice that set his teeth on edge. It would be tiring to live with. Maybe that's why she was on her own.

Swift smiled. 'Probably not. And it's not just the criminals I have to be careful of. During my last investigation, an old lady went for me and whacked me with her stick. Took ages for the bruise to go. But every job has its downsides. I like the element of the unexpected. Plus, I'm my own boss as a private investigator. No one but me in charge of my days. And my three-year-old loves poking at my scars. They provide her with a lot of amusement.'

Orla looked taken aback. 'I like the idea of being my own boss, but I know the reality would scare me. I'm a general assistant in a pharmaceutical lab, you see. I enjoy the structure and routine, putting on my white coat, knowing what tests I have to help with, what's in my sandwich box for lunch.'

Orla rose to let out the black and white cat that was scratching at the door. It shot into the garden as soon as she pulled it back. She stepped outside to check washing on a rotary clothesline that was spinning in the breeze. The sun was pale and misty, slipping through high clouds. Swift realized he'd have to be patient. Trial by tannin. His holiday was racing by, and he didn't even know if there was a job in this, or what it might entail.

He knew the bones of the story from his aunt. The Blacks were distant relatives of his family. Maura had known Orla since she was a child and had told her what he did for a living. His aunt had summed up the background over a glass of late-night whisky.

'They've always been a complicated family. Kelly got married to a man called Neil Dwyer. They were both just eighteen and they fought like cat and dog. She'd always been wayward as a child, a bit of a nuisance and a nosy parker — although a charming one, mind — and I was never sure who I felt sorrier for, her or Neil. They were a pair of rips and both great boozers. The marriage was soon on the rocks and she left him and took off to London. They were never able to repair the relationship. She'd be back and forth but more forth, if you catch my drift. Often, she wasn't back for months at a time. Then one time when she was here in July— must have been four years ago — she and Neil had a huge argument after a drinking session. Neil sped off in his car out on the coast road, and he crashed. There's a dangerous bend and he took it too fast. He was killed outright. Some people said Kelly drove him to it, kept him dangling with the idea that she might come back to him.

'Anyways, Kelly took off again to England and from then on, she visited Orla just once a year. Faith decided to up sticks and get a job in London around two years ago, and she was living with Kelly. Then there was this awful tragedy on the ship last autumn and I believe it's left Faith in a bad way. She stayed with Orla after she came out of hospital, but no one saw her around and Orla was tight-lipped about her. It's awful for Orla that the police haven't come up with any explanation about what happened. I thought you might help her out, given that there's a family connection.'

He wasn't that pleased at the interruption to his brief holiday, but he'd do anything for Maura, so he'd rowed along the river Corrib from her cottage to Orla's house, a couple of miles outside Rossdown. He watched as Orla pulled flapping sheets from the line, folded them carefully into a basket and dropped the pegs into a bag. The kitchen he sat in was neat, shiny and ordered, the draining board empty and gleaming. The cookery books on the shelf beside him were arranged alphabetically. Orla came back through the door, wiped her feet on the mat and set the basket on a chair. Swift seized his opportunity before she could draw breath.

'So, Orla, talk to me about your sisters. It must be very hard, not knowing what happened on the ferry.'

Orla sat back in her chair, sighed and crossed her legs. She was a spry, upright woman with a neat mouth and bright hazel eyes behind rimless glasses. 'You're right. I haven't a clue what happened to Kelly and Faith on that ship, and the police have come up with no explanation. There was gossip around here that maybe they'd had a fight and traded blows, and Kelly had thought Faith was dead, so she committed suicide. Such rubbish! Those two never exchanged a cross word. I don't know how people can be so heartless and cruel. As if I'm not suffering enough. It's a ridiculous idea, and I don't know who started it, but of course there are always people who like to spread a rumour.'

His mother used to wince when she referred to 'country gossip.' He'd heard her say *'Small villages, small minds'* many times. She'd been brought up in an Ireland still firmly in the grip of religious and social conservatism and she'd taken the boat to England herself to escape it. She'd told him that when she arrived in libertarian London in 1968, it was like stepping out of a cage. He could hear her now. *'It was great to be able to stay out late and date who I liked without worrying that Mr Carty would tell Mrs Slane, who'd tell the parish priest.'* He moved his cooling tea aside. 'Presumably there was an autopsy on Kelly?'

'There was. Her body was in a terrible state from being battered by the sea, but there was an injury to the left side of her skull. Faith had been hit around the head too, with something blunt. A hammer, they seemed to think. She couldn't tell the police anything much. To tell you the truth, Ty, I'm feeling terribly troubled and confused. There's Kelly dead, and Faith brain-damaged. She's not right in the head. It's left her with memory problems and poor balance. Her speech is odd sometimes. She gets very tired. She stayed with me for a bit after she came out of hospital last winter, but then she insisted on going back to London. I worry about how she's coping, living on her own. She should have someone helping her. When I ring, I get the answerphone, and sometimes it's days before she calls back. In the meantime, I'm tearing my hair out.'

'Did Faith always respond straight away before?'

'Well no, not always, I suppose. But then I wasn't worrying about her before because Kelly was there. Not that I got much peace of mind knowing that.'

'Was Kelly irresponsible?'

She looked uncomfortable. 'We were never really close. Different temperaments, I suppose. I was always the responsible one, especially after Mum died. Kelly had been away a good while and no matter how hard we tried to stay in touch, it wasn't the same. Faith was quieter. She looked up to Kelly. God knows why — Kelly wasn't much of a role model. But I do worry, especially after some of the things Faith said when she came here from hospital.' She raised her hands and dropped them. 'I've told no one else the details. To be honest, it's a relief to get things off my chest.'

'What details?'

'While Faith was here recuperating, she was uneasy at times. I'd find her pacing up and down, very agitated. Or she'd be sitting out on the wall, staring at the ground and talking to herself. I thought it was to do with the trauma of what had happened. It can take a long time to recover from a shock like that, if you ever do. As I said, she got cross if I asked her what was wrong. Then one night she asked me if I knew of anyone who'd hated Kelly. I didn't understand but I said no, I didn't. But I told her that I wouldn't know, what with Kelly living over in London and me being here. She gave me such a strange look then, and she muttered something about a shadow at her back.'

'What do you think she meant?'

'I've no idea. She repeated it to herself a few times. To be honest with you, I felt out of my depth with her.'

'Was Kelly the kind of person who might have inspired hatred? Or was Faith?'

'Faith? God, no. Kelly was another matter, but hate . . . that's a strong word. There'd be people who didn't approve of Kelly and the way she carried on at times. She was always a jokey sort of person. She was the class clown at school. I always thought that it was a front she hid behind, because deep down, she was insecure. A bit shy, even. I know that sounds like a contradiction.'

'I think that some people who clown around do it to hide self-doubt. It's a kind of armour against the world.'

'Yes, that's how she was. And there was a life force in her. Maybe too much for some people at times! She was persuasive. Faith was lively too, in her own way, before she was harmed. Always interested in new experiences. An inquiring mind. But that's gone now. She's sort of flat. When I've seen her since her injury, she's been moody and distracted. Spends hours just lying on her bed, staring at the ceiling or out of the window. Nothing I do for her is right. Then she apologises, and says she's a pain. Says she's sorry for imposing on me.' She started moving her teacup again.

Swift looked at her pinched face, so loaded with anxiety. The feeling of helplessness, he imagined, would be exhausting. 'So what do you know of Kelly's life in London? She'd lived there for a while. How many years?'

'She left Neil just before she turned twenty, so about six years.'

'Did she have other relationships?'

'To be honest with you, I know next to nothing about her life there. I never visited — well, I was never invited. Faith went over a couple of times before she moved to London herself. When Kelly came here, she hardly ever talked about her life over the water. If I asked her, she just said general stuff about the weather or politics. I could tell she wanted me to mind my own business. She could have been married again three times and I wouldn't have known. She told Faith things when she visited, I know that. They'd go off out together, or they'd be talking upstairs. Those two always had their secrets and confidences, close as twins. Faith would never repeat anything to me that Kelly had told her.'

He thought it must have been lonely being Orla. She'd had responsibilities as the eldest, but her sisters had side-lined her and finally left her alone to fret.

'I suppose that Faith might not recall some of those confidences now, given her memory loss.'

'That's the truth of it. Kelly had a friend, Sarah Ennis, who might be able to tell you more. I know Kelly enjoyed playing camogie and was in a team. Faith joined it too, when she went to live in London.' Orla saw his puzzled look. 'It's the women's equivalent of hurling. Kelly was a great player in her youth, although that went out the window when she started drinking.' She took a breath. 'Our mother died suddenly when Kelly was sixteen, Faith just thirteen. I was twenty-five. It was after that Kelly took to the drink.'

'And your father?'

She pulled a face. 'He was a boozer, too. He took off when our mother was expecting Faith. We never heard from him again. Not even a postcard. Kelly sent me some postcards over the years. I have them here somewhere.' She rummaged in the dresser behind her, and brought out a large brown envelope. It held about twelve postcards. She pushed them towards him. 'They won't tell you much.'

'You never know. Can I take photos of them?'

'Of course.'

He took photos of both sides of the postcards on his phone, thinking that they might provide some information about Kelly's life in England. As he clicked, he asked her more about Kelly's marriage.

Orla sighed. 'Those two could never be together for more than five minutes without a row starting. Not a marriage made in heaven. I knew she was making a big mistake and I tried to persuade her not to go ahead with it, but she never listened to me. They were both blessed with good looks and I'd say they were very taken with the notion of themselves as Rossdown's Harry and Meghan. It was romance and roses all the way for just a few months after the wedding.'

'Then it was thorns and torment?'

She gave a weak smile. 'Spot on. I think Kelly wanted to break away from Neil completely after she left for England, but he kept phoning her, asking her to visit, telling her how much he still loved her. So she was back and forth, as I said. And I do think she still loved him, but it was just impossible. He went over there a couple of times to see her. They always drank too much when they were together. Egged each other on. Then he took the bend too fast in the dark and that was it. Kelly was distraught. That was a difficult time. You know — the sideways glances and people crossing the street when they saw her coming. That's how it is in small places like this. She drank even more after Neil died, if that was possible.'

'Two sudden deaths of people close to Kelly within a short space of time. That was a lot for her to deal with.'

'Well, yes. But drinking herself into a stupor was hardly dealing with it, was it? Just denying it, as far as I'm concerned. And believe me, I had to cope with a lot of the fallout, listening to criticisms, and trying to pour oil on troubled waters.'

Despite her concern for her sister, it was obvious to Swift that Orla also struggled with feelings of deep resentment. Still, families were invented to torment as well as love each other, weren't they?

'Does Neil's family still live here?' From what he'd heard so far, one of them might have held a grudge against the disruptive widow.

'Not anymore. Neil's only family here was his grandmother, Annie. She passed away a year after Neil was killed.

Annie brought him up. Dennis, his father, sent him over from England to be looked after by her after his mother died when he was young. Dennis died when he was in his forties. Neil does have a brother somewhere in England — Dermot. I've only met him twice, once at the wedding and then at Neil's funeral. I think he's in the army.'

'Can you tell me about the day Kelly and Faith left to get the ferry back to England?'

Orla took off her glasses and rubbed her eyes. The picture window behind her showed a vista of tree-lined, blueish hills and small fields separated by dry stone walls. A couple of donkeys were grazing around a small copse of hazel trees. The wide skies, scudding clouds and soft breezes were familiar to Swift, as was the scent of turf that perfumed the air. His mother had often brought him to the area when he was a child, to see his aunt and the house she'd grown up in.

Orla put a hand to her throat. This discussion was clearly causing her pain. 'Kelly was up early that morning, finishing off small jobs here in the house. Sarah Ennis, the friend I mentioned, was in Clifden visiting family and she'd offered to give Kelly and Faith a lift to Dublin. She and Kelly had known each other since their school days. I made them a late breakfast, a good big fry-up, and they went off in high spirits when Sarah arrived. She dropped them off at the port and went on to see family in the city.'

'How long had they been here for?'

'A week. Sometimes Kelly would be back for a bit longer. She'd say she was between jobs. But that time, she had a job waiting.'

'What was her work?'

'She was a gas fitter. She'd always been very practical, good with her hands. Anything she did for me around here lasted for ages. I wish I'd inherited some of those talents. I'm cack-handed about the place. I have to pay other people a fortune for any work in the house.'

'Did Kelly or Faith seem worried about anything during that week?'

'Not at all. I remember they were both on good form and chatting away together. Little jokes between themselves that weren't shared with me. It was the first time Faith had been back since she'd moved to London. She helped me dig the garden over, and Kelly put in new kitchen taps.' Orla reached into another drawer in the dresser and took out a newspaper cutting. 'I know you can see this online, but I found it for you anyway. It's from the local paper.'

Swift had read the article about Kelly and Faith that morning. The photo of Kelly was clearer in the print version. She was a strikingly good-looking woman. Tall and slender but muscular. In the photo, she was grinning and leaning against a gate with hands in her jacket pockets. Her smile was warm and lit up her eyes.

'I took that photo a couple of years ago, out the back.'

Swift glanced through the report again. He knew the effects of a storm at sea. Gales in the Irish Sea were common enough and the cautious person stayed below decks. He'd made the crossing in similar conditions and like Kelly and Faith, he'd thrown caution aside and gone up on deck, lured by the wildness of the weather. He'd gripped the rail and watched the boiling white water, the huge waves with their overhanging crests and the dense foam blowing in the screaming wind and spray. The ship had rolled and ploughed its way through, the engines vibrating as salt-filled rain drenched his face. Falling into those thundering, remorseless waves must have been horrifying. He thought of the well-stocked bars on the ferries. 'Do you think that Kelly might have been drinking that night?'

A firm shake of her head. 'As I said, she developed a drink problem after our mother died, trying to drown her sorrows. She had her wild days, I won't deny it, and then of course after Neil died, she was a real loose cannon. But she managed to give up alcohol a while after he died. Never touched it again. She was looking after herself and keeping fit. I was so relieved that she'd managed to turn things around. So if you were thinking she toppled off the ship in a drunken stupor, you're wrong.' Orla leaned forward, hands flat on the checked oilcloth. 'Kelly loved the sea. It's why she took the ferry usually, rather than flying. She always booked a cabin so she could leave her case there and have a rest if she wanted, but she'd say she spent a good part of every crossing on deck, just watching the waves. I remember her remarking that in another life, she'd have been a sailor. She hated the smell of vomit and booze that you get on the ferries in a storm. She'd have gone on deck for fresh air, and Faith would have gone with her even though I know she'd have been anxious about the wild weather.'

'So Faith usually went along with what Kelly wanted?'

'Oh yes. That was always the way.'

'And as far as you know, Faith hadn't fallen out with anyone?'

'Not that I know of. She's not the type at all to quarrel. She'd always be looking to lend someone a hand, not cross them.'

Swift looked out at the rowan trees that formed a boundary to the garden. They all bent drunkenly to the east, buffeted by the constant Atlantic winds. 'What is it you want me to do?' he asked.

'Well, that's it — I'm not sure. I was talking to Maura after Mass, she told me about you, and she said you'd be visiting. I thought that as you live in London, maybe you'd talk to Faith. See if you can help her. I can see that not knowing what happened on that ferry is eating away at her.'

So far, so vague. 'As you said, Faith's mood and behaviour when she was here might have been a result of trauma and shock. Someone did her terrible damage. Might even have thought they'd killed her.' It occurred to him that maybe Faith was worried that she had been the intended victim.

'I know, but would you do me the favour of just seeing her anyway? I know I annoy her when I try to look after her or get her to talk. She has this shutdown look on her face. If she doesn't want to talk to you, that's that. It'd give me the comfort of knowing I tried.'

'Okay. I'll contact her. That's all I can promise.'

She relaxed for the first time. 'Did you know we're related? Distant cousins, I believe.'

'That's what Maura told me. Through my namesake, Tyrone, who went to Australia many years ago.'

'That's right. He left in 1890 and apart from one letter, he was never heard of again. You know he left behind a wife and three children?'

'No, I didn't know that.'

'Hmm.' She was looking at him shrewdly as if he was the negligent Tyrone, not his ancestor. But then her own father had done a vanishing act, so perhaps the story was a little close to the bone. 'He was supposed to send for them once he got established down under. One letter, then silence.'

'Maybe he died.'

'Maybe. I think that might be a generous slant on it. More likely, the pastures were greener there and there was a girl with a fetching smile. We're linked through his eldest son. Another Tyrone. I've a photo of him somewhere. You have his height. He stayed put and looked out for his family, worked his fingers to the bone.' She nodded and shifted her chair. 'Yes, there are the ones that roam and the ones that stay at home and take care of their own acre.'

CHAPTER 2

The sun grew stronger as Swift rowed back to his aunt's home. The wind had dropped to a soft breeze. The Corrib was the shortest, most powerful river in Europe and he had to concentrate in the strong flow. He was glad that he had recovered now from the parasitic infection he'd caught from the water of the Regent's Canal. Some cases lingered in unwelcome ways, and being drugged and dumped in the canal had made him ill for months. It was good to be rid of the aches and lethargy that cryptosporidium had left in its wake.

The wooden boat, the *Biddy Marie*, was old with peeling blue paint. It belonged to one of Maura's neighbours and it creaked alarmingly as the oars sliced the water. He steered a course down the middle of the river, away from the anglers who dotted the banks, fishing for Atlantic salmon and brown trout. Maura had cooked freshly caught salmon the night before, simply baked with lemon and tasting of the sea. The river was home to an abundance of wildlife and once he was past the anglers, he slowed the boat to watch a couple of pale grey hen harriers swoop low, looking for tasty small mammals. He closed his eyes for a moment. No human sound, just birdsong and the stirring of rushes in the breeze. Peaceful.

When they craved tranquillity, some people went to church, some swam, walked or climbed, and others knitted, meditated, or did yoga. Swift launched his boat on a river.

When he came through the cottage door, he saw Maura looking exhausted. She leaned against a bookcase, her eyes strained. His mother's sister, she was the only surviving sibling in that family. Swift's mother had died of cancer when he was fifteen, and Maura had always showed him a calm, kind affection.

Swift's daughter Branna was sitting on the coffee table, kicking her legs off the edge and eating ginger biscuits from an opened packet beside her. It was half empty. He took it all in in a glance. Maura had had to resort to bribery, then.

'Thank God you're back,' his aunt said with relief. 'I've run out of steam and games to play.'

'Where's Nora?'

'She went off for a walk when Branna started getting a bit excited and loud. Said she had a headache. Then she was gone, like that.' Maura snapped her fingers, the nearest she ever came to sounding tart.

'Hey, Branna. Have you been exhausting your great-aunt?' Swift spoke and signed.

His own cool grey eyes looked back at him, unflinching. She was in her favourite outfit of leggings and T-shirt with a motif of rabbits in hats. It needed a wash, but she'd insisted on wearing it three days running. She shrugged and then signed *Nora was cross.*

'I'm sorry, Ty. I'm not very good at the signing,' Maura said. 'We had a bit of a tiff, me and Branna. My fault, I couldn't understand her. Two deaf girls together. Then she pulled her hearing aids out. Does she do that often?'

'No. It's a phase. She usually does it when she gets frustrated.'

Maura smiled. 'That makes two of us. I take mine out when they're driving me nuts. My excuse is that after seventy years of good hearing, it's hard to adjust. What are we like, Branna?'

Branna gave her an inscrutable stare and took another biscuit.

Swift quickly picked up the packet, folded the top down and put them in his jacket pocket. He could see that his daughter was weighing up the situation and deciding whether to kick up a fuss. He shook his head at her, giving her his best warning look. She folded her arms grumpily but stayed quiet.

'You sit down, Maura, and I'll make you a cup of tea. Then I'll take Branna for a walk to see the horses.'

Branna smiled and put her arms out to him. He lifted her and held her close, kissing the top of her head. She smelled of spices.

'Okay?' he said in her ear.

She laughed and made a thumbs up sign.

'I think you're a lot heavier than you were earlier. Too many biscuits.'

Branna pulled her top up and patted her stomach, sticking it out. 'Nice and full.'

'Hmm.' Swift put her down. 'Are your hearing aids in your pocket?'

Branna nodded.

'Let's put them in.'

She looked at him, head to one side and then decided to cooperate. She stuck her hands in her leggings and pulled the hearing aids out. Swift inserted them, checking that they were positioned correctly.

'Great. Now go and find a storybook while I make a cup of tea for Maura. Then we'll take carrots out for the horses.'

'We take biscuits?' Branna asked.

'Absolutely not. Horses can't have biscuits, and you've had enough. I know your game, Branna Swift.'

She ran away, laughing. He went to the kitchen and filled the kettle.

'I'm sorry about all the biscuits. I know I shouldn't have let her eat so many,' Maura said, following him. She sat down, adjusting a cushion behind her back with a sigh of relief. She had osteoporosis, and Swift knew that she tired easily.

'No problem. Branna's a handful. I wouldn't have been gone for so long if I'd known Nora was going out. You should have phoned me, you know.'

'Well . . . I didn't like to interrupt you. How did it go with Orla?'

'Interesting. I heard about Kelly and Faith. Orla says that Faith sustained a brain injury and it's altered her.'

'Faith was always Kelly's sidekick. Kelly was the strong-willed one. She had a real warmth to her and she was a big name in the youth camogie game. She was such a mischievous young girl. Lively, spirited. A fine athlete. The mother's death was a terrible blow, of course. You know yourself only too well about that kind of loss when you're a teenager. The way it took Orla, it made her stick to her routines and become very rigid in her ways. Everything by the rules. Of course, there's a few years between her and the other two, and she tried to take on the mother's role, getting bossy with Kelly and Faith. That was never going to go well, and I think they fell out a lot, especially after Kelly took to drinking heavily. Given how close Kelly and Faith were, I wasn't surprised when Faith took off to live with her in London. She was the sweet-natured one of the family, always a smile from Faith. I'm sorry to hear she's been left with a bad injury.'

'I said I'd speak to her when I'm back in London. It's all rather vague. Orla told me more about my namesake, Tyrone. She thinks he did a runner.'

'Ah yes, what used to be called an "Irish divorce." It would be easy enough to vanish on the other side of the world. That poor wife of his must have been distraught, left not knowing what had happened to him.'

'I understand that Mr Black did the same. Did his wife try to find him?'

'I don't think so. I always thought she was relieved that he'd gone. He was a drunkard and a blusterer, handy with his fists. Not a popular man.'

She leaned back and closed her eyes. Swift glanced at his watch. He knew that most days, Maura had a nap around half two and now it was gone three.

'What time did Nora go out?' he asked.

She answered faintly with her eyes still closed. 'Must have been soon after two. Branna was no trouble, really. She gets frustrated when I don't hear her or can't understand her. I think she was upset too that Nora went off without her. I think Nora's used to doing her own thing when she wants to.'

'Yes, that's about right.' He felt a snap of anger at Nora. She could be so oblivious to other people. Selfish. He rinsed the dirty crockery stacked by the sink and put it to drain.

'Oh and Ruth rang, just to say hello, so maybe that threw Branna a bit, too. You know, suddenly hearing her mother's voice in another context and in a place she's not familiar with. You never know what goes on in children's minds.'

And Branna had a lot to juggle, he thought. Her deafness, his relationship with Nora, her mother's new partner, Marcel, and dividing her life between these different adults. 'I'll get Branna and head out so you can have a rest,' he said.

There was no reply. He turned and saw that Maura was fast asleep. He took her cardigan from the back of a chair and draped it gently over her shoulders. He heard Branna coming and intercepted her at the door with a finger to his lips. 'Maura's asleep,' he whispered, making the sign with his thumb and forefinger. He helped Branna into her blue raincoat and wellies, and she tiptoed with exaggerated care to the vegetable rack with him, taking carrots and an apple and stuffing them in her pockets. He watched her, thinking that it was good cop, bad cop with his daughter in this phase of her life. You never knew if you'd get saintly cooperation, or outright defiance.

It was as if she'd read his mind when they got outside. She decided that she was having a day when she didn't want to hold his hand. The lanes were quiet, with little traffic, so he insisted that she walk on the inside with no running on ahead. She strode along beside him, hands in her pockets, scuffing her wellies on the tarmac.

'Where you go in boat?' she asked, signing *boat* at the same time.

'To see someone who wanted some help.'

'What help?'

'Something she's worrying about.'

'I go boat with you?'

'Yes. We can take a little trip in the morning, as long as the weather's okay.'

'Not too much rain?' She made the downward sign.

'That's right, and we wouldn't want it stormy.' He'd been studying sign language and made the side-to-side hand movement.

'Oh. Okay. Mummy phoned.'

'Yes, Maura told me. Was it nice to talk to her?'

'S'pose. I said you gone out.'

'Right. Do you miss Mummy?'

'Bit. Look, horses!'

They'd reached the gate to the field. He lifted her onto the bars of the gate, and several of them headed straight over when they saw her. Swift took his penknife and cut chunks of carrot for her to hold out on the palm of her hand. She was bossy with the horses, telling them that they had to take turns and have the same shares. In fact, she was a bossy child, full stop. Bossy and determined. He watched her waving a finger at the greediest horse. To think that he used to worry that her deafness might hold her back or cause shyness!

He looked down the hill, where the road stretched away towards Galway, and saw the bright lime green of Nora's anorak as she strode up towards them. The sun flitted through puffy clouds, casting ripples of light and shade on the fields. She waved, and he waved back.

This was the first time the three of them had taken a break together. Nora was a city girl from Dublin, but she'd fitted in straight away and seemed delighted with Maura's hospitality.

He'd been a little surprised that Nora had agreed to travel with them. She was fond of Branna and got on with her, but a little of any child's company went a long way with her. She didn't want children herself, was upfront about how easily she was bored by them and happily acknowledged that she didn't have a maternal bone in her body. What Swift hadn't realized was that Nora would resolve this by taking her own break within the holiday. Every day she'd had time out on her own with no forewarning, sometimes just disappearing and leaving a note.

'Hi!' she called. 'The weather held after all. Amazing, an afternoon with no rain! I've had a great ramble.'

Branna had her back turned, so hadn't heard Nora arrive. She was patting the chestnut horse, absorbed in her chat with him. Swift stepped away, meeting Nora on the lane. She gave him a quick warm kiss. She looked relaxed and pleased with life, her skin glowing. He thought of Maura's pallor. Whenever he challenged Nora, it didn't go well. She liked to speak her mind when she needed to and had a quick temper, but she reacted badly to being questioned. He tensed, knowing he might provoke her anger and spoke more sharply than he'd intended.

'Maura was completely worn out when I got back. I thought you were staying in with her and Branna.'

'Really? I didn't know. I needed to stretch my legs, and Maura seemed fine when I said I was off out.'

No she didn't. You just didn't want to notice she was tiring because it didn't suit you. 'She's seventy-two and not in the best of health. Could you not see that she needed a hand with Branna?'

Nora frowned. 'No. She could have said if she'd wanted me to stay.'

'You know that's not likely. You're her guest. And anyway, you don't exactly negotiate about your outings, do you?'

'Meaning?'

'You just disappear or declare you're going.'

'I am on holiday, you know! We all went into Clifden together the other day. I don't understand why you're being fierce grumpy. Did it not go well with Orla?'

He shook his head, sensing frustration rise. Sometimes it felt as if he and Nora were at cross purposes. 'It's not about Orla. It's about common courtesy and you not feeling part of us, me and Branna. You could have taken Branna out with you, you know.'

Her expression became closed. 'Oh, right. Well, as you know, because I've never made a secret of it, I have limited tolerance with kids. Being around them makes me feel claustrophobic after a while. Everything moves so slowly and takes so long. It just gets mind-numbing and repetitive. But you do know that, I've always said so.'

'Yes, you have. That's true. I just think you could have been a bit more thoughtful towards Maura, given that she's your host. She looked really done in when I got back. I wasn't gone that long. It wasn't much to ask.'

Nora took a breath. Her voice tightened. 'You shouldn't make assumptions. Maybe you should have stayed with your daughter yourself instead of heading off to scout out a job. I'm not a free childminder, Ty. And I don't fit the job spec. After all, Branna is Maura's family, not mine.'

He shook his head. 'Don't hold back, Nora. Speak your mind.'

She laughed with no amusement. 'Don't start a conversation you don't want to have, Ty. You know, I get fierce fed up of the way people behave about their pets and kids. They're besotted with them. That's all good but they expect you to be, too. Well, I don't want pets or kids, and I don't see why I should have to pretend what I don't feel. I've told you before, Branna's great, but after a while with her, I feel trapped.' She waved a hand. 'I'm fed up with this conversation now, it doesn't go anywhere except round in circles. Thanks for spoiling a lovely afternoon. See you back at the house.'

Swift watched her go, furious that she'd equated Branna with a dog or cat. He turned and kicked a large stone several times, swearing loudly.

'Daddy! What's matter?' Branna was hopping up and down on the gate, making it creak loudly.

'Just something on my boot. No worries.'

'There's Nora.' Branna pointed.

'I know. She's going back to the house.'

Branna looked thoughtful, leaning backwards and forwards and then jumping down from the gate. 'Nora like me?'

'Of course she likes you. Why do you ask that?'

'She look grumpy.' Branna pulled a face, scowling.

'Adults get grumpy sometimes, that's all.' He tipped her nose. 'Do you like Nora?'

'S'pose.'

'Well, then. Nora just needed to get out and have a walk.'

Branna let it go and bent to pull a leaf from a fern, but he could see that she was unconvinced. You couldn't fool children, at least not for long. They were quick to spot leaking emotions.

He reached for her hand, and this time she let him take it. 'Let's head back, the clouds are gathering over there. They're called nimbostratus and they promise rain.'

* * *

The flight back to Heathrow was grim. Branna had enjoyed planes until now. She'd flown several times with her mother to Guernsey, where Ruth's new partner Marcel Vaudin lived, and had been fine on the journey from Heathrow to Galway. But at Galway airport, she went into full meltdown just before they boarded the plane, refusing to embark. Swift cajoled, whispered, cuddled and reasoned. He tensed his biceps and asked her if she wanted to feel them. That was usually a reliable distraction, but this time, it just made her roar even louder. Then he tried bribery with chocolate, but Branna threw it on the floor. Nora stood at the barrier of the departure lounge, remarking helpfully that they'd be popular if they delayed the flight.

Swift knelt on the shiny floor beside his daughter. 'I'm trying to understand, Branna. What's the matter?'

‘Don’t want go plane.’

‘But you like planes. And it’s a lovely one. Look, you can see it through the window.’

‘No. Spell and Hum don’t want go.’

Spell and Hum were her imaginary friends and they usually turned up to help her out when she didn’t want to do or eat something.

‘But they loved it on the plane coming here. They can sit with you by the window.’

She shook her head and hiccupped with rage. Tears spilled down her cheeks. ‘I w . . . w . . . want . . . M . . . M . . . M . . . Mummy!’

‘But that’s why we’re getting on the plane. I’m taking you to Mummy’s when we get back to London. She’s waiting for you at home. You’ll be able to tell her all about your holiday.’

Eventually he managed to get Branna on the plane. The beginning of the flight was punctuated with her bursts of tears and angry yells when a flight attendant attempted to offer her a drink.

‘I think she’s a bit tired after our holiday,’ Swift said.

‘The poor pet, she does look pale,’ the attendant said with sympathy, but Swift could see her eyeing Nora, who was sitting by the aisle, eyes closed and earphones in, and noting his own dismay at his daughter’s distress.

Branna fell asleep after a while, her head against Swift’s arm. He needed the loo, but didn’t want to disturb her. He sat between her and Nora while both of them dozed. Or perhaps Nora was awake, but was just choosing to opt out. Maybe this holiday had been a bad idea. It was hard to see how he, Nora and Branna were ever going to gel. There’d been a coolness between him and Nora since the day she’d left Maura alone, and now Branna seemed to have been upset by it all.

He was puzzled about his feelings for Nora. There was great fondness and he found her witty, engaging. When she was in good spirits, he loved her company. They shared a love of rowing. But the fact that he was unsure told him a truth he knew he had been avoiding. He had known he loved Ruth from the moment he saw her. It had been a mutual, intense chemistry. Overwhelming. When she'd broken their engagement for Emlyn, who she'd quickly married, he'd been distraught for a long time. With Nora, it had been a slow burn and he'd trusted that more tempered emotion after his misery over Ruth. But there were too many times when he was blindsided by Nora's prickliness and quick temper. Then there was what his friend Mark Gill called the toothbrush test. He reckoned that if you'd been seeing someone for more than six months, and neither of you kept a toothbrush in the other's bathroom, things weren't looking optimistic. He and Nora failed that one.

Branna whimpered in her sleep. Ruth was going to meet her tear-stained daughter and wonder what had been going on.

Swift tried to ignore his bladder. He closed his eyes and visualized being out in his boat on a quiet stretch of the Thames, with no sound but his own breathing and the creak of the oars. Then he realized that thinking about water wasn't such a good idea, and distracted himself with a magazine until the plane was ready to land.

When they reached Ruth's flat, Branna threw her arms around her mother on the doorstep and started crying.

'What on earth's the matter?' Ruth picked her up. She stared at Swift while her daughter's hot tears soaked her neck.

'I don't know what's wrong,' Swift said. 'She's been fine on holiday, she really has. She got like this at Galway airport.'

Ruth looked alarmed and cuddled Branna close. She was growing her tawny hair again. When he'd first known her, it had rippled down her back, catching the light. That day they'd met in the British Museum, she'd been sitting with the sun behind her, her hair glinting. She'd had it cut when she escaped the prison of her miserable marriage to Emlyn, but now it was past her shoulders. *Marcel prefers it long*, she'd said to him when he'd commented. Branna pulled Ruth's hair across her face and rubbed it into her eyes. Ruth patted her back in slow, circular movements, making soothing sounds.

'I'll bring Branna's things in if you want to take her through,' Swift said. 'I think she's overtired. She's had a lot of excitement.'

Ruth glanced sideways at him. 'Branna usually copes well with travel and new experiences,' she said coolly. 'I've never known her to get like this when we go away.'

'Well, I don't know, we had a good time with Maura and the horses, and we went to Clifden . . .'

Ruth cut him off. 'Let's not have this conversation now. We do need to talk, but later. I think it's best if you head off, and we'll settle down with a snack and a story. Just leave the bag there, I'll sort it out.'

Turned away at the front door. Clearly, he was to blame. He walked down the pavement, feeling as if he'd been accused of some nameless crime. He got in the car feeling upset and empty. He missed his daughter already. Although he and Ruth had a steady routine for his time with Branna, he always found that leaving her pulled at his heart. He had a moment of self-pity and then glanced at himself in the mirror. The usual wild curling hair and unruly look, not helped by not having had time to shave that morning. He peeled away a tiny scrap of pink plasticine stuck just above his right ear. *Well, if you didn't want this kind of come and go life, you shouldn't have had a child with a woman who told you she didn't love you anymore and left you for someone else. So, get over it,* he told himself.

Suitably admonished, he started the engine.

CHAPTER 3

A couple of evenings later, Swift made a sandwich with some smoked cheese he'd bought in Rossdown, poured himself a glass of merlot and settled down on the sofa with his phone. Upstairs, Elvis was singing 'Always on My Mind'. Swift could never decide if he was a tenor or a baritone. Chand Malla, who rented the top flat from Swift, was a great fan of the King. Sometimes Swift thought that he could do with a bit less of Elvis's crooning, but Chand provided him with delicious Punjabi food via his mother. Swift had never met Mrs Malla, but she sounded like Joyce, his stepmother — determined and full on, with an overwhelmingly kind nature. Chand liked his fish and chips and sausage and mash, but his mother had been convinced since he left home that he would starve. Every time he visited her, he brought back containers of delicious meals, half of which he handed to Swift. Currently, his freezer was replenished with pindi chole, dal makhani, aloo kulcha and paneer pasanda. So there was a quid pro quo in operation concerning the King.

Swift rang Faith Black — his third attempt — and got her voicemail again. He left another message, saying he wouldn't bother her further if she didn't reply in the next couple of days. He was half hoping she wouldn't. Trying to find an attacker who'd struck at sea over six months ago would be tricky, and he didn't like taking on cases that held out little chance of resolution.

He scrolled through the postcards that Kelly had sent to Orla over the years. Most of them were London scenes and the kind you could pick up at shops across the capital — glossy pictures of the Tower of London, Buckingham Palace, St Paul's, Big Ben, the London Eye, Carnaby Street, the Globe Theatre, Battersea Park and the Royal Albert Hall. There were short, uninformative comments on the backs of the cards in clear, upright handwriting.

Great view from here. K x

I went to the top of St Paul's and got giddy. K x

Called at the palace but her Maj was out! K x

Lovely sunset today. K x

Hot here! K x

The last card was of a camogie team, fifteen women in a field dressed in yellow T-shirts and green shorts. They were posed at the front of a wide net. Eight women stood at the back with seven crouched in front of them. They all held long sticks with flattened, curved ends. The woman standing third from the right at the back was Kelly. She'd drawn a little arrow to her head.

We won this one and I have the massive bruises to show for it. K x

Swift sipped his warming wine while 'Heartbreak Hotel' played above, and read them all again. Kelly was a woman of few words.

Nora rang late, just as he was thinking of heading to bed. It was the first time they'd spoken since they'd got back from holiday. He felt both pleased and a little wary when he heard her voice.

'Hi there. No place like home?'

'Sort of. I'm just sitting here and thinking about Kelly Dwyer and her sister, Faith.'

'Ah yes, the woman in the briny. Won't keep you, then. Just wondered if you fancy a row on Saturday. I know I'm going to be straight into a murder case on Monday, so you know, I'll be vanishing for a while.' Nora worked for the Met, as a DI in a serious crime squad. Once she was back at work, she'd be doing long hours.

'Okay. Do you want to come here about midday and we'll take it from there?'

'Great.' There was a pause, and then she said, 'That was a lovely break. I really liked Maura.'

'She's a good woman.'

'She is. I've sent her a card saying as much. I'm ready for my bed, can hardly keep my eyes open. Night.'

He put his phone down. Nora hadn't mentioned Branna or asked if she was okay when she got home. He'd rung Ruth earlier to check, but her phone had gone to voicemail.

He ran his hands through his hair, releasing the lingering sweet scent of turf from Maura's fire. It was good to have breathed the Atlantic-salted Connemara air, but he was glad to be getting back to the routine of work.

* * *

Faith Black had finally responded and left him a curt message in a sleepy, mild voice.

'You can come round tomorrow at half two if it gets Orla off my back.'

She lived in a maisonette in Cricklewood, a fifties block with a front door opening straight onto a steep staircase. When he pushed the bell, the door opened, moving back stiffly. He rang the bell again and called her name. She appeared after a couple of minutes at the top of the stairs.

'I'm Tyrone Swift. Your door was open.'

'Oh bugger, was it? Don't know how that . . . give it a good shove to close it and come on up.'

She looked far more like Kelly than Orla, a more petite version of her dead sister and very thin. A pretty young woman with thick, dark brows, her long chestnut hair fell in soft, full waves over her forehead. She had fine skin, the kind that marks easily. Her expression was sweet but lacked animation, her eyes were dull and there was a heaviness in her body. Something was just off centre about her. Her black tracksuit was crumpled and dotted with fluff, as if she'd slept in it, and her eyes were crusty. He guessed she'd only recently got up. When she brought their coffee in, she staggered slightly and cursed as she mopped up the spillage. She seemed suspicious of him, her glances wary.

'So we're supposed to be related?' she asked.

'Distantly, through another Tyrone who vanished to Australia.'

'Oh yeah. Orla said something about him. She's keen on all that boring ancestry stuff. Spends hours on those websites. She's as bad as a teenager, stuck to a screen, but I suppose it passes the hours for her. Anyway, we're not alike as far as I can see.' She sipped her coffee and yawned.

An animated Orla hadn't stopped talking. Faith seemed moody and distracted. It was months since she'd been attacked, but she looked as if she was still in shock.

'Is this where you lived with Kelly?'

'Yeah. It's rented. Kelly found it the first year she was in London. There's just one bedroom, but it's roomy enough for two single beds. We didn't mind sharing and it saved us money.'

The flat was high-ceilinged and shady. The living room had frayed but comfortable armchairs, and was dusty and untidy with rainbow-coloured exercise resistance bands and dumbbells scattered about. There were at least a dozen blue sticky notes on the back of the door, with lists and dates written on them. The walls were lined with bookshelves and camogie memorabilia.

'It looks as if you've had success in the game.' Swift gestured at the photos and awards. He'd examined them while Faith was in the kitchen. There were a couple of shelves of statuettes, gold plaques, medals, a green and yellow helmet with a faceguard and a stack of camogie balls. Several well-used sticks were propped against a wall beneath rows of team photos. One photo titled *Queen of Camogie* was of a woman in yellow and black stripes balancing a ball on her stick. Below it was an action shot of Kelly running. It showed a vigorous, lean player at full tilt, her stick raised, her eyes alight. A photo of Faith was next to her, showing her swiping the ball, her body poised and focused. There was a terrible contrast when he looked at Faith now.

'Oh yeah. Some of the awards are from Rossdown, back in the day. They're mainly Kelly's. She was a better player than me. I played every week here after I moved to London, in Kelly's team. Until this happened.'

'Can you play now?'

She made a thumbs down gesture. 'Not yet. My coordination's affected. I'm training, going to the gym whenever I feel up to it. I want to get back to full fitness.'

Swift thought that was an unlikely possibility. Faith was staring daggers at him, as if daring him to suggest it.

'It's good to aim for that,' he said.

Faith gestured at the helmet. 'I've always hated having to wear one of those. We didn't have them when I first started playing at school, but now they're compulsory. I've known players to sustain head injuries, so I understand why. Ironic that I've played loads of camogie games with no injury except the odd bruise, and now my brain's fuzzy anyway.' There was a slurring in her speech that came and went.

'Are you having medical treatment?'

She gave a sudden, jarring laugh. 'I've seen a physio and a therapist and I've been referred to a . . .' She paused and frowned, then spoke slowly, spacing the syllables. 'A neuro — psy — chologist. Supposedly, someone who can help me build on my existing skills and abilities. Assuming I've got any. I'll try whatever's on offer. My memory bothers me the most. Feels like there are spaces and gaps in my brain. I've got short-term memory loss and what's called . . . hang on, it's gone. See, I can't even remember my own diagnosis!' She got up and read from one of the blue stickers. 'Retrograde amnesia, which means the past is patchy, too.' She sat back down and knocked her knuckles against her forehead. Her eyes swam with tears. 'Hello, is there anyone there?'

'I'm sorry. It sounds rough.'

'Too right. Chunks of my memory gone AWOL. Years of my life blurry around the edges. I've been looking through photos to try and remind myself, but I just don't recall some of the people in them. I wake up every morning feeling scared in case another bit's gone during the night. Everything's so hit and miss. That's what lack of oxygen does to you.'

'Is there any chance of your memories returning?'

'Possibly. Maybe. Maybe not. And of course, I don't know what's gone missing unless someone tells me.' She brushed tears from her eyes and stopped abruptly, as if thinking she'd revealed too much. 'So anyway, why has Orla sent you my way? She's told me so many times in the last year that I'm just not the same anymore. As if I don't realize! She has a real talent for stating the obvious. Look, I know she means well, but she gets on my nerves.' She laughed again, and he guessed that, like the tears, these emotional outbursts were due to her brain damage. 'Has she been bending your ear?'

'She's worried about you. Concerned that you're struggling and troubled.'

'Yeah. Poking her nose in as usual, I suppose. She's an awful fusspot, that one. Never knows when to leave well alone. She wanted me to stay in Rossdown, so she could fret about me and boss me around like she used to. She should have married and had children instead of spending all her time being a worrywart and obsessing about other people's opinions. Kelly used to call Orla a professional virgin. She reckoned Orla'd never had sex because she'd worry about what the neighbours might say.'

She glanced at him, as if to see what he made of this. He nodded. He'd heard families say much worse about each other.

'You stayed with Orla while you recuperated, so she can't be that bad.'

'She's always okay to start with, but then she can't help overdoing it. She kept making suggestions about work I could do locally when I was better. Pointing out small ads in the paper or drawing rings around them and leaving the paper on the table. Dropping little hints. *"Lottie Moran was saying that she'll need to take on extra staff in the bookshop soon. That would be a great job with regular hours, and the pay's not bad."* I could just imagine the neighbours if I had moved back there, whispering over the fact that I've become a semi-idiot. They've already had a field day picking over Kelly's marriage and her boozing. I couldn't wait to get back here. The blessed anonymity of the city! Now Orla's always leaving messages.'

'Well, you have sustained an injury and you live alone. It's not surprising that she's concerned about you.'

'So what? I can manage. Has she set a private detective on me to check I'm not languishing?' She was restless, moving constantly in her chair, twisting her legs. A couple of times while she was speaking, she half rose and then sank back down.

'As I said, she's anxious. She knows that you're worried about what happened on the ferry and she is, too. She said you spoke about a shadow at your back and that you asked her if anyone hated Kelly. She hoped I'd talk to you in case I can help.'

'How can you help?' The tears brimmed again in her eyes and she looked away.

'I'm not sure I can.'

Her body became rigid. 'Well then, you might as well piss off and stop wasting your time. You don't want to be sitting there looking at a cripple and listening to a sob story.'

She was being eaten up by fear and illness. Swift leaned forward, shaking his head. 'I don't see a cripple. I do see a woman who's had a terrifying experience and is trying her best to overcome it. Someone did you terrible harm, left you for dead, and we don't know who did it or why. Do you worry that they might come back? I would, in your shoes.'

She looked over at him with a kind of relief. 'Yeah. I worry about that sometimes. Except that I got . . .' She looked away.

'You got what?'

'Something. I don't know if I want to tell you.'

A road sweeper rumbled outside, and he waited for the noise to die down. 'Faith, I can see you're grieving because your sister drowned. I almost drowned a while back, in the Regent's Canal. Someone drugged me and threw me in. Luckily a woman jumped in and saved my life. I had nightmares afterwards, still do. I'm sure you do, too, about yourself and Kelly.'

Faith blinked and ran her hands across her brow. She picked up an exercise band and stretched it between her fingers. Swift watched her effort to concentrate and felt a wave of sympathy. She wanted to talk to him, he thought, but her defensiveness about her impairment coupled with suspicion were getting in the way. Most people did want to tell their story, even if they didn't realize it.

'Why don't you tell me about being on the ferry? Then I'll go away if you want.'

She pulled the band to its full length and then dropped it on the floor and stared at it for a moment. 'Might as well, I suppose, if you want to be bored to death, but I think I'd better show you something before I do that. I don't want to mislead you.' She lifted herself up with the kind of groan that old people give when they've been sitting, and went to a bookshelf. She took a piece of paper down and brought it to him. 'This was here waiting for me when I got back from Orla's last December.'

The brief note was printed on white A4 paper:

Your sister got what she deserved. I'm sorry you were injured. Nothing personal, you were in the way. You should have stayed below deck. No apologies about Kelly. Good riddance to bad rubbish.

'Was this in an envelope?'

'Yes, posted in London. The police took the envelope and original. They didn't get anything from it. Orla doesn't know about it. If I'd told her she'd have bombarded me with questions I can't answer, and it would only upset her even more because it's so horrible about Kelly. Please don't tell her about it.'

An apologetic killer who knew where the sisters lived. And at least it cleared up the matter of who had been the intended victim.

'So this is why you hesitated when I asked if you ever worried that your attacker might return.'

She bit at a thumbnail. 'Yeah. I do get chills about it now and again, but after I got that note it seems unlikely they'll be back — doesn't it?'

'That's what the note indicates, but you should stay safety conscious. Better not to trust the word of someone who's already harmed you. I think you should tell Orla about this. She said that there'd been gossip locally that maybe Kelly attacked you and then killed herself. That's very distressing for her. It would put her mind at rest.'

Faith sighed. 'I didn't know about that. Some people are such bastards. It'll probably be coming from the sour-tongued old biddies in the Legion of Mary. I'll mull it over.' She took back the note. 'I read this now and again, looking for any meaning I might have missed in six sentences. Doesn't get me anywhere.'

'So — will you tell me about the ferry journey?'

She nodded, putting the note on the cushion beside her. 'Kelly's friend Sarah gave us a lift, but I can't remember much about the drive. Just chat, and we stopped somewhere for the loo and coffee. We'd booked a cabin, so we must have put our stuff in there when we boarded, although I don't recall it.' She narrowed her eyes, trying to think back. 'We went for a snack. It was crowded in the café, hot and airless. Kids were yelling and running around, making a racket. The ship was lurching once it got out to sea, and I remember someone dropped a tray and food and crockery flew everywhere. Some idiot bloke cheered. After a while, we headed up on deck. It was one of Kelly's favourite places.'

'But not yours, according to Orla.'

'I wasn't so keen, but I did want to get away from the noise and stuffiness and I didn't like the idea of Kelly being on deck on her own in a storm. I remember the wind whipped at the door, and it banged shut behind us. Kelly crossed to the barrier by the rail and looked out to sea. I . . . I stayed behind Kelly because it was so rough. The waves were amazing and the spray lashed us. I took some deep breaths of salt air and I felt light-hearted. A bit scared but giddy, too. Just the wildness of the sea, and the wind gusting and roaring in my ears. That feeling of being glad to be alive, you know?'

'I do know. That's a wonderful feeling.'

'Yeah.' She rubbed an eye. 'Can't imagine having it again. Then . . . I just don't know. I don't remember anything else except a feeling of a presence at my back. Next thing I knew, I was on a stretcher. Then I realized that Kelly wasn't there. I told a paramedic, but she couldn't understand me at first.'

'So someone had come up behind you, probably with a hammer.'

'Yeah.' She shuddered. 'I had a teacher once, used to say, *"I wish I could hammer some sense into you!"* Now I've had the sense hammered out of me.'

'Kelly's back was turned to you at that point.'

'Like I said, she was looking out at the sea. Hands . . . you know, hands on the rail. She had her gloves on.' She pulled a cushion against her chest, hugging it. 'I do dream about Kelly. That long fall into the sea. The police said she was probably unconscious but if she wasn't, she must have been so terrified. I wonder how long she lasted in the water before she died. She was a strong swimmer, but those waves would have exhausted her. One of the worst bits was the waiting — before they found her on that beach. I kept hoping she'd turn up with some weird explanation of where she'd been.' Her eyes had filled up again, and she wiped them with the heels of her hands. 'God, I hate this crying. I'm like a leaky tap. It just happens. It's something I'm stuck with now.'

'This someone at your back — any sense of size or shape?'

'Oh God, I don't know. It's all a blur. You know, when you can feel a shadow, an approach. Like a sudden scent of danger. I just don't know, but it keeps coming back to me, that sensation. It's all confusion.'

'That's what you told the police?'

'What else could I tell them? I was no help to them. They were kind, but I could tell that they disapproved of Kelly and me because we went up on deck in the storm. Like what happened was our fault! I can't stop thinking back to that night. So many times, I wake up and I'm shivering, reliving it. God, the cold! I feel a terrible fear.' Her look was haunted and frozen as she recalled it.

'Did you smell anything? Scent, aftershave?'

'No idea.' She grew irritated again. 'I've been telling you, haven't I? It's all a muddle. Can't you get that?'

'I'm just trying to tease out information. You didn't see anyone you knew on board?'

'No,' she snapped.

'And you and Kelly — had you been arguing, was there any bad feeling between you?'

'The police asked me that. Kelly and I never argued. Only little things like who should buy more toothpaste and bog roll. We were sweet.'

'Have you any idea why someone attacked you and Kelly and then pushed her off the ship? It's unlikely to be a random act.'

There was a long pause before she replied. He could see her trying to remember, struggling. She picked up one of the exercise bands again, twined it around her fingers.

'I don't know. I wish I could think clearly. There's something . . . something there at the back of my mind, but I can't get hold of it. It niggles away at me.' Her voice was full of frustration.

'Maybe it will come to you. That happens sometimes, with memories. They surprise you at odd moments.'

She laughed, a short bark, and shook her head. 'I can remember lots about Kelly and Neil. I wouldn't have minded forgetting all that. Another irony. You know about him? I'm sure Orla enjoyed telling you. She never stopped reminding Kelly that she'd warned her not to marry him.'

'Yes. I heard it was a turbulent marriage, and he died in a car accident.'

'Yeah, that's right.' Another tear slipped down her cheek. She made no move to wipe it away.

'Tell me what you can about Kelly's marriage.' Now that she was opening up, he wanted to keep her talking.

'You call it a turbulent marriage. Kelly used to say it was a magical nightmare. Neil was so handsome, so much fun — to start with. They got together at school. All the girls fancied Neil and all the boys fancied Kelly, so they broke a few hearts. He drove her to distraction, and she couldn't get him out of her system. She never forgave herself for letting him drive off the night he died, but of course, she was plastered. The only good thing that came out of it was that she gave up drinking later that year. Went cold turkey and took up camogie again. The game was her salvation and her . . . oh . . . the thing that steadies . . . secures a ship . . . that's it, anchor.'

'I understand that Kelly was quite a character. Did she get on people's nerves?'

'I suppose she could be a bit of a shit back in the day. She said that herself. She admitted she could be full of herself, opinionated. Out of control when she was drinking. I have a feeling she pissed people off, but that's sort of blurry.'

'But she didn't piss you off, and you were always very fond of her.'

'We sort of got each other. That's the only way I can describe it. I know Orla felt left out sometimes. But she's always been so overbearing, so she's her own worst enemy. If anyone found out me and Kelly shared a bedroom here, they'd be really surprised and like, *"How can you do that? Don't you have terrible arguments?"* Can you understand that we were good mates as well as sisters?'

He nodded. 'I think so. I'm very close to and fond of my cousin Mary. We've always had a bond, ever since we were children.' But he thought the sisters' closeness must have been a tad claustrophobic at times. 'Sharing a bedroom would have cramped your style if either of you wanted to bring someone home.'

'Yeah. We did talk about that but this sofa turns into a bed, so, you know . . .'

'And did the sofa get used?'

She looked vague. 'You asking if we had boyfriends?'

'Yes.'

'I didn't — or at least, no one regular enough to bring home and if Kelly did, I never knew about it. She didn't bring anyone back here. And who'd be interested in me now I'm like this?'

There was no answer to that so he didn't attempt one. 'Do you know if Kelly had any other relationships after she came to London?'

She frowned, pursing her lips. 'I don't think there'd been anyone for a while. She didn't mention seeing anyone after I came to live here. Kelly worked long hours on her own. When she wasn't working, she trained and played camogie, so there wasn't much opportunity for meeting anyone. And I got the impression she didn't want to. Felt too anxious to get involved with anyone else. Didn't trust herself after all the crap that went down.' She sighed deeply. 'There was Sol, Sol Waters. They were together for a while after she left Neil and came to London. Neil suspected that she was seeing someone here and that wound him up. She loved Sol. I think she still did after they split up. She said they never argued, not even once, even though they were drinking. Different dynamic, I suppose.'

'You've met Sol?'

'Hmm. Sol's a messed up happy bunny, lives in a world of his own. One of life's conciliators.'

'So why weren't they still together?'

'Kelly said that after Neil died, she just knew she had to drag herself out of the hole she'd dug, physically and mentally.' Faith seemed to drift away, looking into the distance.

Swift waited, pulling a long loose thread from his shirt cuff. It unravelled a line of stitching and a rip appeared. Should have left well alone. It was one of his favourite shirts, too, a soft, green cotton. 'So she and Sol parted?'

'Hmm? Oh, yeah. Sol was part of her drinking life so, you know, it couldn't work. She knew that if she didn't leave him, she'd go to rock bottom and stay there. She missed him, but staying with him would have been too risky. She saw him now and again, just to check he was okay and sometimes I went with her. He's not okay, he's a wreck. Well, now I match him in the wrecked stakes.' There was something evasive in her voice, but it was hard to tell if it was deliberate or a result of her slowed thinking. She looked perplexed, then carried on. 'I do remember one thing from way back. My mother used to tell me old stories about the sea, that there are as many people living under it as above. People who drowned were living at the bottom of the sea, and sometimes they'd visit the land because they missed it, but they could never stay for long because the power of the sea drew them back. One night when I was in hospital, I thought that maybe Kelly would come and visit from her watery life.'

'It's a lovely story, but I think the reality is better, that you had her body to mourn and hold a funeral for.'

'Thanks. That's kind of reassuring.' She smiled for the first time, a smile of sweetness and warmth.

He thought he might have broken through a barrier and wondered if there'd been someone with a grudge hanging around, someone who'd been on the rough end of Kelly's being a self-confessed bit of a shit. The feeling that Faith had spoken of, that sense of someone at her back on deck had seemed real enough, and the hammer told its own story. Swift could see that she was on edge and tiring. Her fear about what had happened on the ship was palpable. She'd find it hard to get her life back on track while the dread still infected her.

'Do you know if anyone else was aware you'd be on that particular ferry that evening? Apart from Orla and Sarah?'

She shifted, pressed her hands against her cheeks. 'Sorry, I'm not sure. We must have mentioned to people at camogie that we were going away, but I don't know if we gave travel details. Kelly might have mentioned it to people. I don't know who knew in Rossdown. Sorry.' She flushed, looking embarrassed, and flopped sideways, her head on her arm.

The more she told him, the more his heart sank. There was so little to go on. Perhaps he could try to befriend her, offer some support while she was in this weakened state. He felt moved by her situation and there was the other shadow of the vanished Tyrone, who'd reneged on his responsibilities. Payback time.

He leaned forward, touched her arm lightly. 'Faith, do you want me to look into what happened? Clearly, it's worrying you, and the police have made no headway. If you do want me to, I suggest that I start by talking to people you and Kelly worked and socialized with, to see if I come across any disputes or bad feeling. I'll be honest — I'm not at all sure if I can get anywhere, but I can try.'

'Maybe. I don't know. But you do this stuff for a living and I can't pay you. I'm not earning and I'm not sure when I can work again. I can't even drive at the moment.' Her eyes were bloodshot now, the clear blue faded and bleary.

'What did you do for work?'

'I'm . . . I was a professional bridesmaid. Worked for an agency called Bridesmaid Dreams.'

'You mean you were paid to be a bridesmaid?'

'Yeah. There are brides who don't have anyone they can call on, or they don't trust their friends or families to get it right. You'd be amazed how controlling some women are about their weddings. Everything has to be spot on, down to the minutest detail. I knew a bride who banned anyone from wearing . . .' She circled a finger in the air, then jabbed it hard at the side of her head. 'Bloody colour . . . can't think . . . that's it . . . yellow . . . because she hated it. So these brides just need someone who can take care of lots of details, make sure everything goes like clockwork and support them on their big day. But no one wants a bridesmaid who can't walk straight or remember their name, so I'm not sure I'll ever be able to do that again.'

'And was it going well, this work?'

'Yeah! I really enjoyed it and I was good at it.'

'Look — it's okay, forget about payment. After all, we're family, however distant.' And there was something else, too, that made Swift offer. Even in her frail, damaged state, Faith seemed oddly familiar. Now and again, he glimpsed something of his own mother in her, and he felt the warmth of fond memories. Fleeting expressions, the wave of her hair, the rise and fall in her voice.

'Wow — that's generous. I didn't expect that. Let me have a think, anyway. I'll mull it over. I don't want people knowing I'm like this if I can avoid it. There are friends I haven't been in touch with because I don't want them seeing me this way. And people will think I've lost the plot if I'm going on about a cold shadow at my back.' She moved a hand above her head, as if grasping for something.

'Fine. I understand. You know, it might help just as an exercise to fill in some of the gaps for you. Finding and connecting memories.' Of course, there was a risk of resurrecting bad memories about either her sister or herself, but best not to raise that right now. 'When you're ready, and if you want me to help, email me a copy of that note and a list of the main people you and Kelly dealt with in the last couple of years.'

'You mean the ones I remember.'

'It's a place to start. Also, did Kelly use social media, and do you? A lot of your history will be on there.'

'Kelly only used email. Old-fashioned, I know, but she was never able to get the hang of wanting to put your life online. Well, when she was a boozer, she didn't want to advertise the fact. Fair play to Orla, she warned Kelly about that. Best to keep under the radar and not make drunken posts showing yourself up as an arse. I use Facebook and Instagram, mainly for my work and camogie, posts about matches and stuff. I've stayed off it since . . . this crap happened. No point in publicising myself as a moron.'

'But what about Kelly's business — how did she get customers?'

'Just the usual listings on trade websites and word of mouth.'

She showed him to the door and stood with arms crossed, her hands tucked under her armpits. 'Sorry, you know, for being snappy with you. It just takes me that way, comes from nowhere. I'm angry with myself, is the truth of it. Life's a fucking mess. I'd got myself established here and I was really enjoying my life and my job . . .'

He looked at the door lock while she was talking. It seemed okay. He could imagine her wandering off to bed without checking it. 'Had this door been open since last night?'

Faith blushed. 'I must have forgotten to shove it properly. It sticks a bit sometimes. There's a maintenance guy for the block. He's going to look at it. It's the kind of thing I'd have sorted for myself before, but . . .'

'Well, just in case the person who attacked you isn't as contrite as the note suggests, double-check that it's shut and locked. Maybe write one of your sticky notes to remind you.'

'Okay.'

'Look after yourself. Stay in touch, anyway, whatever you decide.'

CHAPTER 4

Ruth rang, sounding terse and tired. 'Hello, Ty.'

'I've been trying to get you,' he said with relief. 'You haven't replied to my messages. I was starting to worry.' He stood at the front window, holding a mug of coffee and looking out on the noonday street. There were few cars parked at this time and rubbish lay exposed by the kerb. This side of the street was stippled with sun, the other side shadowed. He could see that his windows needed cleaning. The house opposite was almost hidden by a tall, gloomy leylandii hedge. It gave the place a foreboding air. Some locals referred to it as 'the Hitchcock house.' It must be as dark as a cave inside. You'd expect to find older or reclusive residents if you knocked on the door, but a cheery young couple with three children lived there.

'Been a bit busy, Ty. Branna's got a very bad ear infection. She had a high temperature last night and was crying so much, I was really frightened. I took her to A&E. They said it had probably been coming on while she was away with you, and it's a pity it wasn't caught earlier, given her hearing loss. Did you notice her pulling at her right ear?'

'No. She took her hearing aids out a couple of times, but she does that now and again, so I didn't think much of it.'

'You didn't think much of it,' she said sarcastically. 'Well, if you had bothered to take more notice, the poor girl wouldn't be in so much pain now. Ty, you know that she stands more chance of getting ear infections with hearing aids. You have to be more careful.'

'Okay, Ruth, I get your point. I'm really sorry. You should have rung me last night. I'd have come to the hospital with you.'

'I didn't have time, I was concentrating on Branna. There's nothing you could have done anyway.'

'Is she on antibiotics?'

'Yes, powerful ones, and paracetamol for the fever. I have to get the GP to check her again tomorrow.'

'I'm so sorry, Ruth. That must explain why she was upset on the way back.'

'Hmm.'

'Shall I come over? I'd like to see her.'

'Best not. She's exhausted and sleeping. She just needs quiet and routine.'

'Okay. I'll ring tonight to see how she is.'

'That's not all, Ty. I spoke to Branna while she was at Maura's. She told me you'd gone out.'

'I was out for a couple of hours.'

'She said she was lonely and bored, and Maura couldn't hear her. I was worried. I don't understand why you take her on holiday and then go off without her.'

'I wasn't gone long. I'm sorry if she was upset.' He thought that maybe suddenly hearing her mother on the phone had disrupted things, but didn't want to suggest it.

'There's more.' Ruth's voice had got tighter and louder. 'Yesterday, Branna told me she doesn't like Nora. She said Nora gets cross with her and tells her off. She said when you went out and left her at Maura's, Nora snapped at her. I could see it had made her unhappy.'

He put his coffee down on the window ledge. 'Nora isn't always the most patient person with children, but they get on well most of the time.' He knew that was an exaggeration even as he said it. 'Nora wouldn't set out to upset Branna, but you know how she can get loud and excitable. Maybe it just got a bit too much for Nora.'

'So this is Branna's fault? I can't believe that you're taking Nora's part rather than your daughter's.'

'That's not what I meant . . .'

'Really? Sounded like it to me. I'm not having my daughter treated like that. And I still don't understand why you left her and went off on your own. You're always going on about spending time with her, but then when you have it, you squander it and she gets anxious.'

'That's not fair, Ruth. Maura asked me to see a friend of hers, Orla — well, she's a distant relative, in fact — who was worried about Faith, her sister. Faith lives in London, and Orla was hoping I'd look into something that happened to her.'

'Oh, right. There was me thinking you wanted precious time with Branna, and you were canvassing for work.'

'Look, it wasn't like that. You're worried and tired and . . .'

'Don't tell me how I am. You need to get your priorities straightened out. And you need to get Nora straightened out while you're at it, or I won't be allowing her to spend time with Branna. Maybe Nora needs to take some tips from Marcel. He knows how to set boundaries with a child without getting irritable. I mean it, Ty. I'm not having it. You can ring tonight.'

The line went dead. He sighed and thought back over the holiday, wondering if he'd missed signs that Branna was unwell. He couldn't think of any. He knew that Ruth was distressed, but he knew also that she wasn't a woman to cross where her daughter's welfare and happiness were concerned. He felt irritable with himself, at Ruth's criticism and with Marcel being held up as a template.

He picked up his coffee. It was a stronger type than he usually bought and he wasn't sure he liked the aromatic tones. He felt guilty about Branna now. He should have realized that her crankiness indicated an underlying problem. A delivery van stopped across the road, outside the hidden house. The driver got no answer when he rang the doorbell. He consulted his phone and tucked the small parcel between the dense branches of the dark green hedge. The van drove away, leaving the street empty again. Swift rubbed with his sleeve at a greasy smudge on the windowpane, making it worse.

He knew he'd have to speak to Nora about her relationship with Branna. That was something to look forward to.

* * *

Faith emailed him as he was having breakfast in the garden and throwing toast crumbs for the sparrows. High up in the converted loft next door, his neighbour Andy Fanning was practising his trumpet — Miles Davis, 'My Funny Valentine'.

Sorry again if I was a pain in the arse. I'd like you to try and find out who did this to Kelly and me. I've been going over and over when we were on the ship deck. The only way I can explain it is to say again that it was like a cold shadow at my back. Thanks for not looking as if you were thinking I'm a headcase when I was talking about it all. That was a relief. But I know it sounds weird. I've checked my phone and made a list. I don't have many friends here. I'd only been in London a while, and I was finding my feet and learning my job. When we weren't working, Kelly and I hung out together. We lived quietly, to be honest. Just playing matches, going to the cinema. Bit of telly.

She'd added a short list of names and contact numbers.

Sarah Ennis

Sol Waters

Una Bassek — runs London Harps camogie club

Kate Pearce at London Harps

Dermot Dwyer — Neil's bro

Amber Oxendon — employed me at Bridesmaid Dreams

The trumpet segued into 'Summertime' while Swift pictured the swaying ferry deck. Kelly watching the roaring waves, Faith hanging back behind her and someone stealthily moving up to Faith. The noise of the ship and the storm would have covered the approach and the attack. Kelly had been oblivious to her sister's distress, still watching the dark raging waters until her killer moved in and threw her into the sea.

He rang Sarah Ennis's number while he finished his toast. She told him that she worked a half day on a Thursday, so he could come tomorrow at one o'clock and she could give him some time then. Now that Faith had given him the green light, he contacted Merseyside police and after several conversations, found his way to a DC Keane who asked him for his number and called him back.

'What do you want to know, Mr Private Detective?' He sounded highly amused.

Swift explained that he was looking into what had happened to the sisters. 'So anything you can give me about where you got with your investigation would be helpful.'

'Right. What can I give you? Let's see. Faith Black was found at six a.m. on the top passenger deck of the ferry. She'd been hit on the head, like, and suffered a blunt instrument trauma, probably from a hammer. She was found shoved by a ventilation funnel. Partly hidden by it. She was unconscious. By the time she regained consciousness and asked after her sister, Kelly Dwyer, all the other passengers had disembarked. Not handy. So, big search all over the ship for Kelly but no trace and their stuff still in their cabin. Conclusion: she'd fallen overboard by accident, been dumped or jumped, but there was nothing to suggest she'd been suicidal. Then she washed up in Anglesey and frightened a jogger on the beach.'

'Were there any injuries sustained prior to drowning?'

'Just checking . . . body'd been bashed about in the Irish Sea and pounded for weeks, so it was hard to tell, but there was an injury to the top left side of her head. Could have been same hammer as used on Faith, obvs. So, maybe the same person bashed Kelly and then chucked her over the side. She died from drowning, but might have already been unconscious as she went into the water. Let's hope so, and we told the family that, in case it was some comfort. Lucky North

Wales manages to cop a few bodies from Ireland. It's the way the current pushes them, like. Yep, they get a good sea harvest from the Emerald Isle.' He chuckled.

Swift hoped he was more circumspect with families. 'I understand you got no lead from the note posted to Faith last December?'

'That's spot on. No forensics. At least it cleared up that Kelly was the intended target. First time I've come across a murderer who sends apologies. The case stalled through lack of evidence. We got nothing from questioning other passengers. No rows witnessed with anyone on board. We talked to a couple of people in the café who'd sat near the sisters and said they were chatting and getting on fine, like, just the two of them. No other company.'

'You got nowhere with questioning Faith?'

'You've got to be kidding. She was as much use as a chocolate fireguard when it came to remembering anything. There was no CCTV on that part of the deck. No DNA, no hammer — bottom of the Irish Sea, presumably. And as I said, all the passengers had left the ferry by the time anyone knew what had happened. We went through the passenger manifest but didn't come up with any names known to the family.'

'Maybe the killer didn't know Faith was going to be on board and was going to use the hammer on Kelly before throwing her over the rail. It came in handy for Faith, too.'

'That's my thinking. 'Course,' DC Keane went on, 'they needed their heads examined anyway, going up on deck in that weather. When I go over to see my grandad, I make sure I stay below. Bloody Irish Sea's like a witch's cauldron a lot of the time.'

'Still, I suppose you should be able to go on deck without worrying that someone will come at you with a hammer or chuck you over the side,' Swift said sarcastically.

'Fair enough, you've got a point there.'

'Yes. You've been very helpful, but just to say, I'm a relative of Kelly and Faith's as well as being a private investigator, so your cheeriness about what happened to them is a tad insensitive.'

'Oh God . . . right . . . look, I didn't know. You might have said!'

'Never make assumptions, DC Keane. And it's usually a good idea to stay respectful about people unless you're certain who you're talking to. Don't forget that some police forces are using "mystery shoppers" these days.'

'Christ! You're not one of them, are you?'

Swift sighed. Keane wasn't the sparkiest match in the box. 'No, I'm not. They don't declare themselves. The clue's in the word "mystery".'

'Right, yeah. Are you going to report me, like?'

'Don't be daft. I've better things to do. But watch your manner and your manners in future.'

He jotted down some notes. So far, it was all about as fluid as the Irish Sea.

* * *

S.J. Ennis dental practice was on the first floor of a handsome Victorian house in Pinner, sandwiched between a law firm at ground level and an architect's on the top. The receptionist showed Swift to a tiny and sunny office at the back of the building, overlooking a walled garden with mature apple trees.

Sarah Ennis rose to greet him and motioned to a chair by the window. 'Hope you don't mind if I eat while we talk. It's been a long time since breakfast and I worked right through the morning without a break. D'you want a tea or coffee?'

'Go ahead with your lunch. I'm fine, thanks.'

She took a bite from a long baguette stuffed with crispy bacon and wiped a dribble of tomato ketchup from her chin. 'No polite way of eating this,' she said cheerfully. She was slim, with a narrow face and downward drooping mouth. A wide, pale scar ran from the middle of her forehead across to her right ear. Her thin brown hair was cut very short with a side parting. The severity of her appearance was offset by a measured, gentle voice. It would reassure nervous patients.

'As I said in my email, Faith Black has asked me to investigate what happened to her and Kelly on the Irish ferry.'

Sarah looked puzzled and put her baguette down on a napkin. 'Isn't that a job for the police?'

'They've had no success with their investigation. Faith is very troubled about what happened.'

'Right. I heard she was badly injured.'

Swift had talked to Faith about how he should play things when he was interviewing. He knew that she was embarrassed by her injuries and uncertain memories, and that she didn't want people to pity her. 'Faith's head injury has caused some memory loss and other weakness. It's upsetting for her and, as you can imagine, she's pretty sensitive about it. Working with me might also help her patch memories back together.'

'I'd have thought that would be a therapist's job. Is that what private investigators do these days?'

'Private investigators take on all kinds of tasks. Some people use my services to get peace of mind, or to feel that they're doing something when they're hurting. And the Blacks and I are related, albeit distantly, so you know, it's helping out family. She's having therapy, of course.'

'I see. Well, how do you think I can help? I haven't seen Faith since the night it all happened.' She didn't sound too eager.

'You weren't at Kelly's funeral?'

'Sadly, no. I just couldn't get the time away from work.'

That sounded a bit limp. 'So you've not been in touch with Faith?' It seemed odd behaviour from a family friend.

'I left her a message, but she didn't respond. We've never socialized as such, so, you know, I assume she has other friends who are helping her.' Sarah ate another chunk of bacon.

'I suppose she's been focusing on getting better and I think she tires easily. Or she might have forgotten that you called. When did you arrange the lift to Dublin with her and Kelly?'

'I was visiting my mother and I bumped into Kelly in Clifden. I offered them a lift when I heard we were leaving on the same date. I was going on to stay with friends in Dublin for a couple of days.'

'Can you recap that journey to Dublin for me, what you talked about, how Kelly and Faith seemed?'

'They were both fine. Faith sat in the back and didn't say much, but then she never did when Kelly was around. She was listening to music through her earbuds for most of the journey. Kelly said Orla had talked her to death. Those two have always rubbed each other up the wrong way. She'd fixed a few things around the place for Orla. Other than that, we chatted a bit about films we'd seen, the changes in Rossdown, people who'd emigrated and those who'd moved in, just general stuff, really.' Sarah poured herself a coffee from a thermos jug. 'Sure you won't join me?'

'I'm fine.'

She stirred three heaped sugars into her coffee. Swift didn't know why he always felt surprised when people in healthcare flouted the rules. He'd come across enough nurses and doctors who smoked like chimneys.

Sarah saw him watching. 'Don't tell the patients about my sweet tooth. They'd be shocked to find I don't practise what I preach. I do extra flossing as penance.'

'Your secret is safe with me. Did Kelly say anything about any relationships she had in London? Orla said she never talked much about her life here.'

'She didn't mention anyone in particular. I didn't see that much of Kelly. I'd never visited her at home. She was always sort of vague about her life in London. Evasive, even. I remember once I asked her if she'd met anyone special here. Given that she's a looker, I'd have expected her to. She said something about marriage to Neil putting her off men for life.'

'That doesn't sound likely. She was only twenty-two when Neil died.'

'Exactly. But that's all I ever got from her.'

'She didn't mention Sol, Sol Waters?'

'Don't think so. I rarely saw her after Neil was killed. She did some work here for me one time and we'd have a coffee now and again. You know, I'm not sure I can help you much.'

'Anything you tell me might be useful.'

'Yes, I see.' She sipped her drink, thinking, and then nodded. 'Look, I have to be frank with you about this. And I don't want you to repeat what I say to Faith — or Orla. I wouldn't want to hurt their feelings, especially if Faith's not well. Have you ever had a friend who isn't really a friend anymore?'

'Do you mean you no longer regarded Kelly as a friend?'

'I wouldn't go that far. It's not that easy to explain.'

He thought that she'd already gone that far. He could see she was struggling to be diplomatic, so left an encouraging silence.

She linked her fingers, moving them up and down. 'I went to school with Kelly and we were great mates back in the day. Messed around together, got on really well. She was bright and funny, always pushing the boundaries. She was an extreme kind of person. Whatever she did, she was full on. I was a quieter type, less confident, so I was sort of carried along in her slipstream. And she was always such a lovely-looking girl. She never went through an ugly duckling stage like most of us. No spots, blemishes, or puppy fat. Kelly was athletic, too. I suppose for a while I had a big crush on her. Yes, I did, no suppose about it.' The memory softened Sarah's voice even more. 'Kelly could never concentrate for long in class. She'd be itching to be out doing things. The teachers used to despair of her, but she had this smile that charmed and disarmed. And she was a terrific camogie player. The school got kudos from her prowess on the field, so they cut her some slack where her studies were concerned. When a teacher told her off, she'd say, *"I don't mean to be difficult, I'm just not made for sitting around."*'

'But that all changed when her mum died, according to Orla.'

'That's right. Kelly's mum was knocked down one morning while she was out shopping in Clifden, dead within the hour. We were at school and Kelly was called out of class. She was in bits. She changed so much after that. She stopped doing sports and dropped camogie. Got into the booze in a big way. Drinking became her new sport, if you like. I was never interested in alcohol. She became sort of wild and all over the place. I started to find her a bit of a bore. Alarming, too. Being around her made me nervous.'

She looked twitchy now, remembering.

'Was she an aggressive drunk?'

'No, never. But she'd be edgy and unpredictable. I'm a conformist by nature, so I started avoiding her.'

'Sounds as if you outgrew the friendship.'

'That about sums it up. Then Kelly married at eighteen and I went away to study in Dublin, then moved to England. We lost touch. I'd see her occasionally when I was visiting and then I heard she'd left Neil and was in London. It didn't surprise me that the marriage didn't last. They hadn't been a couple for all that long when they got hitched. She was still feeling lost after her mother's death and she was swept off her feet by his good looks. Neil was incredibly handsome. A god among men.' She had a tender expression.

'An inebriated god, though.'

'Well . . . yes. They both drank way too much. Anyway, Kelly rang me in London. We hooked up in a bar for a chat. She knocked back wine like a fish, saying that Neil was the love of her life, but she just couldn't live with him. I didn't believe her. If someone's the love of your life, you find a way of hanging on to them, don't you think?'

His thoughts went to Ruth. 'Depends. Sometimes, it's just not possible, no matter what you do.'

She looked unconvinced. 'Well, I had to listen to lots of sentimental stuff about doomed love and I got bored. It was all a bit too *Wuthering Heights* for me. I had to put Kelly into a taxi to get her home safe. I remember going home thinking that we didn't have much in common any more.

Our lives had diverged so much, we didn't have a great deal to talk about. Then a while later, I was moving my practice in here and wanted some refurbishment done. Kelly quoted me a competitive price for the gas system and she did a good job, even though she smelled of booze some days. I nearly told her to leave one morning because she looked the worse for wear but, you know . . . I'd known her a long time and I was still kind of fond of her. Old time's sake and all that. When I heard about Neil's accident, I was sad but not shocked. I'd thought for a long time that as a couple, they courted disaster.'

'So the meeting in Clifden was happenstance?'

'Yes. As I say, I bumped into her. I hadn't seen her for ages.'

'Orla told me that Kelly gave up drinking after Neil died.'

'That's true. It hit her hard. Sometimes an event like that is a turning point in life. I reckon she was shocked into being sober. She took up camogie again once she left off the booze. She found a better class of addiction. Pity she ever swapped one for the other. I met up with her about eighteen months after Neil died. She rang me, and I couldn't think of a way of putting her off. I was relieved when I saw her. She seemed levelled out and much fitter physically. She said that camogie took her mind off wanting alcohol. She'd found the old buzz of the game again.'

This certainly seemed a grudging friendship on Sarah's part. 'So, you must have felt pleased for Kelly.'

'Of course. Who wouldn't be?'

'I can understand that you let the friendship lapse when Kelly was drinking. A lot of people don't want a messed up drunk in their life. But when you knew she was sober, didn't you want to renew it? Given that you'd once been so close.'

She wrapped the crumbs from the baguette in their waxed paper and binned them. 'Things had drifted by then. Life changes, people move on. That time I saw her after Neil's death, when she'd dried out, Kelly was thoughtful — introspective, even. She told me that sometimes she worried about things she might have said or done when she was drunk, things that she had no recollection of. Patches of her life were blank. She wondered what might resurface, come back and bite her. Do you think that's what happened on the ferry?'

'Possibly. Alcoholics often spin complicated, shambolic webs in life that stick to them after they've recovered.'

'Hmm. Nicely put. Even if I'd been tempted to renew the friendship, it put me off when Kelly said that. I wondered who she'd been mixing with, but assumed there could have been some lowlifes. I didn't want to be snagged in one of those shambolic webs. Look, I'm shocked and sorry about what happened to Kelly and Faith. I understand how awful it must be for Faith. She was always much quieter and she looked up to Kelly, big time.'

'Did you meet Faith here, once she'd moved to London?'

'Just the once. Kelly rang me and asked if I'd do Faith a mate's rates price for teeth whitening. She was doing some weird job where she was paid to be a bridesmaid, and someone had suggested she needed to pay attention to her teeth.'

She looked at her watch and pulled a folder across her desk, flicking through papers inside.

'And did you do her teeth for her?'

'Yep, gave her a pearly set. She seemed thrilled with them. She told me brides were extremely pernickety and she had to look just right. Perfect, but not so perfect that she outshone the bride, that is. I remember thinking you must be a bit of a saddo, no-mates bride if you had to pay someone to be your bridesmaid.'

'From what Faith told me, I think it's a role that involves organization as well. Making sure that everything runs smoothly.'

'Okay. I wouldn't know, never having married. I don't think I can tell you anything else and I'm attending a lecture this afternoon, so I'd better get going. Give Faith my best, won't you?' She didn't sound wholehearted and hadn't asked if Faith needed any help.

She saw him out. 'If you want your teeth whitened, make an appointment. I'd give you a discount.'

'You have to wear something in your mouth, don't you?'

'Yes, but it's not painful and most people love the result. We can all do with a lift in life and a bit of sparkle.'

He thought he'd rather get his lift from being out on his boat than having a mouthful of bleach. He found a small café a few doors along from the surgery in which to have some lunch. He ordered a tuna salad and a coffee and sat at a metal table in a tiny patio out the back. He watched jackdaws darting in and out of a broad chimneypot on a nearby roof. They went back and forth busily as if they had a flight schedule. A buddleia had rooted in the side of the chimney and was putting out fresh shoots. One of the jackdaws nipped a twig from it and carried it into the nest.

He went over what Sarah had given him. Not much. Kelly had been a good-looking, bright girl and a skilled athlete. She'd done everything to the max. After her mother's death, she'd had a troubled adolescence, had been a drinker and married unwisely. At times, she'd pushed boundaries, courted disaster. She certainly seemed to have alienated a childhood friend. Maybe there were other people who'd been left disaffected by knowing her. Had she invaded someone else's boundaries in a way that enraged them enough to get rid of her? Maybe she'd courted disaster that night on the Irish Sea, tempting the waves when she'd have been safer below in her snug cabin. Faith was seen as the quiet one, in awe of her big sister and very close to her. She too had been an energetic athlete, but that person had probably vanished for good.

The camogie playing, hard-working Kelly had provoked terrible violence that had rebounded on her sister.

He wasn't at all convinced that he'd make much headway with this investigation. But if he was being honest with himself, the situation had piqued his interest.

CHAPTER 5

Swift was happy to be back in his own familiar boat. He powered it through the water, sensing the burn in his straining muscles. He breathed deep, feeling his lungs expand. It was a windy, humid day. This afternoon, on a full tide, the Thames smelled marshy and oily with a whiff of damp cellars. That familiar, reassuring scent of thousands of years of settlement and the detritus of lives lived. At low tide, the river would have a fishy fragrance. Sometimes it was a steely grey or muddy brown. Today it was light khaki, and a passing dredger had left little rainbows of oil on the surface. He'd been rowing on the Thames for years and knew all its moods and aspects.

The river absorbed his moods, too, and soothed them. He'd rowed out his grief on it when his mother died. Then, his house in Hammersmith had belonged to his great-aunt Lily, and he'd been a frequent visitor to both her and the nearby Thames. Maybe he could have become a career drinker like Kelly if his boat hadn't consoled him. He'd certainly paid more attention to booze than to his lectures when he first went to university. At least he'd had some warning that his mother was leaving him, after her cancer was diagnosed as terminal. Kelly had waved her mother goodbye as she left for school and that was it. No chance to say any last words of love.

He acknowledged another rower who was sculling on the other side of the river and slackened his pace a little. Today, the letter he'd received from his solicitor had frustrated him. He'd expected it, but hoped that it wouldn't arrive. It was brief and dispiriting.

Oliver Sheridan has a new solicitor. She has written to advise me that he is appealing the court's decision regarding his father's will. His solicitor is preparing further information for the court to consider. I will advise you as soon as I have more details and when I hear of a date for the hearing. Please contact me if you would like to discuss this further and also if there is any information we can add to our documents to strengthen our case. We will need to meet anyway before the next hearing.

Swift was caught in a web not of his own making. It had been unintentionally spun by his dear, deceased friend Cedric Sheridan, who'd rented Swift's top flat before Chand became his tenant. Cedric had left a will that enraged his son Oliver and, as the sole executor, Swift was bound by its terms. After Cedric's death, Swift had found the will, written on a form bought from a chain of stationers. Cedric had left twenty thousand pounds to his son Oliver, a hundred and fifty thousand each to Swift and Milo, one of his oldest friends, ten thousand to Yana Ayo, a refugee he had helped and ten thousand to Oxfam.

Cedric had endured a deeply troubled relationship with his son. Oliver had been abusive when he visited his father, usually to demand money. He and Swift had argued many times over his attitude, and Swift had once thrown him out when he bruised Cedric. Oliver had challenged the will, alleging that Swift had prevented him from seeing his father, blocked phone calls and put pressure on Cedric to give him a car. He'd claimed that Swift influenced Cedric into changing his previous will, which named Oliver as the main beneficiary. At the court hearing, the judge decided that there was no evidence that Cedric lacked mental capacity when he had updated his will or that he had been influenced in any way. She stated that Oliver's twenty thousand pounds satisfied the terms about making reasonable financial provision under the 1975 Inheritance Act.

And now it was going to drag drearily on. Swift knew who was behind this latest move: Camilla Finley. Despite being in prison, she must be feeling gleeful. During his last case, Swift had crossed swords with Camilla, a reporter on a local paper in Cornford. He'd discovered that she'd been an accomplice to murder, and she was now on remand, awaiting trial. She'd got her hooks into Oliver while she was conducting a campaign to try and trash Swift's reputation. She'd have encouraged him to lodge the appeal.

Swift spotted a buzzard soaring and gliding. Its broad, rounded wings tipped and tilted as it searched for food below. Swift slowed the boat, wiping sweat from his brow and listening to its mewing. It would be enjoying the warm thermals and a plentiful supply of food in the city. It swooped upriver, towards the tall crane that dominated the skyline carrying its load of concrete blocks.

He put on a burst of speed as he approached Hammersmith and his club Tamesas, revelling in his regained health and energy. He pulled his boat into the clubhouse, washed it down and cleaned carefully around the oarlocks. It would need waxing in the coming months. The ridged scar on his thigh pulled as he bent and stretched. It was a regular reminder of his time working for Interpol, when he'd been stabbed during a raid in a sex trafficking case. He still had vivid dreams about that night, where he relived the sharp, slashing pain and heard the screams and shouts of victims and traffickers. He'd wake with a start, hot and dry mouthed, fingers reaching for the scar.

He massaged it now, resting against his boat. Faith Black must wake with the same sense of panic when recalling the shadow behind her and imagining her sister's long fall into the angry sea.

* * *

It was half ten in the morning, and Sol Waters reeked of the alcohol seeping through his pores. So did the tiny flat he rented above a butcher's shop in Lewisham. The doormat outside stated, *I've Been Expecting You, Mr Bond.* He'd opened the door bleary-eyed, barefoot and wearing stained jeans and an oversized hoodie. Swift thought he'd be good-looking if he had some missing teeth replaced and washed his face and his long greasy hair that trailed down to his waist. Maybe he'd scrubbed up better when Kelly was with him.

'Did you see that Sinéad O'Connor's turned Muslim?' he asked Swift, sinking down into a battered leather sofa and twining one stick-thin leg around the other. He was well spoken and welcoming, though his voice sounded as if he'd swallowed rusty nails and his porridge-coloured pallor indicated a man who rarely saw daylight.

The living room was squalid and dirty, the carpet covered in fluff and ancient-looking grime. A large grey cobweb swayed across a corner of the ceiling. Miss Havisham would feel at home. The room was furnished with an assortment of substantial and once expensive furniture, now worn. There was an impressive collection of spirits on an old mahogany sideboard. Ranks of glass bottles, three deep, caught the sunlight. An amber whisky glowed warmly in a bell-shaped bottle embellished with a stag's head. Waters saw him looking.

'Gin for the morning, whisky in the afternoon,' he said with a wide smile that exhibited receding gums.

Swift sat on an antique winged chair with a curved back and a seat upholstered in grubby purple velvet. 'I didn't know that about Sinéad.'

'I might try it. Good enough for Sinéad, good enough for me.' He sang in a melodic but cracked voice, '*Nothing compares, nothing compares to you . . .*'

'Muslims don't drink.'

'Is that so?' He pulled a face. 'Why didn't I know that? I knew about the pig thing.'

'The Koran forbids any intoxicants.'

'Right. That's it for me, then, I can't convert. I don't know how Sinéad's going to stay dry. Or, you know, maybe that's her way of finding a programme that works. Belief in not getting rat-arsed.'

'You could be right. Maybe she's looking for that self-imposed discipline.' He thought Waters was perceptive enough behind the dishevelled appearance.

'I'll stick with being agnostic. That gives me all the excuses for going on the lash. I suppose Faith told you I'm an alcoholic?'

'Yes.'

He lay back on the sofa, disentangling his legs and crossing one over a crooked knee. 'I'd offer you refreshments, but it's the butler's day orf and the cook left. Can't get the staff, y'know,' he said in a mock upper-class drawl.

'Tell me about it. It's a nightmare these days.'

Waters chuckled, making a noise like a creaking gate. 'Did you say why you wanted to visit me? I was a bit blurry when you rang.'

'I told you that Faith had given me your name because she's asked me to try and find out who attacked her and murdered Kelly.'

'She needs her own policeman? Aren't the real police any good?'

'Not in the sense that they haven't been successful in their investigation.'

'Fair enough.'

'I'm talking to people who knew Kelly and who know Faith. Faith has bad memory loss.'

Waters gave a little shiver. His eyes were sad. 'That's crap, what happened on the ferry. My poor Kelly, chucked over the side as if she was rubbish. I shouldn't think I'll be much help, my memory's hit and miss, like Faith's. Thing is, even when she used to be smashed, Kelly never managed to get herself killed. Just goes to show that sobriety isn't all it's cracked up to be.'

Swift stared at him. 'Sounds as if you're disappointed that Kelly managed to give up drinking.'

'Maybe I am. Thing is, she gave me up as well. I really loved her. Still do. But she got sober and dull. There's no one more boring than a reformed drunk. Know why?'

'Tell me.'

He stood up shakily, stuck his arms out sideways, mimed a balancing act, and then collapsed back on the sofa. Dust puffed up and a spring groaned. 'It's because they're on a tightrope. They're always having to watch themselves because really, deep down, they want the delicious glow that comes with that first glass. The liquid ambrosia that just keeps giving. So, Kelly started exercising all the time as a distraction and batting her little camogie balls around. Working up a virtuous sweat. She still came to see me now and again, like some social worker with a long-term client on their books. Brought me fruit and disgusting vegetable smoothies that looked like liquid mud. Faith came with her once or twice when she moved from Ireland. Nice woman, quiet type. Her job was turning up at weddings as a bridesmaid and keeping everyone sweet. I told Kelly not to come back again last time she visited.'

'Seeing her was too painful?'

'Nail on the head. You know about that, do you, veering between hope and despair?'

'Yes. My fiancée left me for someone else. Took me a long time to get over her.' *Maybe I still haven't*, he thought. 'Faith might not remember that you didn't want visits.'

'Oh well . . . if she turns up, she turns up. I'm rarely at the club or the races these days. I'm usually to be found at home for visitors.'

'How did you meet Kelly?'

'Guess. Where lots of boozers meet.'

'In a bar?'

'Ha ha! Very amusing! But it's actually even funnier than that. We met in rehab. Clearly, it didn't work.'

'When was that?'

'About five years ago. Before the husband died. We were both attempting to dry out so we'd booked into a clinic, a place called Whiteleaf in Surrey. I didn't really want to go there, but my ma paid so I thought I might as well have a holiday on her. Ma has disapproved of me since I grew out of short trousers and opted to go to Cambridge instead of Oxford. The Waters offspring — well, the men, anyway — always go to Oxford, you understand. It's a venerable family tradition. And there was the only son flying in the face of custom! That was bad enough, but then I dropped out halfway through the first year. Just couldn't stomach it. Ma's from the landed gentry in Somerset, you see. One of our ancestors was a Lord of the Treasury in the nineteenth century and we've a coat of arms.' He chuckled, making a noise like a creaky gate. 'Ma keeps it highly polished. She stopped speaking to me after the clinic didn't work out. Sent me an email instructing me not to contact her again. She puts five hundred a month into a bank account for me. I'm one of those disreputable relatives kept at bay with an allowance.'

The background explained the antique furniture sitting in faded splendour amidst the grime. 'So when you went to the clinic, you and Kelly clicked.'

'Yep. We arrived the same day. Went for a long walk in the grounds the first evening. She was genuine about wanting to dry out, unlike me. She told me she really needed to get sober because she was making such a mess of her life and other people's. She was muttering about Neil, getting very teary and saying she had to turn things around, put things right. So, you know, I put my arm around her to console her and . . . cue romantic music. Lush violins for the pair of lushes.' He smiled mistily and coughed. 'We lasted a week there and then we got chucked out, thank goodness. It was torture, pure torture. Inhumane.'

He had a light sheen of sweat on his bleached face. He looked as if he could do with seeing a doctor. 'What happened at the clinic?'

'Well, we were fed up with fruit juice and salads and feeling shitty. Fed up with having to sit in groups and discuss our addiction. I could see that Kelly was wavering and dying to escape dreary reality. I knew exactly how she felt. Funnily enough, she cracked before me and paid a delivery guy to fetch her some bourbon and gin. There was another woman there who we'd got friendly with who was dying to slake her thirst, so we had ourselves a party in her room. Got fubar in there one night.' He laughed at the happy memory and sang in an American twang, '*I just can't lie down without holding on.*'

'I suppose you were discovered in this state of fubar?'

'That's right. Kelly and I were expelled from the Garden of Eden back into the world of pain and sin the next morning. Bliss. D'you want a drink?'

'No, thanks.' He'd wondered when Waters would offer. Most drunks liked a bit of company or at least justification for opening a bottle.

'I need a hair of the dog.' He reached down at the side of the sofa and lifted a half-full bottle of gin. He opened it, took a slug, then poured a liberal amount into a whisky glass. 'That's better. Settles my stomach.'

'How long were you and Kelly together?'

'Couple of years or thereabouts. She had her own place in Cricklewood, but she stayed with me sometimes. It was great. We had such laughs back then. I've never been so happy. We'd have these big cooked breakfasts at the weekends. Irish breakfasts, Kelly called them. She bought this delicious potato bread from somewhere and cooked up a storm. Then she went on one of her trips to Ireland, and it all kicked off with Neil again. He was a pain in the arse, always trying to get her to go back to him.'

'It didn't bother you that she was married?'

'Not really. I reckoned the marriage was over but neither of them could let go. Kelly talked about divorce but in the way an alcoholic considers giving up drink — I'll do it tomorrow, next week, next month. You get the picture. She didn't really love Neil anymore, even though she'd say she did. She just felt guilty about him. He used to ring her at least once a week, and he'd be on the phone for ages. I felt sorry for him because he was still mad about her and it wasn't going anywhere. Then he died in the car crash, and she got attacks of conscience. She obsessed about how he was killed. The whole remorse and guilt trip. The dead can be amazingly powerful, can't they?'

'They can. Especially if they die and leave unfinished business.'

'Too right. So, Kelly got all thoughtful and she decided she was going dry and that was it. She threw all the booze away, poured it down the sink. What a waste! I told her I didn't want to give up. When I brought more home, she said she had to end it. We still saw each other, but gradually . . . you know how it plays. She kicked booze and me.' He drank off the gin and poured another.

'Did Kelly ever mention any other relationships she'd had after she split from you?'

He shook his head. 'But then, she might have and I'd have forgotten. I'm not always paying attention or stuff slips away from me.' He made a fluttering movement with his fingers.

Swift was beginning to feel a little adrift among this accretion of memory loss. His own head was woolly, maybe from inhaling alcohol fumes. 'Was Kelly working as a gas fitter when you were together?'

'Not at first. She was at a small charity, admin of some kind. Yep, do-gooders.' He sounded relaxed, dreamy, his voice growing sluggish as the gin kicked in. 'We had this plan, Kelly and me, that we'd buy a camper van one day and just take off. Travel around. When we had the money. She bought me a toy one for my birthday, until we could get the real thing. Sometime never, as it turned out. It's in the cupboard.'

He struggled up and meandered to a corner cupboard where he rummaged around, bringing out a carrier bag containing the toy. He set it on the floor in front of Swift. It was blue and white with a small navy figure sitting behind the wheel. Waters crouched down and pressed a button on the top of the vehicle. A side panel opened, and the top lifted, exposing the blue and yellow interior. The back of the van was divided in two, one side with a kitchen, complete with sink, cooker, fridge, table and chairs and on the other side, a bathroom with shower and toilet.

'Look,' he said. 'You pull the backs of the two front seats down and beds unfold. Cosy or what?'

'It certainly is. All the home comforts.'

'Kelly and I used to play around with it, arranging it, planning where we'd go. I wanted to head to Cornwall first. Haven't been there since I was a kid. We reckoned we'd park by a remote little cove and just kick back.' He rummaged in the bag and took out several more little figures, arranging them around the table. Then he fell silent, rubbing the top of one thumb with the other.

'I can see you still miss her,' Swift said.

'Every day. All the time.' He nearly fell over as he got up. Swift put a hand out to steady him. 'I've still got my lovely bottles, anyway. Keep me company. Keep me warm. Stay around. Don't try and change me.'

'They can't cook you good breakfasts.'

Waters smiled sadly. 'No. You found the weak point in my argument. That means you have to go. I can't have intelligent people around me.'

Swift laughed. He couldn't help liking this sozzled wreck of a man. He stood. 'You don't remember Kelly ever falling out with anyone while you were together?'

'Kelly? No way. Apart from Neil, who drove her demented. My poor love. I do miss her. Horrible that shitty stuff's happened.'

'One last thing. Did you know that Kelly and Faith were making that trip to Ireland?'

He shook his head. 'No. Hadn't seen them for a while.'

As he left, Swift saw Waters wobbling forwards, shifting the toy figures in the camper van and rearranging the kitchen pans. He didn't doubt the man's sadness but he knew that it would fade quickly, numbed by the spirits lined up on the sideboard. He could see why Kelly had been fond of Sol, despite his grungy appearance and sozzled lifestyle. He was funny and self-aware.

Swift was glad to get out into the air. He took some deep breaths and rubbed his head. He sniffed his arm, sure that his shirt reeked of booze. His phone vibrated as he unlocked the car and he saw that he'd had a couple of emails. He'd sent a message to Orla, saying that he was going to help Faith and asking if she was aware of anyone else around Rossdown who knew that her sisters would be on the ferry that evening.

I'm glad that Faith's seen sense and she's talked to you. It gives me comfort that you're going to be around. It's hard for me to say who knew Kelly and Faith were going to be on that ferry. Anyone around here or even in Clifden might have got to know if I'd mentioned it. Surely, no one we know would have harmed them. Give Faith my love and please ask her to give me a ring. She did email me, but it would be good to hear her voice. God bless you for helping her.

The second email was from Fitz Blackmore.

Hi there Ron. Hope all OK with you and the lovely Nora. My birthday next Saturday, party at mine. Make sure you both come and bring expensive wine.

No one had ever called him Ron but there was no point in trying to dissuade the relentless force that was Blackmore from doing so. Swift had met him during his last case, the murder of a pilot called Greg Roscoe. Blackmore was a DI in Cornford, Hertfordshire and they'd struck up an unlikely friendship. Blackmore was provocative, cynical and abrasive, the kind of man Swift usually avoided. But he was also incisive, with a sharp wit and awareness of his brusque style. He was so macho and politically incorrect that Nora joked that he was in the closet and fancied Swift.

He started the car, slipping into the crawling south London traffic, hoping that Nora would be free to go to the party. Maybe they could relax and mend some fences.

CHAPTER 6

The day brought contact from Swift's two least favourite people. A letter from Camilla Finley arrived in the morning post, blue biro on lined paper torn from a pad. He scanned her cramped handwriting:

Hey Swift,

Hope you're not well. Any of your girlfriends been murdered recently, or any bodies been found in your house? Any sad teenagers tried to jump out of your window before doing a runner? I do hope so. Gosh, that makes strange reading! People might think you're tainted goods if they looked into you thoroughly.

Anyway, enough of the pleasantries. Oliver's been to see me a couple of times. Brought me some books and other stuff like posh chocolate. Such a nice, friendly chap. And he misses his dad so much and talks about him so fondly. You've probably heard by now that he's lodged an appeal about his dad's will. If you think I'm behind it, you're bang on. I find that one of the bonuses of prison is that I've got plenty of time to research and think these days. I'm really enjoying getting into the law and studying case histories. Fascinating stuff. I reckon I might even take a law degree and change career. Given what I've seen of lawyers in my present situation, I could do just as well and the money's eye-watering.

Still, enough of my future career prospects. M'lud, I refer you to "Jameson v Here to Care and others", judgement handed down in

February 2017. You can take it from there. Might give you pause for thought and maybe some sleepless nights. Hope so!

Don't take care.

I'll continue to mentor/advise Oliver and don't worry, I'll be in touch.

CF

Camilla's digging into his past had revealed some events that could certainly put off prospective clients if they didn't know the context. Her articles in the *Cornford Mail* and the spin she had put on the incidents she'd uncovered had nearly caused his previous clients to walk away. He'd noticed a decline in new business in the last months, and was hoping it was just a glitch and not related to Camilla's troublemaking. Havana Roscoe, the troubled young girl who had threatened suicide in Chand's flat, was still missing. Her misery was due to her grief about her murdered father and her mother's unkindness, but Camilla had implied that something had happened in Swift's house to cause the teenager's dramatic disappearance. Now she was sitting in her prison cell sharpening her poisoned arrows.

He opened his laptop and searched for the case she had cited. It concerned an adult, an only child who had contested her mother's will. She had been awarded some money as a result but was dissatisfied and appealed the outcome. After numerous court battles, the Supreme Court had finally ruled in the daughter's favour and awarded her a third of her mother's estate.

Swift threw Camilla's letter in a drawer. She had picked at the scar tissue of some of his most painful memories. He didn't want to let her get to him but she knew his vulnerabilities. A sudden gloom descended on him. He prowled around the living room, full of self-doubt. His skin felt as if it didn't fit. He stopped at a bookshelf and ran his fingers along the spines. He had helped people with his investigations but he'd damaged some as well. Today, he wasn't sure that the positives outweighed the negatives. He still felt deep pain about Kris Jelen, his partner who'd been strangled by a petty criminal engaged to harass him. She'd died because she'd become involved with him, and he'd found her lying lifeless on the floor of her living room. He'd never forget her parents' raw grief when they arrived from Poland to claim her body.

He rubbed his temples, attempting to banish dark thoughts. He just had to deal with Camilla's jibes. Things with Oliver had to run their course and while that was happening, she'd be there in the background like a low-grade fever. He'd never wanted any of Cedric's money anyway, and now he was tangled in this mess with the prospect of a prolonged court case.

He rang his solicitor, made an appointment, and then phoned London Harps, Kelly and Faith's camogie club. A woman with a Kerry accent answered, announcing herself as Una Bassek. He explained why he was ringing and that he was hoping to speak to people who knew the sisters.

'I've been here quite a while,' Una said. 'I've got to know them fairly well, I'd say. It's terrible about what happened. We were so shocked. Kelly was such a marvellous player and Faith is talented, too. She's phoned me just a couple of times since she came out of hospital, but she says she's not ready to play again just yet and I haven't seen her. I asked if I could visit but she refused. She sounded kind of distant and strained. We wanted to have a memorial match for Kelly, but Faith said she'd rather not be involved, she didn't feel well enough. So I respected her wishes and said we'd wait until she felt better. I've been worried about her. I'm glad you've phoned because I was about to call round to her home. She hasn't responded to a couple of messages.'

'I think she's been very tired. Trying to get back on her feet.'

'I'm sure. But, you know, there are things she could be involved in here even if she's not playing, and we'd love to have her help. We miss her and people have been asking after her. If you want to visit, it would be best to come and see us on Saturday morning. That's when we have a lot of members in. You'll ask Faith to phone or come by, won't you?'

He made an appointment and then phoned Faith to update her. She sounded more energetic, saying she'd just been to the gym and the session had gone well.

'I managed a full hour today, that's real progress. Concentrated on balance.'

'Good, well done.'

'Doesn't help the brain, though. I keep trying to fool myself that if I get my physical strength back, my brain will follow suit. As if.'

'You have to try.'

'Hmm. Have you talked to anyone?'

'Sarah, Sol and Una Bassek.'

'You didn't tell them I'm a halfwit now?'

'Faith, that's not true.'

'Wish I could agree with you. How's Sol?'

'Impressively drunk for early morning. We had a general chat. He told me he met Kelly at a rehab place.'

'That's right. Can't remember the name now.'

'Whiteleaf.'

'That's it. That didn't work out. It got messy.'

'Kelly was trying to sort her life out?'

'Yeah.' She sounded vague. 'I suppose. She tried, anyway. I remember she said she might have succeeded if she hadn't met up with Sol. But then she said maybe that was just her making her usual excuses.'

'Sol said she worked for a charity before she took up gas fitting.'

'That's right. She did that for about a year. Then she wanted to learn a trade.'

'Can you give me the name of that employer?'

'Not sure. I'll have a think. But, you know, it was a while ago.'

'Even so, best to cover all bases.'

'I suppose. How did Sol look?'

'As if he'd seen better days. He was very welcoming. Good company. He misses Kelly.'

'What about Sarah?'

'She sent you her best. She couldn't tell me anything in particular, but I have got a question for you. Both Sarah and Orla have said that Kelly never talked much about her life in London. Scant details, like in the postcards she sent Orla. I wondered why.'

'They said that?'

'Both of them.'

'Well . . .' Faith sounded fuddled again, her initial energy dissipated. 'Kelly knew she could trust me to keep shtum so she told me stuff. I suppose for a long time, she was ashamed of the drinking. She reckoned she was a disaster and so was her marriage. And all the stuff with Neil was so complicated. She could hardly introduce Sol to Orla or Sarah, given that he was a career drunk, and she was still married when she met him. She didn't want them judging her. Orla's always been organized and competent, with her life under tight control. And she's so inquisitive and keen on getting into your space given half a chance. She always made Kelly feel like a failure. Then Sarah's made a real success of her life, respected, in a good profession.' Her voice broke. 'Sorry, I'm doing this stupid bloody crying thing again. I hate it so much.'

'I didn't mean to upset you.'

'No, it's not you. It's my bashed-up brain and I can't control it.'

'Let's leave it there. I'm visiting London Harps on Saturday morning. Una Bassek said it would be good to see you. You could come with me.'

'Oh, I don't know. I'm not sure I can face it. I don't want people looking at me and talking behind my back.'

'People mean well, and Una seemed genuinely keen to see you. She said there are things you could do at the club besides playing. Might be a good idea, a way of staying involved.'

There was a silence. 'I would like to go, you know. Just not sure I've got the bottle. The club buzzes on Saturdays.'

'Maybe you could do with that buzz. You must miss it.'

'Get back on the horse?'

'If you like, yes. Better than being at home thinking negatively. Being on your own so much isn't good.'

'I suppose if you're there I might not feel so stupid.'

'I could meet you there.'

'All right. Thanks. You won't mention to anyone there that Kelly used to be a boozer, will you? None of them know and I want it to stay that way.'

'I understand.'

'You're okay. You're growing on me. At first I thought you were Orla's spy, her way of getting the lowdown on me.' She laughed harshly.

'You can relax on that score. See you Saturday.'

Swift hoped this might mean a step forward for Faith. He heard his inbox ping and saw that an email had arrived from Oliver Sheridan.

I expect you were hoping that I'd gone away. Shame, I haven't! I told you I was going to come after you and I am. Camilla Finley's been doing loads of research. She pointed me in the direction of some interesting case law and a better solicitor. I've been to see her in prison, and she's told me about how her mother was raped by that bastard Roscoe. She doesn't deserve to be in jail. She's suffered enough, and it's not as if she actually killed him. But you wouldn't care about that. You're just interested in being the hero, the golden boy who solves another case and succeeds. Doesn't matter what the cost is to other people. You'll have heard by now that I've lodged an appeal. You're going to pay for what you did to my poor dad and me.

Swift saved the email to a folder, as his solicitor had advised. He'd have preferred to delete it, but anything that highlighted Oliver's nastiness was grist to the mill. He pictured Camilla and Oliver getting cosy in the prison visiting room and working up a warm, righteous glow while trashing their common enemy.

He put his phone in his pocket and wandered through his galley kitchen into the small, rectangular garden. The day was blue and hazy, with high, drifting shreds of cloud. He could smell the Thames on the mild breeze, a dank, sedgy scent.

Seedlings had appeared on the sycamore tree, each with its two bright green wings. He hunkered down to where Cedric's ashes were buried under a tea rose. Swift's great-aunt Lily had planted the border of roses when she'd owned the house. He wasn't a great lover of roses himself, he found them showy and their perfume made him drowsy. He preferred delicate wild flowers. Celandine, red campion, wood anemone. Cedric had tended to the garden, so after his death, Swift had had to get some tips from websites on how to care for the plants. He had fed the roses in early April and now pale pink blooms were unfolding above the matt green leaves. He stroked the velvet petals.

'And so it goes on with Oliver, Cedric. Glad you're at rest, old friend, and don't know anything about all this bullshit. With any luck, I'll finally get some peace from your son before I shuffle off!'

* * *

The London Harps club was bustling on Saturday morning. It was housed in a single-storey sixties box of remarkable ugliness, but inside it was cheery, light and surging with energy. It echoed with women's voices while they sped around, calling, laughing, hair tied up in buns, bunches and ponytails. The club backed on to a field that was shared with a school, and Swift could see a camogie game in progress when he parked the car.

Faith was already there, drinking tea with Una Bassek in a small, pine-clad office filled with trophies, stacks of team uniforms and photos of games and players. She sat up straight in her chair, her hair woven in a thick plait and her expression intense. She was clearly trying to maintain focus and give an impression of fitness. Like a child keen to impress her teacher. Swift could see the effort it took for her to sit still and his heart went out to her. She was wearing a dark green tracksuit and a camogie stick lay across her lap. Una offered him tea from a brown earthenware pot and nudged a plate of biscuits towards him.

'I saw Faith hovering outside so I asked her in. I was just telling her how much we've missed her. We have a full list of games coming up for the summer, so it's busy days here.' Una had a beaming smile and large square hands. Her hair was in a bushy afro, held back by a fabric band in the yellow and green team colours.

'That's Una up there,' Faith told him. 'She captained the team that won the 2006 London championships.'

'I was a bit fitter then,' Una said, crunching on a biscuit. 'Are you sporty, Mr Swift? You look as if you might be.'

'Rowing's my thing. I take my boat on the Thames as often as I can.'

'That would keep you fit all right. Faith tells me you're related?'

'That's right.'

'Funny in a way, that we've never met before,' Faith said.

'That's the way it works with emigration,' Una said sagely. 'I have relatives in Cameroon I've never met and I'm probably not likely to. So, you're helping Faith try to find out who's responsible for what happened to her and Kelly?'

Swift waited for Faith to reply, but she was staring wistfully out of the window at the game and running her fingers up and down the edge of her camogie stick. Una cleared her throat.

'Anyway, Faith, you and Mr Swift are working together?'

Faith twitched, laughed her disconnected laugh and patted her stick. 'That's right. Trying to find out who attacked me, and what happened to Kelly. I'm rootling around in the grey matter. I'm feeling stronger every day now. I'm sure I'll be playing again in no time, you know. The demon Black back in the game.' She shifted to the edge of her seat and punched the air with her right fist.

'I'm sure,' Una said. 'That'll put the fear of God in the opposition when they hear!' She glanced quickly at Swift, and then turned again to Faith. 'As I said when you arrived, there's a few new juniors starting with us today, and it would be a great help if you could take them through the rules of the game. They're waiting in the changing room for now, watching a video about famous players. I'd say they'll be just about finished if you want to chat to them.'

'Sure!' Faith said too forcefully. 'How many?'

'Just the four. A nice small group to get started on.'

Faith stood. She hesitated, twirling her stick and then headed out. She knocked against the door as she exited and put a hand out to steady herself.

Swift waited until she'd gone. 'Do you think she'll play again?'

Una rubbed her face with both hands. Now that Faith had left the room, she could show her shock. She stared at him. 'From what I hear and see today, it's unlikely. I'd no idea that she had been affected so badly. It's as if it's Faith but another, slower version of her. A sort of faded version. I can tell you, seeing her has knocked me back. I hope I didn't show it.'

'You handled the situation very well.'

'Oh, I hope so. I wouldn't want to hurt her feelings for the world, and she must be so aware of people's reactions. Now I understand why she's been hiding herself away. Such an awful state of affairs. We'd need a medical certificate before we could allow her back on the field. It's a fast and furious game, the fastest on grass. You need excellent coordination and reactions and ball control is crucial. Never say never and all that, but . . .'

'It's sad because it looks as if she was a good player.'

'Oh yes, and so dedicated. She didn't have Kelly's flair and kiss of genius, but she never missed a training session or a game. We'll support her all the way. We always look after our own. If she can't play again, there are other roles in the club, with coaching and fundraising. I know that won't be the same for her, but we want to keep her involved here.'

'Can you tell me about Kelly — did she have lots of friends in the club?'

Una rubbed her chin in a way that made him think he knew what the answer would be. 'She was always popular and sociable, good at geeing other players up and raising morale. And of course, highly respected for her skills. But I wouldn't say she had close personal friends. Most of the women here chat about themselves, so you get a picture of their families and such. But not Kelly. The only things I found out about her in the time she was a member were her job, and that she came from Connemara and had family there. She'd talk about Faith and she was thrilled when Faith decided to make the move to London. I always thought there was a sadness to Kelly, some burden she carried inside. It's hard to put a finger on. Kate Pearce knew her best. She'll be in from training in a minute. I told her you'd be here and she said she'd be happy to talk to you.'

'Kelly never fell out with anyone?'

'God, no! What makes you ask that?'

'Just part of weaving things together. Someone did attack Faith on the ship and push Kelly overboard.'

She didn't comment but looked saddened. She refolded a club T-shirt, smoothing the edges. 'Isn't it terrible, the things that happen to people? I can hardly believe how this has impacted on Faith. Surely the police must have some idea what happened?'

'It seems not. Do you know if Kelly or Faith had given anyone here their travel details?'

'I've no idea. They always told me any dates they'd be away, of course, so we'd know their match availability. Faith worked some weekends because of the bridesmaid thing. Kelly did occasionally if she needed to finish a job.' She gestured at a year planner on the wall, covered in multicoloured writing. 'I record all the information up there — people, stock deliveries, matches, catering, social events — so it's all available at a glance. I used to have it on a spreadsheet, but then the computer crashed one day and I didn't know if I was coming or going.' Una leaned forward, lowering her voice. 'I don't know how Faith is set financially, and I don't like to ask her. I know she can't work at the moment. We used to love listening to her stories about the weddings she went to — the demanding brides and the tricky mothers, not to mention the insults that got traded once the drink was flowing. We have a small hardship fund here in the club that Faith could access. You might mention it to her.'

'I'll see. We've only just met and I don't want to offend her. Kind of you to offer though.'

'Not at all. She's given so much to the club, as did Kelly. Kelly fitted a new central heating system at cut price, so we'd like to help in any way we can.' She looked up and smiled. 'I can see Kate coming now. You can chat in here if you like. I have to check some catering arrangements.'

Swift looked at the year planner and the different colour inks for the various activities. Then he stood at the window and watched the game while he waited for Kate. He could see what Una meant about it being fast. The players zipped around the field, carrying the ball at times, then whacking it with speed and precision. There were loud cheers as a player sent the ball in a long arcing loop over the crossbar. There was plenty of physical contact, shoving, shouldering and the occasional pile-up. Groans and laughter echoed in equal measure. He understood why helmets had been introduced.

When Kate breezed in, she brought an aroma of fresh sweat and grass. She had a towel around her shoulders and the healthy flush of exertion.

'I haven't showered because I have a game in the next half hour, so forgive the pong,' she said, not sounding at all apologetic. 'I haven't seen Faith yet, is she with the juniors?'

'Yes, taking them through the rules of the game. Thanks for making time to see me.' He explained about his investigation.

Kate had an open, kindly expression but she frowned as she listened. 'I've been feeling a bit put out, you know. Faith hasn't been in touch since the attack. I didn't even know they were going to Ireland, and I had no idea Kelly had drowned until Una told me. It was an awful shock. I've left messages since, but Faith didn't reply.'

'I think she's embarrassed about the impact the attack has had on her. I'd guess she hasn't been seeing people much.'

'Oh, okay. I get that, I suppose.' She rubbed her neck with her towel.

'You're friends with Faith?'

'Yes, but I knew Kelly better. We started in the team around the same time. She was a skilled player compared to me, and she was always really supportive, helped me out a lot. We'd go for lunch after a match, that kind of thing. She was really happy that Faith was moving here. Kelly said it would do her good to get out of the backwater she was living in and away from their bossy older sister. Then when Faith joined the club, she'd come for lunch with us.' She looked around. 'It feels weird to be talking about her like this when she's in the building.'

He thought it seemed weird himself, but then Faith's life had taken a very strange turn. 'I understand, but Faith has given me permission to talk to the people who know her and Kelly. I get the impression that Kelly and Faith were close.'

'Oh yes. Best friends as well as sisters. I think that's rare. Sisters often fall out. I know I do with mine. You know too much about each other, all the dirty secrets!' She laughed and then covered her mouth, as if remembering that one of the sisters was dead.

'Did you ever meet any of Kelly's other friends, any partners?'

'No. I only ever saw her around here. Camogie-based friendship, you know. She never talked about anyone. Said she'd had a crap marriage and it had put her off men. She talked about her work and camogie. She lived and breathed the game. She travelled to watch matches all over the country and in Europe. She'd talked about maybe heading for America sometime. Camogie's been growing in popularity there. We hosted a team from Boston a while back.'

'So she never told you about any problems or worries she had?'

'No, but she wasn't the kind who confided in other people. She was always good company and generous. Very sociable and funny but you never really got past the outer skin. I always thought that there was a shy person hiding behind the gregarious front. There was one time when she talked about a charity she'd worked at. Something had gone wrong. I think that bothered her.'

'What was that about?'

'I don't really know. It happened before I met her. She didn't give details. We were talking about jobs. I work in HR for a major bank and I was telling her about a tribunal I'd had to attend because we'd suspended someone. It was doing my head in so much, my game was off. Kelly told me she'd once had some trouble at work, and she'd decided to leave and train as a gas engineer. Is Faith back at work yet? I always thought it was great what she did, a pretend bridesmaid, getting paid to have her hair styled and wear gorgeous dresses.'

'No, not yet. She needs more recovery time.'

'I'd like to see her before I start my match. I'm not sure I can help you with anything else.'

He didn't think so either. People at the club had known only one version of Kelly, a newly minted one. She'd had to keep herself under wraps in order to conceal her previous drinking habit. Maybe she'd kept Faith so close and loyal because her sister knew all about Kelly mark one. He opened the office window and continued to watch the match until Faith reappeared, looking tired but more at ease.

'How did that go?' he asked.

'Okay. Yes, okay. And it was good to see Una and Kate again. I said I'd come back next Saturday.'

'That's good. I wondered if you'd like lunch.'

She cradled her camogie stick. 'Okay, but not here. I'm not ready for any more people today.' Her eyes brimmed and she rubbed at them, swallowing. She seemed very young. And, it seemed, very alone. A great deal had happened to her in her twenty-four years and he thought that it had forced her into a protective shell.

He drove her to the Silver Mermaid, his local pub in Hammersmith. She was silent on the journey. When he glanced at her, her eyes were closed with pale mauve rings of exhaustion in the hollows beneath. Her hair curled damply on her forehead. The pub was busy, but they found a table tucked in a corner. They ordered food, and he sipped a beer while Faith drank bitter lemon.

'Sol rang me yesterday, told me you'd been round and he'd been thinking about me,' she said. 'Wanted to know how I was doing. It was nice to hear his voice. We talked for a while about Kelly. I'm going round to see him this week. I've been feeling guilty because I know Kelly would have kept on visiting him, even though he wasn't always keen on seeing her.'

'I could tell how much he loved her.'

'Yeah. I know.'

'I realize that this morning wasn't easy for you, but I think you did the right thing,' he said.

She nodded. 'Hmm. I doubt I'd have done it if you hadn't encouraged me. I think I did okay with the juniors. They seemed to follow what I said. Funny, isn't it? I can remember all the rules of camogie but if I hadn't written a note about today, I might have forgotten to come.' She smoothed her plait between her fingers, twisting the end. 'When I'm in camogie world, I feel like a whole person. As if I'm where I'm supposed to be.'

'I get it. That's how I feel when I'm in my boat.'

She nodded. 'But what if I never play again? What will happen to me then?' Tears slipped down her cheeks and pooled in the hollow of her neck.

He was lost for words. He reached out and held her hand, squeezing it.

She shook her head. 'You're a decent man, Ty. And fit. How come you're not married?'

'I was almost, once. Then she left me.' He told her about Ruth and Branna. 'My daughter was born with significant hearing loss, so Ruth and I work together to do our best for her.'

'We'll have to get Branna playing camogie. It's a great confidence builder and it's never too early to start.' She gave her raucous laugh and several people looked across. 'The game's been promoted recently as "chicks with sticks". You can get her a T-shirt with the slogan.'

He liked the fact that Faith hadn't offered sympathy, even if the thought of Branna wielding a camogie stick was a tad alarming. 'That's an idea. Although I have to say, confidence is one thing Branna doesn't lack. I worried about how she'd manage socially, but so far, nothing seems to deter her.'

'Sounds like I could learn a lesson or two from her.'

'You're not doing so badly. That wasn't easy, walking back in there this morning.' He decided to ask her the question which had been bothering him since they had left the club. 'Kate Pearce told me that Kelly had had some trouble at the charity she worked at. Do you remember what that was about?'

She sat back in her chair and pressed her fingers to her temples. 'The charity was called Live . . . hold on . . . Live Local. Sorry, I was supposed to give you that info but I forgot. It's not as if I've anything else to do, but the hours vanish and I can't think where they've gone.' She yawned, her body slumping. 'It was all about promoting regeneration in poor city areas. Kelly liked it there.'

'What was her role?'

'Admin stuff — letters, setting up meetings, coordinating diaries. I'm not sure why she left. Something about arguing with the manager. Sorry, my brain's such a sieve. If we are our memories, what does that make me? Some kind of half-filled vacancy. This therapist I saw last week told me that brain cells don't regenerate when they're destroyed. That was the bad news.'

'Was there good news?'

'Not sure you could call it that. She said that the brain has flexibility and can sometimes reorganize to an extent. It's called something like . . . hold on, I wrote it down 'cos I knew I'd forget.' She took her phone from her bag and checked it. 'That's it, brain "plasticity". I might regain some lost function and memory. But of course, that comes with the rider that every brain injury is unique, so there's no template. It's all unpredictable. It'll be months before the picture is clearer, and she advised that I wait for a year before making any important decisions about the future. I definitely can't work for another year. No more manicures and posh dresses for a while. If ever.'

'Do you have a programme for therapy?'

She had become restless again, moving in her chair and rubbing the tabletop. 'Hmm. Baby steps. Being active is important, so I'm trying to stay on top of that. Some days it's hard to get out of bed, though. Can't get motivated and the blues kick in. Malika, the therapist, says to do crosswords, puzzles, word games, all that kind of stuff. Make a schedule for the day and stick to it.' She yawned and slumped. 'All good advice, but some days I don't get up until the afternoon.'

He thought that she shouldn't be on her own, that she needed people around her to gee her up and distract her, give her things to do. Maybe she'd have been better staying with Orla, no matter how much her sister annoyed her. She had no mother to turn to.

'I heard about how your mother died,' he said. 'That was hard for you. My mum died of cancer when I was fifteen so I know a bit about it.'

'Hmm. It was tough all right. We all deal with things like that in different ways. I climbed into a shell, Orla became a sergeant major and Kelly started the slide into booze world. She was bright, you know, even if she wasn't academic. Reckon she could have gone to college, got a degree. There are camogie scholarships, and her teachers wanted her to apply for one. They'd discussed that route with her and Mum. But then Mum was killed and she lost the plot.'

He savoured his beer, thinking. 'The cousin I mentioned to you lives in London, so you know, she's also another distant relative of yours. Her name's Mary Adair. She's a great woman. Maybe you'd like to meet her sometime?'

'Maybe. But not just yet. When I've made more progress.'

The drag was back in her voice, and he saw that her eyes had become glazed, so he tapped her hand. 'Food's coming this way. Let's eat before you topple over, and then I'll drive you home.'

She ate her roast chicken slowly, picking at vegetables, disinterested. Her face looked thinner than the first time they'd met, and he wondered if she was forgetting to eat or couldn't be bothered. She spoke so quietly, he had to lean forward to catch her words.

'Sometimes I just want my mum. Pathetic, isn't it?'

He knew how she felt.

CHAPTER 7

He'd built himself up to Nora storming off and him having to turn up solo at Blackmore's party. But she seemed to have taken his comments about Branna remarkably calmly. That was the thing about her — he never knew which way she might blow. It was like being in his boat and wondering if the wind would veer. He'd suggested a walk at Cornford Marina before heading to the party nearby. It was a still, mild evening as they idled by the river, watching a family of swans. A woman sat on the deck of a houseboat, feet up, knitting with two balls of wool.

'I'd never have the patience for that,' Nora said. 'My sister tried to teach me once, but I got in a terrible tangle. No matter how hard I concentrated, I never had the same number of stitches at the end of the next row.'

'You mean you dropped them?'

'No, funnily enough, I'd always add extra ones and I could never work out how I'd done it. So I had strangely expanding garments.' She laughed at the memory. 'Is Branna better now?'

'She's fine, completely recovered. I saw her yesterday and she was back on form. I had to tell you what Ruth said because she was cross and upset about what Branna told her.'

'Hmm. Snitched on by a three-year-old.' She stopped on the path and looked at him with a preoccupied gaze. He knew that look. It meant that she was deep into an investigation and finding it hard to switch off. 'I'm not sure what you want me to say, Ty. I'm sorry that Branna got sick. That was rotten for her. But I didn't cause her ear infection.'

'I suppose I'd like you to say that you understand. That you'll try to respond to Branna without getting cross with her and raising your voice.'

'Listen, there was always someone sounding off in my house when I was growing up. That's what families are like. Doors slamming, name-calling, arguments. We were always thumping each other. If social services had seen the bruises, we'd all have been in care. My parents used to yell at us when they got cross, especially my mam. She was moody, always up and down and she'd turn on you before you knew what was happening. She'd get fierce snappy and holler the house down. Sometimes I got a clip round the ear. Didn't do me any harm.'

'If you say so. But that was your family. Families differ and their rules and customs differ.' Although he thought that her description of her childhood explained a lot about Nora. But no way was he going to open that Pandora's box.

'Now you sound like Ruth, coming out with the old psychological angle.'

'They're my thoughts, not Ruth's.'

'I bet she'd echo them, though.' Nora gestured at a bench. 'I have to sit down. I've grit in my shoe.'

They sat and she eased her right shoe off and shook it out. She was looking lovely in the rose light of the evening sun, her grey-green eyes shining. Nora didn't really do dressing up but her black jeans and mustard velvet shirt with black buttons suited her.

'You know, Ty, you were an only child. It was all very civilized and quiet in your house. From what you've told me about it, I'd have died of boredom. I think it gave you strange ideas about family life always being mannerly and tranquil.

I'm not claiming that I never get impatient, but there's nothing intrinsically wrong in getting cross with a kid now and then. It helps them understand that the grown-up world is tricky and bloody tiring.'

'I know, but . . .'

'And maybe Branna was starting to feel unwell and mistook my mood. I mean, she can add a touch of drama herself to things. I know she's the apple of your eye and most of the time she's a poppet, but she can lay it on thick.'

'I'm not saying Branna's an angel but she is only three and she asked me if you liked her. That indicates that she's thinking about it. Anxious about it.'

'Look, next time I see her I'll make a fuss of her, buy her some sweets — that milk chocolate she likes. That'll sort it.'

He took a breath. This was going nowhere and he could see that Nora was never going to be on his wavelength. He held back from telling her that Ruth had threatened not to let her see Branna. Partly because he worried that Nora wouldn't much mind.

'Shall we leave it there?' he said.

'Sure. Storm in a teacup. It'll blow over, me and Branna can share a bar of chocolate, and Ruth will have something better to fret about.' She leaned forward and kissed him, running a hand through his curls.

'Don't,' he said. 'I spent hours styling my hair and you'll spoil the look.'

She chuckled. 'You're looking very handsome in yourself tonight. I'm glad you're over that parasite. You were far too pale and haunted-looking. You looked like a man who'd just come from a funeral. Come on, let's be party animals. I'm dying to see what Fitz's friends are like. I'm picturing glamorous women in dresses and stilettos and predatory men.'

Blackmore's house was heaving. For a man with such a blunt, pugnacious manner, his modern home was tastefully furnished and full of smart gadgets. He opened the door waving a champagne flute. He looked casual in a close-fitting grey linen suit and dark grey T-shirt. He kissed Nora's cheek, told her he'd never seen a more delightful advertisement for mustard and clapped Swift on the arm.

'Glad to see you've put a bit of weight back on, Ron. Was worried you were fading away. Come and get introduced. My friends are mainly cops but there's a smattering of rowers and some skiers.'

Blackmore had hired two waiters for the evening who circulated among the guests, offering savoury snacks and refilling glasses. Swift and Nora were staying the night in the spare room, so Swift helped himself to the flowing wine while he chatted to an earnest man about rowing in the Wye valley. Looking around, he saw that Nora had been right about the women guests, more or less. There weren't many dresses, but they looked groomed and styled. The men were equally smart and glossy. There'd been a sea change in the police since his days in the Met, when a do like this would have involved paunchy, drunken men in ill-fitting, tired suits and women with glazed expressions, wearing too much make-up and looking as if they'd rather be anywhere else.

Blackmore drifted towards him with his arm around a dark-haired, slender woman in blue silk. He introduced her as Carly, adding that she was a terrific skier. Swift found himself distracted by the fullness of her Botox-filled lips. They dominated her small face and were painted deep purple. She resembled a cartoon character. Blackmore left them together, and they spoke about ski slopes for a while. Swift had only been skiing once, so his knowledge was limited. Carly spoke animatedly about snow conditions, hotels and ski runs while his mind drifted to Faith and Kelly's social media.

Faith had given him access to their accounts, and he could find nothing out of the ordinary or worrying in hers. He'd trawled through Kelly's emails that morning, spending several hours reading and sifting. Kelly's inbox and sent folders had messages concerning camogie training and games and queries about jobs. There was the odd one from Orla, about holiday arrangements, saying things like *long time no hear* and passing on bits of news from Rossdown. There was one other folder named *JOBS*, containing emails with quotes for work, dates and arrangements, and others with invoices for completed work attached. Just one email in that folder caught his eye. It was dated September 2016 and when he'd read it, he forwarded it to himself.

From jsheppard16@mercury.com

To dwyerkp@sayitnow.com

22 September. 10.05 p.m.

Dear Ms Dwyer,

I accept that you have rectified the problem with the boiler and that you seem to have made a genuine mistake. You're bloody lucky that I haven't reported you, or gone to the police about your serious error. You have my daughter to thank for that. She is kind-hearted and persuaded me that I should give you the benefit of the doubt. She told me that you offered to return some of your fee, but that's not necessary. I'd never employ you again and hope you've learned a lesson. You're lucky to have a job still.

Jon Sheppard

He tuned back in to Carly, realizing that she'd stopped speaking and was looking at him expectantly.

'Sorry? It's noisy in here.'

'So which is your favourite resort?' She raised her voice, running her tongue along her lips.

'I liked Courchevel.'

'Really? Give me Chamonix any time. That's where I met Fitz back in January.' She moved closer. Her scent was slightly peppery and pungent, and he breathed through his mouth, hoping to avoid a fit of sneezes. 'Do you know him well?'

'Not that well. We've worked together and socialized a bit. I've been here once before.'

She glanced quickly across the room to where Blackmore was chatting. 'Do you think he's a keeper?'

There was a look in her eyes that dismayed him. An anxious look, seeking reassurance. 'I've no idea. You're a better judge of that than me.'

She moved even closer. 'But as a man, you must have some instinct about it. You've talked to him and been in his company. What would you guess?'

He took a deep draught of wine. Well, she was keen for him to answer and he thought she didn't deserve the inevitable bumpy ride that Blackmore would give her. 'Okay, Carly, if you want my honest opinion—'

'I do, yes.'

'From the things I've heard Fitz say, I'd guess not. Not yet, anyway.'

'Oh.' She pressed her lips into a pout and turned away.

The stirring of the air caused an extra waft of scent, and he sneezed loudly several times. He stepped through the open patio door into the empty garden. The last time he'd been at the house, Blackmore had offered him a bed for the night because of heavy snowfall, and the garden had been in darkness or whited out. He saw now that it was oblong and fully decked with half a dozen stone urns containing low-maintenance bamboo and yuccas. He blew his nose and saw Blackmore weaving towards him in the dusk.

'Ron, mate! What you doing loitering out here on your own? Hope you're not spreading cold germs around my guests!'

'Allergy. Carly's perfume.'

'Got that close to her, did you? Poaching on my turf?' Blackmore was very drunk now, his eyes glinting, head up. He resembled a lean grey wolf.

'The other way round. She got a bit close to me.'

'You accusing my girlfriend of coming on to you?' Blackmore shrugged his jacket back and made a feint with his right fist. He was grinning lazily but there was an edge to his voice.

'Hardly.'

'What, you saying now that she's not attractive enough?' He made the feint move again, now on the balls of his feet.

'Cut it out, Fitz. You're boring me. Carly was quizzing me.'

'Oh yeah? About what? I know understated, good-looking blokes like you. You draw women in with your progressive views and listening ears. Touchy-feely crap.' He adopted a falsetto. 'I'm what a feminist looks like. I'm with you in the fight against the patriarchy.'

'Careful, Fitz. You're revealing the dinosaur skin underneath the elegant suit.'

Blackmore made another one-two feint, and the momentum propelled him against the fence. He banged his elbow and swore.

Swift laughed. 'Own goal. You needn't worry. It was all about you. I wasn't in the frame. She asked me if I think you're a keeper.'

That stopped him in his tracks. He groaned and leaned against the fence. 'That's it, then. Despite her wondrous charms — and they're many — she'll have to go. Once women start on that jag, there's no peace. It all heads downhill.'

'Like a ski run.'

'Nice one. I've missed you, Ron. You're as dry as an extra dry martini. So where's the lovely Nora? Why aren't you two smooching out here?'

'Last time I saw her, she was talking to your sergeant.'

'He bores for England, that one. Still, I'm flamboyant enough for both of us. You two getting along okay? The river of love flowing smoothly?'

The night Swift had stayed, he'd had a lot to drink, and he'd told Blackmore some of his and Nora's difficulties. He'd regretted it afterwards, knowing how gossip travelled in the police, even between different forces.

'We're okay,' he lied. 'We had a holiday in Ireland recently.'

Blackmore stepped closer. His breath was laden with oaky wine but Swift knew how astute he was, even when inebriated. 'Hmm. Bet hot-tempered Nora gives you a run for your money, keeps you on your toes. Couples not spending any time together at parties. Not a good sign. Visual evidence of detachment.'

'You should get back to Carly, then.'

Swift made for the door. Blackmore followed, threw an arm around his neck and whispered.

'So what did you reply to Carly's question?'

Swift looked him in the eye and adopted an innocent expression. 'I said I'd guess not.'

Blackmore laughed loudly and placed a smacking kiss on his forehead. 'Good man, Ron! Ten out of ten!'

Later in Blackmore's spare bedroom, Nora snuggled up to him. 'I saw Fitz kissing you. Was he proposing? Am I in the way?'

'I turned him down for tonight. Said I didn't want to hurt your feelings.'

She jabbed him in the ribs, slurring her words. 'Maybe I should try Botox. Did you see Carly's lips? Fierce plumped up. I was wondering if they might explode. She's keen on Fitz. Kept seeking him out and draping herself around him.'

'I think she's doomed to disappointment with him.'

'Hmm. Too keen. Off-putting to a bloke like that. The best way to deal with the likes of him is to make yourself unavailable. Keep him interested and hungry. It's all about the chase with Fitz.'

'You seem to know a lot about it.'

'I've read the mags, Ron.'

'Don't talk so loud. How can I have a hangover before it's morning?'

'It's the drink coming round on trays. Hard to keep count.'

At three in the morning, they were both woken by enthusiastic noises from Blackmore's room.

'I don't think he's disappointing her tonight.' Nora buried her head under a pillow.

The noises had abated and Swift had just drifted back to sleep when his phone pinged. A message from Faith:

I've just remembered that Kelly did see someone she recognized on the ferry. But I can't remember who. There's a shape. It was in the café. Can you ring me tomorrow?

* * *

When he woke in the morning, Nora was already up and about. He could hear her downstairs, talking to Fitz and laughing. There was a rattle of crockery, the delicious aroma of coffee and croissants. His head was fuzzy. He sat up in bed, drank a bottle of water and rang Faith. She picked up immediately.

'I'm sorry about the time I texted. Did I wake you?'

'Yes, but it doesn't matter. Tell me exactly what you remembered.'

She sighed. 'That's the trouble. It was like a half-memory. I woke up and couldn't get back to sleep. Then from nowhere, I had a flashback to the ferry. We were queueing at the till in the café, and Kelly saw someone. She knew them from somewhere. That's all I can say.'

'Man or woman?'

'I'm not sure. Sorry, I just don't know. I felt so excited that I'd had that memory, but it's not much, is it?'

'No, but it's something and more might follow. Do you think Kelly spoke to the person?'

'I don't think so.'

'Okay. Just let it simmer.'

'I finished a couple of crosswords last night. First time I've been able to concentrate that long.'

'That mental exercise and recall might have stimulated your memory. You never know.'

'I didn't think of that. I'm going to the gym soon. Doing my best.'

'You're doing fine. Listen, I need to tell you something that might worry you. Kelly might never have told you about the incident.'

'Hmm?'

'I looked through her emails yesterday and found one about a job she did for a Jon Sheppard some time around September 2016. It reads as if there was a problem with a boiler she installed. She'd made a mistake, and she had to rectify it. Sheppard wasn't happy.'

'Oh, right. It doesn't ring any bells. I was still living in Rossdown then.'

'I haven't had a chance to crosscheck the email with any others with the same name. The client said his daughter had persuaded him not to report Kelly.'

'I don't think Kelly ever mentioned it, but I can't be sure.' Her voice became quieter, trailing over the words as if she was picking her way slowly along a stony path. 'She was still drinking then, a complete shambles. I used to . . . used to worry in case she ever made a mistake at work. I mean, you can't mess around with gas. She once told me that she'd had her last drink a couple of months after Neil died. A gin and tonic. You see, I can remember that exactly. She rang me that night to tell me. I was so delighted. She said she'd never forget the taste of that final drink. When she finished it, she poured the rest of the bottle away, picked up her camogie stick and went for a practice in the park. She was so unfit and exhausted after ten minutes, but she built up every day for three months and then she contacted London Harps . . .' She seemed to be fading away in that distracted way she had, then rallied. 'So, you say this guy Sheppard was angry with Kelly?'

'Yes. I'll send you the email. Have a look at it. But go to the gym first. It's not urgent.'

'Okay.' She sounded as if she was crying now. 'You know, Ty, this is the kind of thing that really worries me. Stuff that's happened or things Kelly did when she was still drinking heavily. They're out there and I don't know about them, or I can't remember. And someone came at us out of the dark and murdered Kelly and they're still out there, too.'

'I know this is hard. Sarah Ennis said that Kelly had had the same worries about things that might come back and bite her from her drinking days.'

'Did she? I expect Kelly talked to me about that, too, but if so, it's gone through the holes in the sieve that used to be my brain.'

'I won't advise you not to worry because that's pointless. But remember I'm here to help. Take care of your security. Have you had your door fixed?'

'I told the maintenance guy. He said he'll do it next week.'

'Good. Talk again soon. Okay?'

'Hmm. Okay. Thanks.'

He stretched and his neck clicked. That had been difficult. He'd heard Faith's voice sink into despondency. Any effort at reassurance sounded phony.

There was loud laughter downstairs, as if the party was continuing. He needed a lot of coffee and a couple of aspirin.

* * *

Dermot Dwyer, Neil's brother, lived in a neat ground-floor studio flat in Orpington, opposite a grand red brick Methodist church. His bed folded out from the wall and was tidy, with an old-fashioned tartan eiderdown. A large pinboard hung on the wall behind the bed. It was covered with army regimental and cap badges and other military insignia.

Swift took one of a pair of dining chairs while Dwyer sat on the bed. He was medium height and skinny, with bloodshot eyes and the waxy skin of the very ill. His misshapen nose looked as if it had been broken several times. He was wearing a short-sleeved shirt and had a tattoo on each forearm. One was of two crossed swords, the other a pair of khaki army boots.

'D'you want a brew? Be warned, there's cheapo teabags and coffee from Costcutter. Or have you brought your own? A lot of people seem to be doing that these days. This bloke comes now and again from army welfare and he's got peppermint teabags in his pocket. Says they're good for digestion. I threaten I'll charge him for the hot water.'

'I'm fine, thanks. I appreciate your time. Can you tell me what you know about Kelly and her sister Faith?'

'I'm not sure the journey's been worth your while. I can't tell you much because I hardly knew either of them.'

'Anything you can tell me might be helpful.'

Dwyer pulled his feet up and sat cross-legged on the bed. Two of the nails on his right hand were blackened, as if he had injured his fingers. 'What I knew of Kelly I didn't like. Beautiful-looking girl and bubbly, outgoing but I dunno . . . seemed sort of unstable to me. Like she had no off switch. Lots of nervous energy. There was a bloke like that in my squad once and I never trusted him to have my back, which isn't reassuring when you're down an alley in Helmand. I always thought Kelly was bad for Neil. He needed a woman who could ground him, help him sort himself out, face his alcoholism. Not one who was trying to drink Ireland dry with him.'

'Were you close to your brother?'

'Not close, no. We spent a lot of time apart. But we kept in touch. He went off to live in Ireland with our gran when he was eight and I stayed with Dad. I joined the army after school and I was abroad a lot. If I hadn't been away with my regiment in Afghanistan, I might have tried to persuade him not to marry Kelly, but it was all a done deal by the time I got wind of it.'

The army years accounted for the orderliness and sparseness of the flat, the exactness of the ironed creases in his jeans.

'When did you meet Kelly?'

'First time was at the wedding. Neil asked me to be best man. As I said, she was lovely-looking so I got why Neil fell for her. But there was definitely something a bit frantic about her. They were both pretty much off their faces and falling around by the time they'd had the first dance. They were propping each other up. It was a fiasco when they cut the cake. It nearly ended up on the floor – I just caught it as it was sliding off the table. Embarrassing for the guests. Our gran was disgusted because the priest was there, and she didn't know where to look. She left early. I remember thinking then that it wouldn't last. Kelly had an older sister who looked as if she was attending a wake rather than a wedding. I vaguely remember Faith. Pretty-looking girl, nice smile.'

'Did you see much of Neil and Kelly when they were married?'

'Nah. I was away most of the time, tours of duty. I visited them once in Rossdown about a year or so after they married and they were shouting the house down. They were living with my gran and it really got to her. She said they were drinking every night and picking fights over the smallest things. I went out with them for dinner one evening and it was bloody awful. One minute they were all loved up and kissing, next thing a row would kick off from nowhere and glasses would go flying. I'd rather have been out on patrol.'

'Sounds like they were very hard work to be around.'

'You can say that again. Next thing I heard, Kelly had legged it to London. Neil emailed me, really cut up, but I was glad in a way. I thought it meant there'd be a divorce, and maybe Neil could sort himself out. Meet a woman who really cared about him. But of course, the marriage lingered on long distance. Then I got sick in Afghanistan and invalided out and, well . . .' He sounded breathless and lowered his head.

Someone was playing an organ in the Methodist church, a complex, soothing harmony. Swift listened, giving Dwyer time. Buses ran along the street outside and the air was smoky and bitter. The fumes wouldn't be doing Dwyer's health any good, but otherwise it wasn't a bad place to live, with the organ pipes sounding their rich melody across the road.

'I'm sorry your health has suffered,' Swift said.

'Yeah. Nothing as dramatic or gallant as being blown up or wounded in action. I caught Q fever. Don't recommend it.'

'I've not heard of it.'

'No, well, there's not much of it about here. It's a bacterial infection. Humans can pick it up where there are infected animals. I must have breathed it in from dust. Probably from goats, the bloody things were everywhere out there. Or maybe it was the Taliban's secret weapon. Who knows? It was like flu to start with and then it got severe and recurrent, high temperatures and shivers. I was in hospital for months.

Damaged my heart in the end.' He reached for a photo and handed it to Swift. 'That's me when I was fitter.'

He was in his uniform and beret, muscly, strong-looking, a stark contrast to the figure sitting on the bed. He and Faith had something in common, both having been brought down by random events. Together, Faith, Sol and Dwyer resembled a trio of patients from a hospital ward, the kind of sickly people you saw in sepia photos from sanatoriums.

'That's rough.'

'Not exactly being covered in glory and medals, is it? You join up and you know you might get shot or blown up. You don't expect goat fever. Not much to brag about in the pub. I suppose there's even a funny side to it although I can't see it myself. Just when I thought I might be over the worst of it, the medics told me my heart had been affected and I had to have a stent.' He sat back against a pillow, pulling it up behind his shoulders.

'Did you ever see Kelly in London?'

'No. I didn't seek out her company. Neil was so upset about her leaving and always hoped she'd go back to him. You don't want to get involved in a messy marriage. People have to sort out their own crap. I saw Neil once, when he came over here to try and get her back. He was in a right state. Shaking, in fact. I've always wondered what went down that day.'

'Can you tell me a bit more? What did Neil say?'

'Not much. He'd been to visit Kelly and he said it had been a nightmare. He was sober but really pale and jumpy. I'd never seen him as bad as that before. Then we went out for a curry and he got blotto. I heard him crying in the bathroom when we got back. Sobbing. He fell asleep on the bathroom floor and left early the next morning. Next thing I heard was that he'd been killed in a car crash. Kelly was at the funeral. At least she stayed sober for that.'

'Did people blame her for Neil's death?'

'I don't know. Our gran did. She said she never wanted to hear Kelly's name again, and she was looking daggers at her in the church. I didn't stay around to listen to the fallout. I'd started to feel sick by then. I'd only just managed to make it to the funeral. The doctors didn't want me to go but, you know — my only brother. There was a nice woman there, Sarah. She could see I wasn't well, and she brought me a cup of tea. She was another of Kelly's victims, in a way.'

Swift lifted his head. Maybe there was a useful nugget in this depressing tale of illness and disaster. 'What do you mean?'

'The scar Sarah has on her face — she got that when she and Kelly were larking around as kids. They were balancing on boulders by the river and Sarah fell, gashed her head open. Gran told me after the funeral. She was keen to list Kelly's sins. Said that Kelly was leaping on the rocks and daring Sarah to jump, winding her up. According to Gran, people around there held Kelly responsible. Mind you, you had to take some of the things Gran said with a pinch of salt. But it does sound exactly like the kind of stupid thing Kelly would have done.'

'Did you blame Kelly for Neil's death?' It would be a strong motive. Although he couldn't see the sickly man in front of him managing to go further than the local shop, let alone wield a hammer and push someone off a ship.

Dwyer traced a finger over his sword tattoo. 'In a way. I thought she had the upper hand in the marriage, and she should have just refused to see Neil again. Seemed to me that she liked having him pursue her and plead with her. She got off on popping over to Rossdown for a hopeless reunion every now and again. If she'd ended it properly, that would have hurt him, but at least then he'd have stopped with the false hopes.'

'Faith told me that Kelly did love Neil, and that's why she found it hard to finish the marriage.'

Dwyer gave a cynical laugh. 'Yeah. Well, people like to give a good impression to their families, don't they? Kelly wouldn't have wanted to admit to being a selfish bitch.'

'Going back to that time when Neil was here and so upset, do you know where he met Kelly?' He wondered if

Neil had somehow found his way to Lewisham and discovered her relationship with Sol. That might well account for his shock and tears.

'I'm not sure. He'd asked me how to get to Willesden from here, so I assume that's where she was. From what you say, it sounds as if poor Faith's a sickly has-been like me now?'

'She sustained a bad injury.'

'Was Kelly pissed out of her head on the ferry?'

'No. She gave up drinking soon after Neil died and took up sport again. She played camogie.'

'Oh, right. Well, good for her. Pity she couldn't have given up booze before he died. He might still be here.' An edge of bitterness had crept into his voice. He shook his head. 'Pity you can't swap illnesses with other people. I'd rather not have quite a lot of my memories. I could give Faith some of my brain cells. Except I wouldn't give her the time of day after what her sister did to my brother.'

No point in playing the blame game. Swift stood up. 'Well . . . it's hard when you've lost someone close to you. I wish you luck with your health. Like Faith, you must find it hard to get up some mornings.'

'Tell me about it. Once a soldier, always a soldier, though. I'm always up with the lark, whatever I feel like. I've got a reveille call on my phone. Keeps me sharp, hearing that bugle. I make myself go out a couple of days a week, to Costcutter and the pub. Then I spend the next day recovering. But thanks for the good wishes. I envy you, you know. We're about the same age, but you look fit and healthy.'

'Believe me, I don't take it for granted. If you do think of anything else, let me know.'

CHAPTER 8

Faith had checked through her emails for 2016 and found one that Kelly had sent her about the job she'd done for Jon Sheppard. She'd fitted a new boiler and thermostat for the central heating in a flat in Fulham.

I messed up. I was probably still drunk/hungover, and I'm lucky he didn't report me. I didn't finish off the cap on the flue pipe properly, and there was a build-up of carbon monoxide. I'm mortified even thinking about it. Such a basic and stupid mistake.

Swift suspected that it had played a part in Kelly's decision to kick the booze. He'd phoned the number for Jon Sheppard, and when he explained the reason for the contact, Sheppard had said his office was in Putney and he'd drop by to see Swift after work.

He'd rowed for a couple of hours in the afternoon sun. The air was muggy and sticky, the Thames idling along drowsily. The sky seemed uncertain and bruised-looking clouds hung overhead. It was the kind of close atmosphere that needed a thunderstorm.

He jogged home just after four p.m., his skin slicked with sweat. His house was ten minutes from the river, so he had time for a shower before Sheppard was due. He stuffed his clammy gear in the washing machine, dressed in jeans and a shirt and then headed to his office in the basement. It used to smell a bit like the river down there, but he'd had it decorated and the painter had applied a damp proofing layer under the new paintwork. The fresh décor was pleasanter for clients, but he missed the old, familiar aroma, both marshy and doggy, which he'd always associated with Lily. She'd run her chiropractic clinic in the basement and would deal with aches and pains while her dogs snoozed in the corner.

He brewed coffee on the posh machine his cousin Mary had bought him and was just pouring it when he saw Sheppard thumping down the steps outside, a motorcycle helmet under his arm. Sheppard accepted a coffee and looked around appraisingly. He was dressed in black bike leathers and heavy black boots. Not comfortable clothing for such an oppressive day, as the light sheen of sweat on his broad face suggested. He unzipped his jacket and pushed his cropped sandy hair back from his forehead. He was a hefty man with large thighs, and the chair creaked beneath him. He smelled of diesel and traffic, that warm, gritty aroma of the city.

'Thanks for coming,' Swift said.

Sheppard nodded. 'It was on my way home. Looks like your business is doing okay. Newly decorated premises, upmarket coffee.'

'Yes, I do okay.'

'Interesting line of work. So, you contacted me about Kelly Dwyer. Did she manage to kill someone before she drowned? I always wondered if she might.' He had a deep voice and testy manner.

'Not as far as I know. Kelly was travelling on a ferry with her sister who was attacked on board and left with memory loss. The police enquiry stalled.'

Sheppard raised his eyebrows. 'Why do you want to know about her previous botched work? How does that help your investigation?'

'I don't know if it will. It's just part of piecing together Kelly's recent past.'

‘Right. Well, I’m sorry the young woman died in such a horrible way, but my son or daughter could have been killed by her error, you know.’ He drank his coffee straight down.

‘Could you tell me what happened?’ There seemed to be less oxygen in the room now Sheppard was in it. Swift turned on a small desk fan and set it to rotate.

Sheppard placed his mug on the desk and folded his arms. ‘It’s a straightforward fuck-up story. My son Cameron and my daughter Emilia wanted to live in London. He’s a marine scientist and she was waiting to start a job teaching. I bought them a flat in Fulham to give them a leg up and it needed some work to get it up to scratch. Kelly Dwyer submitted a competitive quote for a new boiler and Emmy was keen on the idea of a woman taking on the men at gas fitting, so I gave her the job. I was there once while she was working, and I thought I smelled alcohol on her breath but I was busy, just in and out to check on the work, so I let it go. I suppose I thought she partied hard in her own time. And Emmy got on well with her, the two of them were chatting away when I saw them together. It was a top of the range boiler, and Kelly seemed to have done an efficient job. Can I have another of this excellent coffee?’

When Swift had given him his second mug, he stretched his legs out. He had a smooth, fluent delivery when he spoke. A man used to holding his ground. ‘Soon after Kelly finished the work, Cameron and Emmy started getting headaches and feeling sick. She was worse than him because he travels for work, so he’s away regularly. After a couple of weeks, she went to her doctor, and he got her to have a blood test. That showed she’d been exposed to carbon monoxide and she was advised to get any home gas appliances checked out. When Cameron was tested, he had a lower level of carbon monoxide, but then he’d been working abroad. The cooker and hob were electric, so I got Kelly back to check the boiler. I was busy at work, so Emmy dealt with it and once Kelly looked, she admitted straight away that she’d forgotten to attach a cap to the flue. She fixed it there and then.’

'You weren't tempted to get an independent inspection of the boiler?'

'I did think of it, but I reckoned if Kelly had made a mistake, she should be the one to fix it. When Emmy told Cameron and me about it, we were livid. I wanted to report her straight away, and I thought Emmy would be all for it because she's pretty tough in that way. Chip off the old block when it comes to not putting up with any nonsense and holding people to account. But Emmy said that Kelly had been really upset and apologetic. There was a sob story about her husband dying in a car crash in Ireland, and she was still grieving for him. She offered to return half of her fee, but I didn't want to go down that road, let her think she'd bought her way out of trouble. Anyway, what Emmy wants Emmy gets, and she's very persuasive with the men in her family, so I backed off.'

'I think Kelly was very lucky that you did.'

'Well, she had Emmy to thank, not me. The sisterhood kicking in. We men are just putty in women's hands when they're determined, aren't we?' He stood and pulled his jacket on. 'That's it. I have to be on my way. I googled you before I came round. Mostly positive, impressive stuff but some negatives as well. I saw a couple of hostile articles by a Camilla Finley, saying that one of your girlfriends was stabbed by a man who was harassing you, and that a young man who helped you with a case was killed in your home. Does that mean this house?'

'Sadly, yes. His name was Ben Ramsay. Someone who was a suspect in a case I was investigating suffocated him. The murderer hoped I'd get the blame.' Ruth had found the body, with Branna in her arms. He knew that she still hadn't forgiven him. He couldn't blame her. It had been a terrible sight, with Ben stuffed into a wardrobe and left to die.

Sheppard rubbed his chin. 'Wow. That's quite a story. Think I'd move house if that had happened to me.'

'I don't feel the need to do that. If I reacted to every threat and stumbling block in my line of work, I'd never get anything done. Camilla Finley, the reporter who wrote that stuff, is a nasty piece of work and has a grudge against me. That's her retaliation. I discovered her role in a murder. She was an accomplice and stuck a pin through the dead man's genitals. She's on remand in prison. So she has an angle.'

'Right. She sounds a nice piece of work. Her angle's out there, though. Some people might think no smoke without fire and all that.'

'Yes, I know, and mud can stick. A detective's path is never smooth. But I think my track record of solving cases speaks for itself.' He sounded more confident than he felt. Sheppard's comments were just the kind of negative response he'd been worrying about.

When Sheppard had gone, he sat making notes and thinking. There was something about the man that rang false. He was assertive and sure of himself, the kind who wouldn't suffer fools gladly. When Swift googled him, he saw that he was Chief Executive of a finance company, with homes in Chelsea, Nice and Miami. His son and daughter could have died of carbon monoxide poisoning because of someone he'd employed, and yet he had let Kelly off the hook with a slap on the wrists. If he'd reported her, it could have resulted in a criminal investigation.

It didn't seem to add up.

* * *

Swift sat at right angles to Marcel Vaudin in the clinic's waiting room. They were surrounded by brightly coloured toys and walls festooned with information posters, photos of smiling children wearing hearing aids and parents in support groups. He was feeling annoyed and wrong-footed. He'd arranged to meet Ruth and Branna at the audiology clinic. Branna was having a final health check and hearing test before an operation for cochlear implants in a couple of months. When he'd arrived, he'd found Vaudin there with them. Ruth hadn't mentioned that her partner would be coming and Swift resented his presence. It was unnecessary and an intrusion. Branna was in with her mother and the specialist nurse for a hearing test while he and Vaudin waited.

'Would you like a coffee?' Vaudin asked. He was smartly dressed and sleek-looking with a trim beard and treacle-coloured eyes.

Swift was suddenly aware of the missing button on his jacket and the worn knees of his jeans. He'd have loved a coffee, even the hospital kind. 'No, thanks.'

'I'm just going to get one. I won't be long.'

Swift watched him get up. 'I don't understand what you're doing here.'

Vaudin adjusted his dark-framed glasses on the bony bridge of his nose. 'I'm supporting Ruth and Branna, of course.'

'That's my role. I'm Branna's father. There was no need for you to come. I've got it covered.' *God, I sound like a kid in the playground.*

'And I'm Ruth's partner. I'm involved in her life and Branna's. I was able to be here today, and I thought it right.' Vaudin spoke slowly, as if Swift was a dull student.

'I don't. This is stressful enough for Branna without extra people being here. It should just be her parents with her. That's why I haven't brought Nora.' As soon as he mentioned her name, he wished he hadn't. Own goal.

Vaudin gave a little half-smile, aware of his discomfort. 'I can't imagine that you had to restrain an eager Nora from coming!' He headed to the door. 'Don't be petty, Ty. This isn't a competition. I have some professional knowledge of deafness and implants, as you know. I'm only here to help. By the way, have you addressed Nora's attitude to Branna with her?'

Swift stared. 'That's nothing to do with you.'

Vaudin shrugged and went out, letting the door swing shut. Swift shifted his chair. Bloody man. Interfering know-it-all. He knew that whatever he said was going to sound grudging. The decision to go ahead with Branna's digital implants had been complex and agonizing. There were numerous pros and cons. Her hearing aids, paired with signing, had been working well for her, and the implants might not prove successful. If they weren't, she'd have been put through surgery for nothing. If they were successful, they would make her part of the hearing world, which would be a huge change for her. There was also a chance that they might upset and confuse her. In the end, Ruth had been keen to go ahead, supported and encouraged by Vaudin, so Swift had agreed. He still felt uncertain, though, and his extensive reading on the subject had given him sleepless nights. He could only hope that this was the right decision and that Branna would benefit.

Nora had told him that one of the reasons she didn't want children was that she knew how brave you had to be as a parent, and she lacked that courage. Today, he didn't feel particularly brave himself.

Ruth came out of the clinic and sat beside him. Her hair was in a sleek chignon. 'The nurse wants to observe Branna on her own for a bit. Where's Marcel?'

'Gone to get coffee. Why is he here?'

'Why shouldn't he be here?'

'Just seems unnecessary. I told him so.'

Ruth gave him a long look that made him feel uncomfortable. 'Did you, Ty? That was useful behaviour. And I don't think it's unnecessary. I appreciate the support. Marcel is knowledgeable about deafness and implants from his work in education.'

'So you've said before. But he's not Branna's parent and I can support you with this.'

'Oh, get over yourself, Ty. What if I'm with Marcel long-term? What if we marry? He'll be Branna's stepfather and you'll just have to reconcile yourself to that. Surely it's better for her that he's interested in her and engaged in her welfare. They get on well, but maybe that's the problem as far as you're concerned.'

'What does that mean?' As if he didn't know.

'Come on, Marcel's attitude tends to show up your girlfriend's distinct lack of care and interest.'

She'd hit home and she knew it.

He looked down at the floor. 'Are you thinking of marrying him?' Swift knew that her divorce from Emlyn, her first husband, was complete. He hated himself for asking the question, showing that he minded.

Ruth shook her head. 'None of your business, but don't worry, I'll let you know if it's on the cards. Did you speak to Nora about her behaviour towards Branna?'

'Yes. She understands.'

'Really?'

'Really. Let's focus on Branna. How is she dealing with today?'

'She's fine. Seems to enjoy the attention, if anything, and the nurse can sign. She's really good at explaining everything to her. If all goes well today, the operation should be on schedule.'

He listened as Ruth talked about the details of the surgery. She was dressed smartly, her skirt and jacket in the same muted shades of grey as Vaudin wore. When they'd been together, she'd enjoyed wearing bright jewel colours that reflected the light. Now she absorbed it. As he watched the face that he'd once loved so dearly, he knew that his real dread was that Ruth might move with Branna to Guernsey, where Vaudin lived. When he thought about that prospect — usually in the early hours — he was engulfed in a dull, hopeless anxiety. It had to be a possibility, but he hadn't been able to name his fear with Ruth. Not yet. It would feel like tempting fate.

Vaudin came back in with a tray of coffee. Ruth looked up at him and smiled, holding out a hand. At that moment, Branna shot through the consulting room door, saw her father and ran to him, climbing onto his lap. Swift couldn't help feeling a small, albeit mean-spirited ripple of satisfaction as she reached up and threw her arms around his neck.

* * *

Trying to get hold of Faith was frustrating. Swift had left a couple of voicemail messages, asking her if she knew whether Kelly had ever had a connection to Willesden. He avoided the tube when he could, so he was on a bus, on his way to visit the charity Kelly had worked for. He emailed Faith, asking again for a response. The charity had changed its name and was now called Locality, but it was still at the same address in Kensal Green.

Thunderstorms had brought fresher air and the early summer day was warm and bright. The sun glinted on the dirt and grease on the bus windows. Someone had written *wanker* in the dust beside him. He listened to Aretha Franklin while the double decker grumbled through the snarled traffic on Ladbroke Grove. A steel band was playing outside the tube station. He could hear 'All You Need is Love' competing with Aretha singing 'Nobody Like You' through his earbuds. A toddler in front of him was dancing on the seat, waving his arms in the air. Swift gave him a thumbs up, and he smiled, showing tiny, perfect teeth.

Locality's offices were on a side road running parallel to Kensal Green cemetery. The charity was based on the first floor of a converted factory that had produced milk bottles from the mid-nineteenth century until the 1980s. Swift had read that there was a growing demand for milk in bottles again as part of the fight against plastic waste. Maybe the factory would experience another conversion and revert to its original use. One of his earliest memories was of the gentle whine of the milk float as it stopped outside his home and the comforting chink of bottles clustering on the step.

A notice by the gleaming main door announced that this was a conservation area. He was buzzed in and climbed wide stone steps to the first floor, where he entered through a double door to a poky reception that smelled of fried food. There was a large green and white notice above the front desk featuring a tall tree. Beneath the tree's branches was the slogan *Locality. Grow Where You Live.*

He announced himself to the immensely fat and grumpy-looking woman behind the desk. According to her badge, she rejoiced in the name of Sweetie. He could see a game involving castles on her ancient-looking computer screen. She was giving her full attention to a large bag of pork scratchings and threw him a surly sideways glance. She waved to a seat without speaking, tapped on her keyboard and popped a large handful of crispy pork into her mouth. There was a moist, chomping sound.

Swift sat beside a cheese plant that had seen better days, noting that the thin, grey carpet tiles were stained and worn and a window blind was broken, the chain trailing. Locality didn't look as if its growth was too successful, and the space didn't fit with the well-kept appearance of the rest of the building.

Sweetie's phone rang, and she embarked on a loud conversation about childminding problems, the cost of a new washing machine, her husband's snoring and the misdeeds of someone called Junior. Swift thought he might be in for a lengthy wait and checked out some new apps for his phone, for use with Branna. She was staying with him at the weekend and he wanted to work on numbers with her, so he downloaded one for numeracy skills and a play app with games and puzzles.

A man with a saffron orange turban, a luxurious beard and a harassed look appeared. Sweetie ended her call. The man wrinkled his nose at the pong in the air and stepped over to Swift, introducing himself as Daler Ayer.

'Sorry about the wait. Manic morning. Do come through.' He paused at the door. 'Sweetie, have you got those printouts I asked for?'

'Just doing it now. Won't be long.'

'I needed them an hour ago. Please make sure they're ready when I finish this meeting.'

Swift didn't look back but he reckoned that if he did, Sweetie would be scowling and reaching for another whiffy snack. He followed Ayer into a narrow room that looked out onto the cemetery. There was just about space to sit down among the ranks of filing cabinets and white boards with plans and designs on.

‘I don’t suppose Sweetie offered you a drink. I have herbal tea if you’d like some.’

‘I’m fine, thanks. I can see that you struggle to get her to do some work, what with the computer games, the running buffet and the personal phone calls.’ She’d been rude and dismissive. He felt no compunction about dishing the dirt on her.

Ayer threw his eyes upwards. ‘She’s hard work in herself. And she keeps eating out there, leaving food smells. It makes a bad impression. And . . .’ He looked sheepish. ‘I feel foolish every time I use her name.’

‘Can’t you get rid of her?’

‘If only! She’ll still be here when I’ve had my nineteenth nervous breakdown. I saw the Stones at the O2 recently. Can’t get that song out of my head.’

His eyes were strained and he did look agitated, constantly running his fingers through his beard. A homegrown comfort blanket, Swift thought.

‘I won’t keep you long. I just wanted to know about Kelly Dwyer’s time here. Did you work with her?’

Ayer’s expression softened. ‘Oh dear, poor Kelly. So sad, what happened to her. We replaced her with Sweetie. Out of the frying pan into the fire. Kelly was a skilled and dedicated pro in comparison. On her good days, anyway.’

‘Why did she leave the charity?’

He pressed a hand to his stomach. ‘It was such a fiasco. She messed up a grant application. I don’t know about subsequently, but back then she had a drink problem.’

‘I know about that. Is that what caused the mess?’

‘I’m afraid so. Soon after Kelly started here, it became obvious that she had an alcohol dependency. Some days, she wasn’t quite with it. She had a boyfriend who used to turn up sometimes to meet her after work, and he reeked of spirits. When she was on form, she was great and well-liked but . . . we wanted to keep her, support her, so we gave her special leave to go to a rehab clinic at one point, but it didn’t work out.’

'I've heard about the rehab. It was a place called Whiteleaf.'

'That's right. I was deputy manager then. The manager was Chantelle Lowick. It was Chantelle who found the clinic and most of the funding for Kelly and encouraged her to go. She was a motherly sort. Took Kelly under her wing a bit. She was disappointed when Kelly didn't last at Whiteleaf, but she knew how hard it can be to break addiction. I used to think she was a bit *too* understanding with Kelly. Some tough love might not have gone amiss.' He laughed at himself. 'Says the man who puts up with Sweetie's bolshiness and several thousand daily excuses for never getting anything done.'

Swift smiled. He reckoned that Ayer was frightened of Sweetie. She was terrifying. 'It's good to know your own shortcomings.'

'So they say. I think Chantelle might have regretted helping Kelly go to rehab because a guy turned up here a couple of months later, shouting and cursing about his wife and looking for Kelly. She was in a meeting so he didn't see her. Chantelle had to be called to reception to deal with him. She managed to calm him down, took him to a side room, gave him a cup of tea. He went away after that.'

'What was the problem?'

'I don't know the details. Chantelle was tight-lipped about it but I could tell she was furious with Kelly. The guy's wife had been in rehab at Whiteleaf, so it was something to do with when Kelly was there. That's all I know.'

'Any idea of his name?'

'Sorry, no.'

'Okay. So — what happened about this grant application?'

'Yes, right. After Kelly came back from rehab, we were applying for a major grant for a project we'd designed. A community hub with space for small businesses and shops, a crèche and drop-in for advice and support. We'd put a lot of time and effort in, as you can imagine. Months of hard work.' He winced, remembering, touched his stomach again and pressed a large pink tablet from a foil wrapper. 'Sorry, I have gastric trouble. Doctor says it's stress.' He crunched the pill. 'We had to submit paper copies of the grant application and all the plans plus costings, signed off by our trustees. It was Kelly's responsibility to send them special delivery. She took them out of the office with her, but she segued into a bar on the way home and left them under a chair. Forgot all about them. By the time we were alerted, it was too late, the deadline had passed. It was awful. Kelly was in floods of tears and kept apologizing. But in the end, I felt sorrier for us than I did for her. We'd stood an excellent chance of securing the money. Staff were very disappointed and demoralized. The charity took such a hit. Lost credibility. Chantelle had to take the blame, as the manager.'

'Was Chantelle sacked?'

'No, but she was given to understand that it might be better if she looked for a new job. She was gutted because she'd built the charity up from inception and devoted years to it. Chantelle was always the first person here and the last to leave. A real grafter, with high standards. But she didn't really want to stay after that. She felt as if she'd looked incompetent. She was terribly upset, especially after all she'd done to reach out to Kelly. She applied for the first job she saw and moved to Hastings. She did sack Kelly before she left. Kelly was pleading with her but really, she had to go.' He sighed. 'What did Kelly do when she left here?'

'She managed to kick alcohol in the end and she trained as a gas fitter.'

Ayer smiled. 'That makes sense. That's one of the things we missed when she left. She was good at fixing things around the place. I did regret having to lose her, but in a way, we've never recovered from that blow with the grant.'

'It damaged your reputation?' He couldn't help thinking of Camilla Finley and how mud sticks.

'Well — it didn't do it any good. Some staff left through frustration. We merged with another small charity the following year to try and reestablish ourselves. Hence the name change. Rebranding, trying to put the past behind us. That's when I became manager.'

'How are you doing now?'

'Okay . . . ish. As you can see, we have old equipment and it's always breaking down. We should be a paperless office by now, but . . .' He waved at the filing cabinets. 'It can be hard to keep up with some of the more streamlined charities in a competitive market. I'm putting together a grant application right now, and I'll post this one myself and hand deliver a copy.' He crunched on another tablet. 'Actually, I've just accepted a new job. I'm working three months' notice, so I hope to secure this new grant and leave on a high.'

That explained why he was willing to be so frank about his staff and the history of the charity. 'You said that Kelly was liked here. Did she have any close friends?' From what he'd learned about her so far, he expected a negative answer.

'I'm not sure.' Ayer checked in again with his beard. 'We had a part-timer, Mia. She and Kelly seemed to get on well. Mia was having problems with her marriage. I heard Kelly talking to her about it a couple of times, and I got the impression they hooked up outside of work. I'm not sure, though. My job took me out a lot to meetings. Still does. That's why I could do with a reliable admin.'

'Does Mia still work here?'

'No, she left soon after Kelly. I don't know where she went.'

'What was her surname?'

He rubbed his forehead. 'Let me think . . . Wilson. Yes, that was it. There's no one left here who worked with Kelly except for me, so you're lucky to have caught me before I exit.'

'Are you still in touch with Chantelle Lowick?'

'No, but she shouldn't be hard to find. She went to work for a charity for the homeless.'

Sweetie was on her phone again as Swift left the offices. She leaned back in her chair, her short, stout legs propped up on an open drawer. Her dress had rucked up, exposing the elastic tops of her knee socks. She was swigging back a can of fizzy drink and talking about a hair conditioning treatment. Her cackling laugh followed him down the stairs.

Back on the bus, Swift reflected on the information he'd got so far. Kelly had managed to anger a number of people when her drinking had clashed with her work and other lives. Jon Sheppard could have found himself with a dead son or daughter and Chantelle Lowick had lost her job because of Kelly's error. Dermot Dwyer clearly blamed her for his brother's death. An angry man had turned up at the charity and had had to be pacified by the manager. Then there was the matter of Sarah Ennis's accident and scar.

All of these events were some time ago. Why would any of them wait so long if they were going to kill Kelly?

And who was the person she'd recognized on the ferry?

CHAPTER 9

Faith phoned him while he was heating up Mrs Malla's delicious dal with roasted aubergines and peppers. The kitchen was full of wonderful aromas, and his mouth was watering. He listened while he stirred.

'Sorry I haven't been in touch, Ty. I went to see Sol and I stayed over on his sofa for a couple of nights. He's not well, some sort of horrible flu. God, he looks so awful. Made me feel almost healthy. I got him aspirin and soup and then I crashed out. He said we were the invalid looking after the invalid. But when we were chatting, he told me something I thought you should know.'

Swift turned the gas down and checked on the samosas in the oven. 'Go on.'

'It's about Jon Sheppard. Well, about his son and daughter. It's . . . erm . . . well, really embarrassing, to be honest.'

'Sounds fascinating. I'm not easily shocked.'

'Right. Well . . . I mentioned to Sol that you'd asked me about that email Kelly had received from Jon Sheppard and the error with the gas boiler. Sol started laughing and said Kelly had turned up at his place one evening after work, all red in the face. She told him she'd seen . . . well . . . this is weird and awkward . . .'

'Take a breath and say it. Usually the best way.'

'Okay, she saw the brother and sister who lived there — she saw them, erm, having sex.' She said it in a rush, tripping over the words.

That was unexpected. Swift gave the saucepan a stir. The spicy steam was putting his sinuses on alert. 'Was this when Kelly was fitting the boiler in their flat in Fulham?'

'That's right. Sol was really enjoying telling me about it. I didn't know where to look. Kelly told him that the sex was an up-against-the-wall job in the living room, half-undressed. She'd gone out one lunchtime to get a bite to eat, but had hurried back because she was keen to get on with the work. The sister, Emmy, had given her a key, so that she didn't have to be around for access. When Kelly let herself in, she saw them.'

'Did they realize?'

'Not sure. Sol knows more, I think, but I didn't want to listen to him going on about it with relish.'

'And Kelly never mentioned what she'd seen to you?'

'Don't think so. I had another look back at my emails from that time, but there was nothing. I suppose she might have told me on the phone and I've forgotten. Although it seems the kind of strange thing that would stick in your memory.' She yawned deeply. 'I'm so tired now. It was good to see Sol. We talked a lot about Kelly. It was nice to hear a bit more about their life together.'

'Maybe looking after him took your mind off your own problems, freed you up. It can work that way.'

'You might be right. Maybe if I talk to him some more, other memories might come back. Just hope they're not as embarrassing as what Kelly told him!'

'I went to visit Kelly's old workplace.' He told her about Daler Ayer's information.

'Oh God, more mess that Kelly left behind. I'm sure she never told me about that. Probably didn't want to admit to what had happened. I worry about talking to you. Frightened what I might hear about her. Expecting bad news. I've set the hare running, but I don't know where it's going.' Her speech was slurring again.

'I know it's hard. I never know what I'll turn over once I start asking questions. Does the name Mia Wilson mean anything to you? Ayer mentioned her. Kelly worked with her at the charity and they were friendly. Mia was having marital problems.'

'Mia . . . Mia . . . that's right. Kelly said she was like a pixie with freckles. She liked cashew nuts. How come I remember something that random? This memory thing is so weird. I think Kelly helped Mia move into a flat and get away from her husband. Hang on . . . yes, she found her a place in Willesden. She stayed over there on and off for a couple of weeks when she was helping Mia decorate it.'

He recalled what Dermot Dwyer had said about Neil asking for directions. 'Can you remember if Neil visited Kelly there?'

'What, in Willesden? No idea. I suppose he might have, but I can't think why he'd have been there. I think they usually met in pubs or bars. She liked to try and keep it on neutral territory. He came here to see her in Cricklewood a couple of times, wanting to stay over with her, but she wouldn't let him.'

'One more thing. I saw Dermot Dwyer. He told me that Sarah Ennis's facial scar was caused when she fell on rocks. She was out playing with Kelly. Do you recall anything about that?'

'Hang on, I need to think.' There was the sound of a finger tapping. 'I think so. It was years ago. I remember Kelly running into the house, yelling at the top of her voice and my mother phoning Sarah's family. Sarah was in hospital for a while. Orla could tell you more. Why do you want to know?'

'It might be of interest.'

'Oh, I see. Or maybe I don't.' Her voice was cracking and fading. 'Sorry, I'm a bit emotional again. I think my brain gets tired or something once I remember, or try to.'

'Let's leave it there, then. I don't want to overload you, or worry you more than I have already. Get some rest.'

He turned off the dal and licked the wooden spoon clean before phoning Sol Waters. Sol sounded mellow but alert enough.

'I was talking to Faith. She told me that you were entertaining her with a story of how Kelly had once witnessed incest.'

Sol chuckled and had a coughing fit. He sounded like a wheezing set of bagpipes. 'Yeah, the Fulham fuckers. Poor old Kelly went on about that for days. I told her there was probably plenty of it going on under her nose in the west of Ireland. Remote country areas, lack of company, poteen, long chilly nights, shared beds, needing a bit of spice, boredom . . .'

'And you're quite sure that this happened when she was working for the Sheppards in Fulham?'

'If they're siblings called Cameron and Emmy, yes.'

'Can you recall exactly what Kelly told you?'

'Certainly can. She went on about it enough, like a broken record.' Sol snickered again. Swift heard liquid being poured and more coughing. 'Let's see . . . well, she said she heard them before she saw them. They were amazingly noisy. She was just inside the front door of their flat, and she froze for a minute. You know, shocked, holding her breath. Couldn't believe her eyes, a brother and sister going at it. I think she said she slipped out again for half an hour. Closed the door quietly and walked around a bit. She was pinching herself. Then she nipped into a pub for a drink to calm her nerves. Poor love was really shaky. I reckon they must have thought it would be safe to have a quickie while she was at lunch, and they didn't expect her back that soon. When she got back to the flat, they'd both gone.'

'So they didn't know she'd seen them?'

'Ah, well, that was partly why Kelly was so upset. Emmy knew. Cameron had his back to Kelly.' He snorted. 'And his furry bum. I think Kelly was as amazed by that as what they were up to. She said she didn't know a bum could be so hairy. So, Emmy saw Kelly over his shoulder. This was all in a split second, and then Kelly went back out. She tried to complete the job when she got back that afternoon, because she didn't want to have to go there again the next day, but there was too much still to do. She said she didn't know where she'd look if Cameron was there, so I suggested at his arse!'

'Was he there?'

'No, I think he'd gone away working. He and sis had been having an overfond farewell, from the sound of it. Kelly didn't know what she was going to say if Emmy talked about it. I couldn't offer any suggestions, or at least not any that Kelly found acceptable. I mean, what do you say about witnessing incest? Comment that they seem a very close family?' He wheezed long and loudly. 'I just told her to try not to think about it. Kelly kept going on that this Emmy seemed a really decent, honest person. Kelly'd told her a bit about Neil while she was working there, and Emmy had been very sympathetic by all accounts.'

'So do you know if Emmy broached the subject with Kelly?'

'No, she didn't. Kelly was relieved! She rang me the following lunchtime. I'd asked for an update, could hardly wait. Better than watching a soap on TV! Emmy was there the next day, in and out of the flat. She was bright and breezy, but in an artificial kind of way, and Kelly felt that she was watching her. Or waiting to see if she'd say anything. Kelly felt so uncomfortable, she managed to put in a long day and finish the work. I think that's probably why she forgot the flue cap. She was so desperate to get out of there, she rushed towards the end. She'd never done an unsafe installation before that, and as far as I know, she never did again.'

'It must have been difficult for her, going back when they discovered the problem with carbon monoxide.'

'It was the last thing she wanted to have to do. Luckily, it took less than an hour to fix the cap and test the system. She was so upset when she realized her mistake. I remember her face was burning, and she thought Emmy would be furious because she'd been feeling ill. But Emmy kept reassuring her that as long as Kelly made it all safe, she was okay with it. Kelly said that Emmy came up close, put a hand on her shoulder and said something about the two of them calling it quits.'

'So that was an oblique reference to the sex scene. Kelly had caught her out, now she'd been caught out, so it was honours even.'

'That's what Kelly understood. Emmy said she'd talk to her dad and square it with him. Do you think they're still . . . you know . . .'

'No idea. Possibly. I think some incestuous relationships can be long-term.'

'Wow! Well, I suppose it's handy, and you don't have to go through all the hard work of looking on the market. Economic, too — you wouldn't have to bother much with romantic dinners and stuff. I never fancied either of my sisters. They're outdoor, sturdy types. More mannish than me, not that that's difficult.'

'One other thing. Kelly was friendly with a Mia Wilson who worked at the charity with her. Did Kelly talk about her?'

'Hmm. Not sure. Think so. Something about a dodgy marriage? Yeah, she wanted to get away from her husband and Kelly helped her look for a place to live. That's all I knew about it.'

'Thanks for that. Hope you feel better soon.'

'Ta. I've heard whisky's good for flu so I'm about to pour a large one.'

The evening was settling into a hazy calm, so Swift took his meal out to the garden and sat on the old swing seat. He'd thought that Faith had been slow in returning his calls because of her injury and fatigue. It hadn't occurred to him that she might be avoiding him because she was anxious about what he might reveal about Kelly's past.

He didn't feel much like a running hare with this case. More like a tortoise, inching forwards, possibly on a wild goose chase. He shook his head at himself. Hares, tortoises, geese . . . and now here was Nigel the plump cat from next door, popping over the wall to see what he could poke his nose into. He circled the seat a couple of times, jumped up beside Swift, wrinkled his nose at the spicy food and then sat with his paws tucked under his chest.

Swift finished his food and googled Emilia Sheppard on his phone. He found a woman of that name in Fulham, and followed a link to an article about her in a West London paper, dated eight weeks ago. It informed him that she had recently been elected as local councillor and was taking a strong stand against knife crime.

Emilia Sheppard, 29, is causing quite a stir in her local council. Many see her open, accessible and frank style as a breath of fresh air at a time when many voters are cynical about politicians. People clearly like the fact that she answers questions directly without trying to hedge her bets. Some MPs and ministers, take note!

Ms Sheppard makes no effort to hide her ambition to stand as an MP before too long. She has given up her teaching job to concentrate on politics. She says that she hopes to bring youth, commitment and vigour to her role in the local community. She is particularly interested in the plague of knife crime in the capital. She told us, "There is now a terrible climate of fear among young people on our streets. We have to intervene, educate young people and most of all, ensure that we promote and encourage strong family units, so that these young men have good role models and a sense of belonging in society."

Her brother and father have been active in campaigning tirelessly on her behalf. Ms Sheppard acknowledges their help, saying that they are her rock, and that she couldn't manage without the support of her own strong family unit. Cameron Sheppard told us proudly that he's sure his sister can make it all the way to No 10 Downing Street.

There was a photo of Emilia, showing a dark-haired, round-shouldered woman with an intense gaze. Her family unit might be a little less supportive if her activities with her brother ever came to light, and especially if they were ongoing. Swift wondered if Emilia had ever told Cameron about the day Kelly had seen them. He searched local election results, and saw that she had been standing for election eight weeks after Kelly's drowning. It may have rung alarm bells when he got in touch with Jon Sheppard asking about the incident with the boiler and revealing his investigation into Kelly's death.

Chand raised the window high above him and leaned out, releasing strains of Elvis singing 'Burning Love'.

'Lovely evening! Fancy a drink?'

'Definitely. I could do with a beer to cool my mouth. Just had a portion of your mum's dal with samosas. Delicious, but my tongue's been taken hostage. Think she made the samosas hotter this time.'

'She's a devil with the spices. She'll be giving me another massive batch of meals next weekend. I'll drop some off. Ready in ten.'

They walked to the Silver Mermaid and sat in the back garden. Chand talked about Havana Roscoe, the girl who'd had a crush on him and threatened to jump from his window before she ran away. There'd been no news of her since, apart from a Christmas card she'd sent to her grandmother. Chand checked the missing persons database regularly and updated Swift.

'Still nothing. It was her birthday last week. She was fifteen.'

'I hope she was able to celebrate it. She's never far from my mind.'

'Nor mine. I keep hoping she might get in touch with us. Leave a message, anything.'

'It's been months. It's unlikely.'

'Do you know the worst thing? Her mum put a sugary birthday message on her Facebook page. Chand made inverted commas with his fingers. *"To my darling Havana. I love you so much. Please, please come home. We miss you, and your little baby brother wants to meet you. He sends you big kisses."* That woman is such a hypocrite. She neglected Havana and iced her out of her home, and now she's pretending she gives a toss.'

'She is a hypocrite and she's awful, but that doesn't mean she hasn't got regrets. I expect feelings of guilt have finally kicked in.'

Chand raised an eyebrow. 'You're kinder than me, that's all I can say.'

Swift wasn't sure about that. He had Kris Jelen, Ben Ramsay and Havana Roscoe as constant guilt companions. Rather than kindness, he reckoned it was simply that he knew how self-reproach could intensify rather than fade as time went on.

Chand interrupted his thoughts. 'What are you working on now?'

He described Kelly's death and Faith's injuries. 'Truth is, I'm not sure where I am with it. It feels as if I'm trying to grasp fog. Of course, foggy sums up Faith's memory.'

'Tricky.'

'Exactly. So, I'll just carry on doing the detective thing. Ask questions, gather information, link it up, see if I have any suspects.'

'Who knew they'd be on the ship that night?'

'I've considered that. Their elder sister and Kelly's friend Sarah, for definite. I can't see any reason why either of them would want rid of Kelly. There might have been other people who knew their movements. Any number of people in Rossdown. In that kind of small community, word gets around, and I don't know who Kelly had told in London — and of course, Faith's memory is unreliable.'

'I see what you mean about fog.'

'Yeah. And of course, without any hard evidence, forensics or witnesses, proving that someone is the perpetrator is going to be difficult, even if I can place them on board the ferry.'

'Realistically, it would have to be a confession.'

'And that's not very likely.'

They chatted for a while, then Chand went off to meet Bella, his partner. Swift walked home, pausing by Hammersmith Bridge to look out at the river. He had decided years ago that it was the most attractive of London's bridges, with its wrought iron structure, magnificent cupolas and coats of arms. He'd lost track of how many times he'd rowed beneath it. There were coloured lights on the far shore, dancing in the breeze, their reflection rippling in the water below. The tide was high, the river swirling against the struts of the bridge, carrying debris. He was lucky. He'd caught a parasite in canal water and recovered. Nearby was a plaque to a man who'd dived in to the Thames to save a drowning woman. He'd succeeded, but had died afterwards from tetanus contracted from his injuries.

Faith rang as he was heading for home. She was excited, stumbling over her words. 'I've remem . . . remembered! About the ferry. It was a dark-haired person Kelly saw in the café on board. A dark-haired person in a blue anorak.'

He felt a kick of interest. 'You're sure?'

'Positive. I had a rest and did what my therapist has been teaching me. She told me some stuff about experimental evidence regarding the brain. It's probable that quite a few of my memories are still stored but not accessible. Getting stressed about it makes retrieval even harder. She showed me a routine. I suppose it's like a kind of self-hypnotism. I take deep breaths, count to thirty, relax and visualize. So I did that with the café on the ship. Sort of watched and listened to Kelly and myself. I heard Kelly saying, *"Oh God, just my luck."* That's it. We were paying at the till, and Kelly was looking at someone sitting at a table near the door. I glanced across. Kelly wanted us to go and sit on the other side of the café.'

'So she wanted to avoid this person.'

'Yeah, that's right.'

'And you can't recall if Kelly told you who this person was?'

'Sorry. I'm so useless. I've tried but I can't get it. Maybe she didn't tell me. And I can't remember if it was a man or a woman, or anything about what the person looked like apart from the hair being dark and their blue anorak. As I said, useless.'

'You're not useless. It's another step, another bit of information. Maybe try that technique again tomorrow, see if you can get anything else. Have you been back to camogie?'

'Yep, I went last Saturday, and I'm going on Wednesday evening to help with training.'

'Good. Keep on with the visualization. Talk soon. And Faith . . . don't forget your home security. Has your door been fixed?'

'Yeah, the guy did it yesterday.'

'Good. Lock up at night.'

Swift carried on home. Perhaps the person Kelly had spotted on the ship had been on board with the intent of doing her harm, or had seen her and seized an opportunity. He wondered about Emilia Sheppard. The incident that Kelly had witnessed might have been some time ago, but Emilia hadn't been an aspiring politician then. Incest was illegal. If you were an ambitious person with a public profile, the reminder that someone had information about you that might lead to your arrest and detonate your career could be a provocation to violence. There was only one way to find out if Emilia had helped Kelly fall into the waves.

At home, he found Emilia Sheppard's name on a list of local councillors for her area. There was an email address below it, so he messaged her, considering the wording carefully so as not to frighten her off.

I met with your father recently about the problem with the gas boiler in your flat, and he was very helpful. He's probably mentioned seeing me. I'm investigating how Kelly Dwyer, a family member, drowned at sea and how her sister Faith sustained a bad injury. I have a few more questions and I'd like a quick chat. I'm sure you have a busy schedule, but hope you can fit me in ASAP so that I needn't bother you again.

He thought the implied threat in the last sentence was worthy of Camilla Finley. He pressed send and went to bed.

CHAPTER 10

He was on his way to Hastings to see Chantelle Lowick when Orla emailed him. He'd contacted her to ask about Sarah Ennis's accident. He read the email on a garage forecourt, where he'd stopped to fill up and buy a coffee:

That accident happened when Sarah and Kelly were about nine years old. They were larking around down by the river one afternoon in the school holidays. No doubt Kelly egged Sarah on, although Sarah never blamed her for what happened, and the girls stayed friends. Mrs Ennis, Sarah's mother, was raging about it. She came to the house, spitting nails. Sarah was in hospital for several weeks, and it was touch and go if she'd need plastic surgery, but the wound did heal. She was left with the scar, though. I think she's always been self-conscious about it.

Faith told me about the note she was sent from the person responsible for this terrible thing. I know I have you to thank for that. At least it means I can stamp on the horrible gossip about suicide. Small mercies.

Sarah Ennis would be self-conscious, he thought. A significant facial scar would have an impact on anyone. Perhaps Sarah had blamed Kelly without ever saying so. He drove on, thinking about Sarah and checking his route. Maybe her offer of a lift to the ferry had been more complicated than a friendly gesture. Sure, revenge was a dish best served cold — but so many years later? He couldn't see it. A few sharp rain showers whipped the windscreen as he drove into Sussex. The sky looked busy with watery grey clouds scudding through the blue.

He'd found Chantelle Lowick easily enough. She was now director of a help centre for homeless people in Hastings. Getting to speak to her wasn't as easy. He'd left several messages with a courteous, apologetic receptionist who could have taught Sweetie a few lessons in manners. Finally, the receptionist had emailed him and offered him a half hour slot with Ms Lowick at her office in Hastings town centre.

He'd decided not to tell Faith that he was trying to contact Chantelle. He was aware of how fragile she was, and there was no point overloading her with information. The angry man who'd turned up at Live Local might not be of any importance.

He'd never been to Hastings. A huge hoarding informed him that he was entering '1066 Country'. Driving into the town in sun and showers, he felt as if he was passing in and out of two different locations. There was grand, imposing architecture, timber-framed, medieval and Victorian structures, and then roads with buildings that were shabby or boarded up.

He parked the car and walked along wide streets. Rough sleepers occupied many of the doorways, oblivious to the cries of the seagulls. There was a market in the centre, making an effort to be jolly, and he stopped to buy a cheese and ham roll. While he ate, he strolled around the stalls, which offered mainly tat, interspersed with some charcuterie, chocolate and artisan breads. When Cedric was alive, he'd have bought him a loaf of the rye or the seeded sourdough. He'd loved good bread. *Dear boy, how kind of you and what a treat!* Today he bought a tiny white chocolate mouse for Branna, to have by as bribery when needed. It was so well-made, with detailed whiskers, ears and tail, he thought it would almost be a shame to eat it. Branna would have no such reservations.

The help centre was behind the market, down a narrow, grimy alley where odours of urine, garbage and dog mess fought for priority. Swift thought that it must have smelled like this in 1066. The centre itself was a bleak, modern affair of steel and plate glass. Effort had been made with the reception area, which was crammed with plants and bright, framed posters of Hastings in its heyday — bucolic scenes of people larking on the beach, fisher folk repairing nets and the elegant pier in its Victorian glory. A stark contrast to some of the streets outside.

'Is the pier open these days?' Swift asked the young man called Ronan on the front desk, who'd given him a friendly greeting and huge smile. He had a vague memory of reading that it had been damaged by fire, but if it was open, he'd visit it. He had a soft spot for British seaside piers, and he liked them a bit melancholy and run down, with kiosks selling junk alongside fish and chips and candyfloss.

'Sensitive subject alert. Someone bought it and did it up, and not everyone is happy with the alterations. There's been public arguments, letters to the papers, online protests.' Ronan's tone darkened. 'It boasts a gold baby hippo among other attractions.'

'Sounds like I should take a look.'

'Wear your sunglasses if you do, protect your eyes from the bling. Now, Chantelle's got a busy day so best not hang about.'

He showed Swift into a square, plain office. It was overshadowed by a tall hotel that blocked it in, making it appear sepia-tinted. The strip lights were on but did little to alleviate the oppressive shadows and gloom. If he had to work in this dismal space all day, he'd be on medication. Chantelle Lowick greeted him but didn't stand up as she gestured to a chair. She was a stocky woman in her fifties with wide cheeks, dark eyes and a small, sculptured nose. Her dark chocolate hair was clipped up, and she wore an ill-fitting yellow shirt with a black skirt. Her foundation ended in a line above her jaw.

'How can I help you, Mr Swift?'

'I'm looking into Kelly Dwyer's death and an attack on her sister, Faith. I'm speaking to people who knew them.'

'Yes, I saw your email. I was very sorry to hear that Kelly died and in such an awful way. A double tragedy for the family. Please give them my condolences.'

She spoke kindly but firmly. Maybe in her line of work, like the police, she had to navigate difficult situations frequently.

'Faith sustained a brain injury.'

'Dreadful. Kelly rarely talked about her family but she did mention her sister a couple of times. I knew Kelly was from the west of Ireland and that her marriage had failed, and that's how she'd ended up in London.'

'Did you know Kelly well?'

She was composed, leaning back in her chair, hands clasped lightly in her lap. 'At first, I thought I knew her. But then I realized she was an alcoholic, and I don't think you ever do get to know an alcoholic. They're so camouflaged, you see.'

'Did you like her?'

Her eyes flickered at the question and she gave a sharp sigh. 'Probably too much. I grew fond of her. Kelly was very engaging and bright. That's why her drinking was so awful. It got in the way of who she could have been. Her addiction was a terrible waste of her young life, and that really saddened me.' She looked and sounded as Daler Ayer had described her — a mature, protective woman. So why was he feeling as if he didn't quite believe her?

'Daler Ayer told me about how you tried to help Kelly. That was kind of you. Not every employer would make those efforts.'

'As I said, I was fond of her. She was young, with a lot of promise and living on her own, away from family. I knew her mother had died in an accident. I felt for her because of that. You see, it took me a while to realize what a mess Kelly's life was in when she came to work for us. She was good at masking her alcoholism and associated problems and projected a confident persona.'

'That's why you helped her access rehab at Whiteleaf?'

'Yes. I was really hoping that rehab would help her.' She grimaced, her lips pressed hard together. 'You come across people sometimes, and you want to try to save them. It rarely works, because in the end, people have to save themselves, but you have to give it your best shot. I talked to Kelly at length, pointed out that her drinking was going to damage both her health and her job prospects. She told me that she wanted to try and kick the addiction. I helped her look up clinics and agreed time off work for her with management. I secured some funding for her, too. She couldn't have afforded Whiteleaf on her own.'

'But the clinic didn't work out.'

She cleared her throat. 'Sadly, no. And unfortunately, Kelly met a man there, also an alcoholic who she got involved with, and that only served to prop up her addiction. I can't remember his name.'

'Sol. Sol Waters.'

'That's right. He hung around to meet her from work a couple of times. Seemed a nice enough man, but of course with two people in a relationship drinking . . .' She shrugged. 'Kelly was just repeating the dynamic she'd had with her husband. That often happens with people who have addictions. They seek out others who'll accompany them on the journey.'

He'd wondered if she was going to volunteer anything about why Kelly's rehab attempt had failed. 'When I spoke to Daler Ayer, he mentioned that Kelly was asked to leave Whiteleaf because she brought drink in and got another patient drunk with her. Sol Waters told me about that, too.'

'Yes, that's right. As I said, people have to help themselves and if they can't . . .' She glanced at her watch.

He felt that she was waiting him out, dishing out her information gradually, wanting to see how much he knew. 'What can you tell me about the fallout from that drunken party at the clinic?'

'Fallout? I'm not sure what you mean.'

'Mr Ayer mentioned that you once dealt with a man who turned up at your office. He was angry with Kelly. It was related to the time she spent at rehab in Whiteleaf. He wanted to see Kelly, but you side-tracked him.' He could hear her intake of breath as he finished speaking.

'Oh,' she said. 'That was very difficult. The man was grieving and yes, very angry. I thought I was going to have to call the police, but once I'd spoken to him and he calmed down a little, I was glad I didn't.'

'Can you tell me a bit more?'

'Possibly. You say you're a family member as well as a private investigator?'

'A distant cousin of Kelly's.'

'Well then — I suppose I can divulge the information. I never told Kelly about that man's visit. It was a deliberate choice. I thought it better that she didn't know. I couldn't see that knowing about it would do her any good.'

'If you could tell me now, that would be helpful.'

'I'm not sure how, but I see no reason not to. Whiteleaf didn't work out, but I didn't know all the details of what had happened until that man, Mr Greeve, came to the office. He was so distraught about his wife and what had gone on at the clinic.'

Swift recalled what Sol Waters had told him. 'Was Mrs Greeve the woman who got very drunk with Kelly?'

'Yes, that's right. Kelly had supplied her with alcohol. Sadly, Mrs Greeve died of a stroke not long after. She'd suffered atrial fibrillation before entering the clinic, and that can lead to strokes. I got the impression that she'd been told by her doctor that if she didn't stop drinking, she wouldn't make old age. Her husband blamed Kelly. Mrs Greeve had been in the clinic for a month at the point when Kelly arrived, and she'd been doing well. She lived locally and Ellis, her husband, had visited her every day. He'd been seeing the improvement. She'd got through the worst of her withdrawal symptoms. After the drinking session with Kelly, she discharged herself and started bingeing again.'

'Did Mr Greeve threaten Kelly?'

'Not as such. He was terribly upset and wanted to confront and blame her for his wife's death. He was convinced that Kelly had caused the stroke by supplying her with alcohol. I talked to him for quite a while, and in the end, he seemed to accept that his wife's death couldn't be attributed directly to Kelly. I suggested he contact a bereavement counsellor to try and work through his grief. He had a cup of tea with me, and when he left, he was a lot calmer. He didn't come back.'

Maybe Ellis Greeve had come back at another time and in another place. Grief and anger were good companions.

'I know about the problems regarding the grant application and the effect it had on your workplace. Kelly forgot to post the papers, and you had to sack her. You must have felt very let down by her, especially after the efforts you'd made on her behalf.'

'I admit I did feel let down. But then when you manage people, you know that some of them will disappoint you.'

She seemed too glib. It was raining outside now, the sky a dirty grey and the light in the office had dimmed further to a sulphurous yellow. He felt that he was in a place where secrets might be whispered, or hidden. It was hard to see Chantelle Lowick's expression clearly. 'And is that what your managers thought when they invited you to find another job?'

She drew herself up, and her tone dropped down the thermometer to ice. 'You're sounding offensive now.'

He held his hands out. 'It's only what Mr Ayer told me. A kind of fall-on-your-sword scenario. Better than being dismissed, surely? I've known of that kind of deal. *"If you go willingly, we'll give you good references"* et cetera.'

'My employment history is my affair, not yours. We're out of time. I wish you well with your enquiries.'

'Just a quick question — have you ever taken a ferry from Ireland?'

'Even more insulting. I know what you're getting at. The answer is no.'

She tutted, picked up a bag and crossed to the door, wrenching it open. She hurried away, calling to Ronan to show their visitor out.

Swift walked through light drizzle, down a steep hill to the seafront and the pier, where he admired the gold hippo and a fibreglass elk and skirted amusement arcades. He climbed to the upper deck, where he bought fish and chips and sat under a canopy. Grey sky, grey sea, with just a suggestion of clouds breaking to the east. He gazed at the raindrops dimpling the channel. His parents had brought him on seaside trips from London a couple of times a year to Whitstable, Deal or Margate. *It's good to feel on the edge of things, like I used to be in Connemara,* his mother would say, while his father shooed away seagulls.

He dipped his chips in ketchup. Something about Chantelle Lowick didn't ring true. She was no pushover and he didn't get why she'd been so generous to Kelly about Mrs Greeve, so careful of her feelings. Especially after she'd dropped the charity in it by leaving a crucial document in a bar and had lost Chantelle her job. A lot of people — most people, surely — would have been furious and confronted Kelly with her snowballing disaster trail at that point. It might have done her good. Perhaps Chantelle, like other people — Sarah, and, from what he'd heard, Emilia Sheppard — had had conflicted emotions about Kelly and that had made them cut her some slack. He reckoned he'd have found Kelly bewildering if he'd known her in her drinking years. Such an engaging yet combustible mix.

He watched gulls dive-bombing a wastepaper bin for food scraps and rang the homeless centre again.

'Hi Ronan, we met earlier. I meant to check something with Ms Lowick and once we got chatting, I forgot. I wonder if I could ask you instead. I appreciate how busy she is, and she's already been so helpful, I don't want to bother her again.'

'Depends. What d'you want to know?'

'I just wondered if she had any time off work last October, the first week or so.'

‘Ahm . . .’ He sounded doubtful.

‘Don’t worry if you can’t tell me. It’s just that if I know, I won’t need to contact her again.’

‘Well . . . okay. Don’t see that’s a problem. Hang on . . . yeah. She had a week or so’s leave then.’

‘Know if she went anywhere nice? We were talking about good holiday destinations.’

‘No idea. Might have been a staycation and working from home, knowing Chantelle.’

‘Great, thanks. I’ve looked at the hippo, by the way. Eye-catching.’

Ronan chuckled. ‘But not necessarily in a good way.’

So Chantelle could have been sailing the Irish Sea with a hammer in her bag. A look at the passenger manifest for 2 October would be handy. He made a note, finished a wedge of crisp batter and rang Sarah Ennis.

‘Is this a good time? I just wanted to check a few things.’

‘I have a short break between patients.’

‘Okay. As you know, I’ve been talking to people about Kelly. I understand that you had an accident when you were playing by the beach with her.’

‘Goodness, that was years ago. I cut my head, hence the scar.’

‘How did it happen?’

‘I slipped and fell when we were playing. What’s this got to do with Kelly drowning?’

He could hear the whine of a drill in the background. It made him clench his jaw. ‘It’s part of the picture about her. I understand that your mother blamed Kelly for what happened.’

‘Who told you that?’

‘Kelly’s brother-in-law.’

‘How would he know anything about it?’

‘He said Neil’s gran told him about it at Neil’s funeral. Orla gave me the information as well.’

She made an impatient, tutting noise. ‘Tittle-tattle. You must hear a lot of that when you’re snooping in family business.’

'You're right, I do. Was it Kelly's fault?'

'No, if it was anyone's "fault", it was my own. We were messing about and I lost my footing on slime from seaweed. Kids have accidents.'

'But yours put you in hospital, and there was a chance you'd need plastic surgery.'

'That's true, but I didn't and I healed and have a scar. It all happened a long time ago, and I never think about it, so it would be good if other people didn't. Fancy raising that with you!'

'People start chatting. They rake over stuff. Sometimes it's useful.'

'Well I can assure you that my childhood misadventure isn't. Now, I have a crown to fit, so I must leave you.'

He bought a coffee and walked back to the station. Sarah hadn't asked anything about his enquiries or whether he was making any progress. She hadn't even asked how Faith was doing. That could mean something or nothing.

In the meantime, he thought that Ellis Greeve might bear further investigation.

* * *

The Parterre was Nora's favourite London bar. Situated off Portobello Road, it was a cosy, dim cave of scatter cushions, rag rugs, woven wall hangings in primary colours and distressed leather armchairs. Swift and his cousin Mary were tucked in a corner, drinking red wine, nibbling at a dish of olives and waiting for Nora. A candle sputtered on the chunky wooden table.

'Seems ages since I saw you,' Swift said. Mary's company always did him good. They'd been close friends since childhood and had joined the Met at the same time. She was now an Assistant Commissioner and married to Simone, with one son, Louis, who was the same age as Branna.

She ran a hand through her brunette curls. 'Tell me about it. Work's been mad, then Simone had a nasty flu that

Louis caught, so it felt like we were in quarantine for weeks. Why does flu in summer seem so much worse than in winter? Anyway, I was last woman standing and luckily, I didn't get it. Then you were in Ireland so . . . how did it go?'

'Okay. It was good to see Maura, and Branna had a great time. Unfortunately, she got an ear infection towards the end and had a meltdown on the plane coming back.'

'Poor little mite! She's okay now?'

'Fine, all cleared up. We're going ahead with cochlear implants soon. I'm on tenterhooks about that. It's been hard, weighing up the benefits and risks. I hope it's the right decision. The success rates in children her age are high.'

'I understand your concerns but, you know, I think in your place, that's the decision I'd have made, too. Otherwise, you'd always be wondering if you'd deprived Branna of opportunities.'

'Hmm. And there's a much lower risk of ear infections with implants. So, fingers crossed.'

'And how did Nora enjoy Branna's company?'

'Fine up to a point. They had a bit of a falling out. Branna told Ruth, and Ruth gave me grief.'

Mary was nobody's fool and knew well his propensity for understatement where his personal life was concerned. She tapped his arm. 'Spill. What exactly did Ruth say?'

'Hmm . . . that if Nora didn't stop being snappy, Ruth might put an embargo on her seeing Branna.'

'Oh, I see. What did Nora say or do to cause that reaction?'

'I don't know exactly. I wasn't there at Maura's when it happened. I was meeting up with the new family connection I emailed you about. Branna was playing up, and Nora shouted at her. Branna thinks Nora doesn't like her, and she said that to Ruth.'

'That's not good. And is Branna right?' Her eyes were boring into him from behind her dark-framed glasses.

He flinched. 'That's a bit strong. I don't believe that. It's just that Nora is impatient around children.'

'But if that's what Branna feels and thinks . . .'

'I know, I know. I've reassured Branna and I've spoken to Nora about it.'

'Right. Well, hopefully it can be resolved. One of the things that would concern me is if Branna starts copying Nora's behaviour, as in losing her temper and raising her voice.'

He paused with his glass in hand. 'I hadn't considered that. I haven't noticed it happening.'

'It could over time. Kids mimic adult behaviour. I know that Branna doesn't spend a lot of time with Nora, but she's a significant person in your life, so there's potential for it. Still, I'm sure you're on top of it. Branna knows you're her champion.' But there was hesitation in her voice. 'Nora's a bit late, isn't she?'

'She texted to say she's on her way in a cab, but traffic's snarled up.'

'The curse of London. So, what's happening with this appeal that Oliver's lodged about Cedric's will?'

'It's grinding through. I had another letter from Camilla Finley. She's egging him on.'

Mary frowned. 'Surely you can contact the prison to stop her sending malicious letters to you. There must be a rule about that. Want me to pull a few strings?'

'Let me think about it. I don't want to do anything that gives her even more ammunition. At the moment she's a nuisance, but no more than that.'

'I think you should . . .' Mary's phone rang and she checked the screen. 'Simone. I'd better take this.'

He nodded and sipped his wine. These days, he rarely got to see his cousin on her own. Simone was the kind of partner who thought that couples should do everything together. Even when Mary did manage to meet up, Simone always phoned or texted so that she was present, if not in person.

Mary ended the call. 'Oh dear,' she said. 'We were hoping to have some time together on Sunday, go for a tandem ride. Simone's been planning the route. It's been ages since we managed some "us" time. Our babysitter's just let us down and Simone's really disappointed.'

'I've got Branna for the weekend. Louis could spend some time with us if he'd like to.'

'Ty, you're an angel! That would be great. Ah, here's Nora.'

Nora was heading towards them, followed by Fitz Blackmore. 'Look who I've picked up like a bit of flotsam,' she said.

'Hope you don't mind me barging in,' Blackmore said, sounding unapologetic. 'I had a meeting in Lambeth that finished early and texted you both on the off chance that you might be free to meet. Didn't you get my text, Ron?'

Swift checked his phone. 'Sorry, it's there. I just didn't see it.'

'Hmm. Says you. You just don't want me outshining you with the lovely ladies.'

Mary was looking askance at Blackmore as he and Nora settled themselves. Blackmore stretched his legs out and snapped his fingers for a waiter. For a slim man, he took up a lot of space.

'I need nuts, bread and more olives,' Nora said, tucking her rucksack under her chair and leaning over to kiss Swift. She was wearing her usual work gear of dark suit, string bow tie — today's a bright cherry — and smart trainers. She wriggled her shoes off, as was her custom as soon as she relaxed, stretched and rolled her head.

Swift made introductions after Blackmore had placed his order.

'Better behave myself then, with top rank present,' Blackmore said. He was looking particularly sharp, in a fine black wool suit and snowy white shirt.

'That's advisable,' Mary agreed. 'Especially with *ladies* around.'

'Oh, another verbal gaffe. Hush my mouth. Comes from living in the backward shires. A thousand pardons.' His insincerity was palpable.

Oh God, this could be a long evening if Blackmore got into full swing. Swift avoided Mary's perplexed glance and drank his wine. She got up to leave after another half hour, saying she didn't want to be late for dinner.

As Swift kissed her, she muttered, 'Who's the Neanderthal?'

'I met him in Cornford. He's not quite the throwback he makes out to be.'

'He puts up a good pretence, then. Nora seems to find him amusing.'

They were laughing as Swift sat back down.

'Ron, my man, I've been missing you,' Blackmore said. 'Let's get another bottle in and plan a river trip. You up for that, Nora?'

'Certainly am. Will Carly be coming with us?' she asked innocently.

'Sadly, we had to part company. I heard a ball and chain rattling in the background whenever I saw her. I've seen a new companion called Tasha once or twice, but she's not the outdoorsy type.'

'You don't let the grass grow,' Swift told him.

'You know me, Ron. Move fast, move smart. Let me top you up. Got any good murders on the go? You know, ones that slow plods like me have failed to solve.'

'I have, since you ask. Police have got nowhere. Speaking of which, has either of you ever dealt with a case involving incest?'

'OMG!' Blackmore pulled a mock disgusted face. 'Is that a hot conversational topic in trendy West London these days?'

'I've always thought that's an interesting area,' Nora said. 'I've never worked with it, but I had a friend at school who once told me she fancied her uncle. Family attraction isn't uncommon, is it?'

Swift took an olive. 'Maybe, but most people don't act on it. Something to do with how we're drawn to others who look like ourselves. I suppose proximity helps. Most cultures have a strong taboo against it.'

'Don't think I could ever have fancied any of my aunts. A bit like shopping in the family store.' Blackmore laughed dirtily. 'You don't hear it talked about much. Uncomfortable subject for most people. I reckon it's perverted. Makes me feel sick.'

'It depends on where you live. In parts of Europe and some states in America, incest isn't illegal, and some countries allow half-siblings to marry,' Swift told him.

Nora shuddered. 'Ugh, I couldn't be doing with that. Isn't that knitting the gene pool a bit tightly?'

'I've never really given it any thought until recently,' Swift said. 'I can't get worked up about it, as long as it's between consenting adults and doesn't result in abuse or impaired children. But parent–child incest, even an adult child, makes me feel queasy.'

'You think it might be a motive for a crime?' Blackmore asked.

'Could be. I'm looking into it.'

'Well, the sex would have to be pretty amazing to do time inside for, is all I'm saying.' Blackmore grinned. 'I once knew a bloke who got two years for having it off with his daughter. I reckon they should have thrown away the key.'

'You're well known for your liberal views,' Swift said, earning a playful but painful punch on the arm.

After another couple of glasses of wine, a shared plate of mezze and a whisky chaser, Swift felt as if he hadn't a care in the world. When they left the Parterre just before midnight, Nora snuggled under his arm. The taxi lights danced and shimmered in a way he found delightful.

CHAPTER 11

Emilia Sheppard had sent him a terse email, saying she could spare him half an hour. She'd opted to meet him mid-afternoon in the café of a dingy department store in Acton. Swift rode grubby escalators past sad racks and shelves of cheap clothes, kitchen utensils, toys, bedding and curtains. Tinny muzak played faintly. Bored-looking assistants folded and neatened for something to do. The heavy, chemical smell of acrylic fibres filled the air, sucking out oxygen. *SALE* signs covered every area, but the place was almost empty.

The café was called Cozee and was anything but. It was small and on the top floor, tucked around a corner by the toilets. It had no external windows and low, yellowish lighting of the kind that casts a jaundiced hue. The worn plastic seating and chipped melamine tables were in a shade that could only be called vomit. The marble effect floor was sticky underfoot. There was one elderly man in a corner surrounded by three bulging, striped bags, the type used for carrying laundry. He was eating a plate of chips covered in brown sauce. Despite the warmth of the day, he wore a heavy overcoat and scarf. Homeless, Swift thought, as he approached the counter and surveyed the tired tarts and scones. A fly was enjoying the raspberry jam on top of a doughnut. A single limp slice of quiche lay on a plate filled with crumbs. He didn't want anything, but decided a bottle of water would be safe, so he bought one from a girl with a runny nose and moist fingers.

He sat near the entrance, clearing bits of debris from a chair and the table with a paper napkin. Emilia must have chosen this godforsaken venue because she knew it would be almost empty at this time of day, and she was unlikely to be seen by anyone she knew. You might almost think she had something to hide. He was interested in seeing how she was going to play the meeting. She must be worried that he might know about her incestuous relationship. He expected she'd deal her cards carefully, trying to gauge his responses.

While he waited, he read an email from the ferry company that Kelly and Faith had travelled with. It informed him that he couldn't have a copy of their passenger manifest for the sailing on 2 October. He'd expected the refusal because of data protection. He'd tried Liverpool police with the same request and had been told it wasn't possible. It was frustrating. He'd have liked to check the names he'd been acquiring against that list, especially Chantelle Lowick.

Emilia Sheppard was ten minutes late but looked unhurried. Her hair was in a neat, glossy bob and she wore a plain navy, sleeveless dress with a grey tailored jacket, teamed with tiny blue topaz earrings and a fine topaz necklace. She was an unlikely-looking customer for Cozee, and resembled a woman you might see on the evening news, striding along Downing Street with a briefcase full of important papers.

'Mr Swift?' Her voice was low pitched but clear. He thought of Margaret Thatcher after her voice training.

'Yes.' He stood and pulled a chair out. 'This a regular haunt of yours?'

There was a shadow of a smile. 'Not regular, no. It was handy for my diary today.' She inspected the chair, and then sat, smoothing her skirt and placing her bag on her lap.

'Are you having anything?'

'No. I don't have long. What is it you want to talk to me about?'

'Did your father mention that I'd seen him?'

'He did, and as far as he was concerned, he'd said all that needed to be said. I don't quite understand why the issue about the gas boiler is being raised again. That was all resolved. Ms Dwyer corrected her error and we were satisfied. I was terribly saddened to hear about her death.' She spoke carefully, weighing her words. Her make-up, like everything else about her, was discreet and skilfully done.

'Well, I just wanted to nail a few stray things down. I understand that you got on well with Kelly when she was doing the work for you.'

She touched her necklace. 'That's putting it a little strongly. We chatted a bit. She told me something about her husband's death, and of course, I felt for her.'

'But you liked her enough to persuade your father not to take the issue of her error with the boiler any further?'

She blinked and cleared her throat. 'I was sorry for her because she'd had her problems. It seemed the fair thing to do.'

'Even though you could have died of carbon monoxide poisoning?'

'The point is that I didn't and we all moved on, including Ms Dwyer. People make mistakes.'

He shook his head. 'I don't know. There are mistakes and mistakes. It puzzles me. It was very generous of you.' *And looking into your unforgiving eyes, not your usual style.*

She frowned. 'We seem to be going round in circles now. This had all been put to bed. I think you've had a wasted journey.' She straightened her bag strap, ready to get up.

'Have you been to Ireland recently?'

'Pardon?'

'Ireland. Have you travelled there by boat recently?'

She widened her eyes. 'Why do you ask?'

The woman was beginning to irritate him. 'I just wondered. Kelly saw someone she recognized on board the ferry. The ferry she was thrown from, into the sea.'

'How do you know that?'

'Someone told me.' He was pleased to see that his vagueness was now annoying her. He could also see her weighing up, making calculations.

'Who? Who told you?'

He shrugged. 'I can't reveal all my informants, it wouldn't be professional.'

'Have you spoken to the police about their investigation?'

'I've been in touch with Liverpool police, yes.'

'I didn't know that the police liaised with private investigators.'

'It happens sometimes. Depends on the police force involved. Liverpool were very helpful.'

'In what way?'

This cat and mouse game could go on and on. There were a number of tried and tested ways of breaking the dynamic. He decided on a lie.

'They shared the passenger manifest with me.'

It didn't occur to her that this was unlikely. She was too busy repositioning. She cleared her throat, a little murmur. 'Then you know that I was on the ferry that Kelly travelled back on. I didn't see her. I had no idea that she was on board or that she'd vanished until the police contacted me a week or so later.'

'Why were you on the ferry?'

'It's none of your business, but I'd been to a friend's engagement party in Wicklow.'

'Did you go to the café?'

She wrinkled her nose. 'Not likely. Those places are awful — noisy and hot. I had a drink in one of the bars and read a newspaper.'

'Humour me now — what were you wearing when you were in the bar?'

'Humour you? Hardly! What's my clothing got to do with anything?'

'Just go with it. It's quick and painless. Did you have a coat on?'

She tutted. 'No. I'd left it in my cabin because it was so warm on board. I was wearing jeans and a thin jumper — a pale green one, I think.' Her gaze held and he thought that bit of information was honest.

'Where were you after you left the bar?'

She gave him a measuring look and drew a little circle on the table with her forefinger. He hoped she'd wash her hand afterwards.

'As I said, I had a cabin and I went down there and fell asleep. I always take a sleeping tablet on journeys and I made sure I did on that one. We were warned that it would be a rough crossing.'

'You didn't see anything on the news about what happened to Kelly and her sister?'

'No. I don't always catch the news, life's so busy.'

He didn't think that sounded right. Whenever he read about politicians' routines, there was usually something about keeping up with daily news reports. 'Did you tell the police that you knew Kelly from before, when she'd worked for you?'

'No, they didn't ask me if I knew her, only if I'd seen her or her sister on board and I didn't think it was relevant. As I've told you, the fact that we were on the same ferry was pure coincidence.' She seemed relaxed, unworried.

'I'm not sure the police would have found it irrelevant. That could be described as withholding information.'

Her eyes flashed. 'I don't see why. An error with a boiler some time ago was nothing to do with what happened to Kelly.'

'Your father didn't seem to know about what had happened to her until I told him. Didn't you mention it to him?'

'No. I saw no reason to. He was away on business at the time. He didn't even know I'd popped to Ireland. When he said you'd been in touch about Kelly, I told him I'd heard that she died.'

'But you didn't tell him you were on the ferry?'

'I didn't think that was necessary. We're both very busy people and it was a quick chat.'

'Why didn't you fly?'

'Pardon?'

'I wondered why you didn't travel by plane.'

'I don't understand.'

'It's a simple enough question. Flying would have been much quicker.'

She leaned forward slightly, her eyes glittering. 'I don't like your attitude. Don't try to bully me, it won't get you anywhere. My travel arrangements are none of your business, and I don't understand why you're asking me all these questions. What's this got to do with a gas boiler from several years ago?'

He leaned back. 'What happened to Kelly and her sister is my business. I can't see why my question would cause offence.'

She gave an exasperated sigh, but visibly shifted gear and softened her tone. 'I went by ferry because I wanted to travel around for a couple of days while I was in Ireland. I'd never been there before, so it was an opportunity. Are we done now?'

'I'm not sure. You didn't see Kelly and Faith on deck?'

'No, of course not! Only a fool went up on deck on a night like that. The ship was pitching. When my stomach pitched with it, I did regret not flying!' She was all conciliatory smiles now, but the warmth didn't reach her eyes. 'I'm sorry about what happened to Ms Dwyer and her sister but frankly, I can't imagine why they didn't stay safely below like all the other passengers and I said that to the police at the time. Now, Mr Swift, I really must go, I have a punishing schedule . . .'

He pulled his chair in closer to her. 'Did you ever tell your brother Cameron that Kelly saw the two of you having sex in your flat?'

There was a silence. Emilia looked down, threading her fingers together. She was a politician, albeit only a local one for now. She'd have prepared a response in case she needed it. He knew what he'd say in her position. She was a canny woman, and she didn't disappoint.

She put her shoulders back and looked him straight in the eye, her own gaze full of challenge. 'What makes you come out with that outrageous statement?'

'Information I acquired. Kelly reported that she came back from an early lunch one day when she was working in your flat, and you were having sex with Cameron in the living room. Against the wall.'

'That's a disgusting thing to say and I can't imagine why she would make up such a thing. I can't believe you've repeated it.' She touched her necklace again. Some adviser was going to have to talk her through behavioural tells if she was aiming for parliament. 'I suppose it's her sister who's told you this. From what you've said, I understand that she has memory problems.'

'She has, yes.'

'Then I'm afraid that her memory is playing tricks on her. Cameron and I are very fond of each other. We have a close but entirely healthy brother–sister relationship. I recall that Ms Dwyer came in as Cameron was helping me with the zip on my dress. It was stuck and we were trying to release it. It never occurred to me that she might think that anything else was going on. Perhaps it says a lot about her that she jumped to such a bizarre conclusion at the time, and that her sister would pass it on to you. If I err on the side of kindness, I believe that brain injuries can have strange effects.'

'What Kelly described would have been hard to mistake. It seemed pretty graphic. Your brother's trousers were lowered.'

Emilia shook her head. 'She was mistaken. That's all I can say. And it's all I'm prepared to say. I'm sorry that Kelly's sister is so sick and that her memory is unreliable. That must be very hard for her. Brain injury is so difficult to judge, and memory is a tricky area. Perhaps Ms Black is recalling some other traumatic incident in her life and placing it at the wrong scene. And you're no clinician, Mr Swift, so you need to take care about what you parrot.' She was more confident again, thinking that she was on firmer ground.

'I didn't say that Faith Black gave me the information. You've jumped to that conclusion yourself,' he said.

Her neck reddened. 'Who did, then?'

'That's my business. You told Kelly that you'd call it quits over her mistake with the boiler. It seems that you didn't want to take the issue further because she'd seen something intimate that she shouldn't have. You reckoned she'd stay quiet if her own error was, as you say, put to bed with no professional repercussions.'

She shook her head. 'That's nonsense. As I've said, and I'm tired of repeating myself, I felt sorry for her because of the tragedy with her husband.'

Swift shook his bottle of water, watching the bubbles fizz. 'Did you tell Cameron that Kelly had seen the two of you? Does he know you're meeting me?' He gave her an understanding smile. 'We'll call it the "zip incident" for now, if it makes you more comfortable.'

That got her riled. 'We won't call it anything, thank you very much. If you or anyone else dare to repeat this slander, there will be consequences. Do you understand?'

'I'll tell you what I don't understand. You didn't seem that shocked when I described Kelly's tale of what she'd seen. Most people would have reacted much more. Most people would have looked horrified and then got angry. After all, I was accusing you of a taboo and illegal act that you could go to prison for. You took it in your stride. I think you were expecting it. And because your brain was so busy with anticipation and organizing a reaction, you forgot to look appalled. It's harder than you think to juggle lots of balls when you're under pressure, and you're still on the starter steps of politics. And by the way, I don't care who you're having sex with, as long as it's consensual and with an adult.'

She pushed her chair back. 'How dare you! Sorry I haven't been a drama queen for you! I refute these slanderous comments, and I can't believe that you're repeating them. If you come anywhere near my family or me again, I will take legal action. And from what I understand about you and your personal affairs, you don't need any more legal activity or bad publicity in your life.'

She stood, took a breath and then nodded at the startled girl behind the counter before walking away with measured steps. She'd prepared well, briefed herself and thought ahead. She might yet have what it took to get to Downing Street. As long as she or her brother hadn't killed Kelly to keep themselves safe. Voters might well take a dim view of a public figure who had had an incestuous relationship, especially one who made such a big deal out of family strength and support. It was a motive that might have driven either Emilia or Cameron to want to dispose of that threat.

Swift sat for a while, watching the homeless man eat a wedge of cake with a plastic fork. Tiny nibbles, eking out the cake and the time indoors. The waitress wandered over, flicking at tables with a grubby cloth.

'Think I've seen that woman on the telly,' she said nasally. 'She famous?'

'Not yet. She hopes to be prime minister one day. She's in local politics.'

'What's her name?'

'Emilia Sheppard.'

'Oh, right. Should've got her autograph. I got Tess Daly's last year when I saw her on Oxford Street. Think she'll be in here again?'

'She might be. I'm sure she'd give you her autograph.'

The girl flicked her way back to the counter. Swift drank his water. Emilia was weaselly. She'd be wondering now if he was going to tell the police that she'd known Kelly. If he did, they might not be that interested, but she couldn't be sure. And she had been on the ferry, albeit not wearing a blue anorak and possibly not in the café, which meant that if Faith's memory was correct, she wasn't the person Kelly had wanted to avoid. But had Cameron been with her? Did he know about what Kelly had seen? It was hard to believe that Emilia wouldn't have shared her anxieties with her very close sibling.

* * *

Branna's bottom lip was trembling with rage. Her cousin Louis was sitting by the window with his back to them, playing with the toy he'd wrestled from her. Swift looked at his watch. Mary would be here in the next hour and it couldn't come soon enough. He felt exhausted.

'Thanks for the cuppa, Ty, I think I'll head off now,' Faith said, reaching for her jacket.

'Are you sure? I was hoping you'd meet Mary. She won't be long,' he said, although he did think she looked as if she needed to rest. Her speech was starting to slide, and she looked pallid.

'I'm a bit done in now, Ty. It's been a long day and I want to call in to Sol's. He's got a chest infection and he's been wobbly. Tell Mary I look forward to meeting her another time.'

'Mummy?' Louis turned his head hopefully.

'She'll be here soon,' Swift reassured him.

He'd taken the children to London Harps where they'd met Faith and watched a camogie match before heading back to Hammersmith. Louis was a placid, careful boy and looked askance at the thudding players, whereas Branna had jumped up and down, cheering them on. The two children usually got along well. Louis was even-tempered, a good balance for Branna's louder, more boisterous personality. Today they'd decided they didn't like each other's company and had bickered on and off throughout. Whatever one had, the other wanted. When Faith had given them presents of two small camogie sticks, Branna had decided that she preferred Louis' green and red one to her own, which was orange and blue, and proceeded to arm-wrestle him for it. It had taken a while to sort that one out and mop up the tears of rage. Faith had seemed to take it all in her stride and had looked the liveliest Swift had seen her. Now he could see that she was worn out and fading.

'We'll have a little camogie knockabout of our own next time,' Faith said to the children. 'Team Toddler, way to go! Would you like that?'

Branna nodded, continuing to give her cousin a death stare. Louis shrugged.

‘I think Branna’s interested. Not so sure about Louis,’ Swift said.

‘No problem. It’ll be chicks with sticks, right Branna?’

‘Chicks wiv sticks!’ Branna stuck a thumb up.

‘You horrible.’ Louis scowled at her.

‘Take no notice of them,’ Swift said. ‘Today, hell is a pair of three-year-olds. Next time, they’ll probably be a couple of angels. Sorry they’ve been hard work.’

‘It’s okay. I was made to play with some visiting girl when I was little and I hated her guts. Kids change. One day you like someone, next day you don’t. Kelly and Sarah used to be like that — inseparable, and then there’d be weeks when they’d have fallen out big time. To be honest, I really enjoyed being with the kids today. They’re a great distraction from life’s problems. It’s good to be around that fizzing energy. All that young promise.’ She gazed at the children and he thought she was seeing her much younger self, before her life got so tortuous. She yawned and shook her head. ‘I should probably get tucked up soon, like these two.’

When she’d gone, Swift thought that divide and rule might be the best option. He took Branna to the kitchen to help get some drinks, leaving the door open so that he could keep an eye on Louis. He’d been worrying about Mary’s comment, that Branna might mimic Nora’s behaviour.

‘I talked to Nora about when she upset you. She’s sorry about that. She didn’t mean to. She really likes you.’

Branna was fiddling with plastic cups, deciding which colour she wanted. She didn’t reply.

He bent down. ‘Did you hear what I said?’

‘Yeah.’

‘Do you like Nora?’

She gave that some thought. ‘Sometimes. When we went Kew was good.’

‘Okay.’

‘Like Marcel. He funny,’ she offered.

‘That’s good.’ He took a breath. Lies were crucial at times like this. ‘I’m glad you like him.’

'Are you going to marry Nora?'

He looked down. She was anxious, twisting the top of a cup on and off.

'I'm not planning to marry anyone.'

She brightened. 'Good. I going marry you!'

'You're daft.'

'You daft!' She burst out laughing.

Louis had pressed the lever on a lorry that played nursery tunes. 'The Wheels on the Bus' jangled loudly and Branna rolled her eyes.

'Are you fed up with Louis today?' Swift signed. Sometimes, silent communication was handy.

'Don't know. He stupid.'

'Why is he stupid?'

'Don't know. Just is. Spell wants a biscuit.' Her beady eyes were on the cupboard door.

'Oh, I see. Well, no biscuits right now. Louis isn't allowed biscuits and it wouldn't be fair to him.'

'Why can't he?'

'His mums don't like him having sugary stuff.' It was Simone's rule but Mary went along with it. Simone ensured that Louis ate only organic foods and no sugar or ready meals.

'No sweets?' Branna looked dejected.

'No. You can have one of these mango and coconut bars. Simone made them. They're tasty.'

'Don't like mango.'

Inevitable. 'Okay, don't have one then.'

'I want biscuit.'

'When Louis has gone. Then just one.'

'Marcel let me have two.'

'I doubt it. I'm your dad and I say one. You can have an apple for now.'

'Apples smell.'

'That's right. They smell of apples. Do you want one?'

Branna didn't reply but stomped away, arms folded, and threw herself into a chair. She proceeded to kick her legs and sing '*La la la*' in competition with 'Old MacDonald'. Louis objected and it took several minutes to restore peace. As soon as they were focused on guzzling apple juice, he hid the annoying lorry behind the sofa. He was relieved when the doorbell rang.

Once Louis had gone with Mary, Branna morphed into a winsome, delightful child, cuddling up for stories. She was in the bath, creating mayhem with bubbles, when Swift's phone rang. It was Faith, sobbing.

'Ty, it's Sol. He's . . . he's really ill. I found him collapsed.'

'Oh, Faith. I'm so sorry. What's happened?'

'I don't know. I thought he was dead.'

'Where are you?'

'At the hospital. Doctors are with him. He was on his bedroom floor. Oh Ty, he was so cold, I really thought he was dead. Thank God he'd given me a key. The paramedic said it might be pneumonia. I don't know what to do. I'm just . . . I don't know . . .'

He could hear her desperation and jumbled words. The last thing she needed was for the hospital staff to think she was drunk or drugged up. 'I'll see if I can get over there.'

'Can you? What about Branna?'

'Leave it with me. I'll ring back soon.'

He knew that Ruth and Marcel were away for the weekend, not back until tomorrow evening, but he'd heard Elvis singing upstairs earlier. He knelt down beside the bath as Branna popped bubbles and giggled.

'Faith's a bit upset and I need to go and help her. Is it okay if I see if Chand from upstairs can look after you for a couple of hours?' He was expecting immediate protests but as so often happened, she wrong-footed him.

She furrowed her brows and stared at him. 'Here?'

'Yes, here. I won't be long. Chand's nice. You like him.'

'He found fruit gum behind my ear.'

Thank goodness for Chand's basic magic tricks. 'That's right, and his mum made the lovely bhajis we had for tea.'

She thought about it. 'Two biscuits for supper?'

'Yes, okay. But no more. I worry that you're going to grow up into a serial blackmailer.' *A very fat one with no teeth*, he thought.

'What's blackmailer?'

'Tell you later.'

He rang Chand, who said he was fine to babysit for a couple of hours. Swift dried Branna, got her into her pyjamas, left instructions regarding supper with Chand, wished him luck, and headed for his car.

CHAPTER 12

Faith was pale and subdued. She was slumped in a chair by a water dispenser and looked up at him with raw eyes.

'Any news?'

'They think it's fungal pneumonia. It's serious and his immune system is weak. They asked me if Sol ever had heart problems. I don't know. He never mentioned that he had.'

'He has a long history of alcohol abuse and that would have affected his immune system,' Swift said.

'I know. I don't know what to do.'

'Do you know his mother's address?'

Faith shook her head. 'I've never met her. I believe his mum refuses to speak to him because of his drinking. She cut him out of the family after he gave up on rehab.'

'He told me that,' Swift confirmed. 'He said that his mother lives in Somerset and pays him an allowance. She won't be hard to find.'

'She paid him to stay away!' Faith gave a wild laugh, shuddered and then leaned forward with her face in her hands.

A doctor came through swing doors, asked Faith if she was okay and invited them to step into a side cubicle. Faith looked distraught.

'Your friend is very ill and we're admitting him,' the doctor said. 'We've started him on antibiotics. He's very dehydrated.'

'Will he be okay?' Faith asked.

'We'll hope for the best but his condition is serious. Also, he looks malnourished. We'll be able to tell you more after further tests.'

'Can I see him?' Faith was drooping. Swift put an arm about her and she leaned against him with a grateful sigh.

The doctor gave her a measuring look. 'Not now. You've had a bad shock. I suggest you go home and come back in the morning. We'll ring you if there's any change.'

Swift thought the doctor looked as worn out as Faith. 'Mr Waters once told me that his mother lives in Somerset. He mentioned two sisters. I got the impression he doesn't have much family contact.'

'Okay, thanks. I'll pass that on.' Her bleeper sounded and she turned away.

'Come on, I can take you home,' Swift said, keeping a hand under Faith's elbow in case she folded to the floor.

She sank into the car. Her hair was loose and she wrapped it around her neck, tugging on it. The street was busy with Saturday night traffic. A pub opposite had its front windows open to the balmy evening air. Light spilled out, reflecting on raised glasses and women's pale, shiny dresses. Customers lounged outside in the inky shadows, glasses and bottles clinking, laughter soaring. Faith wanted to talk, so he left the key in the ignition and turned to her.

'I can't believe this,' she said. 'This is like another bad dream. My life is full of them. I saw Sol two days ago and he seemed better.'

'Maybe he had an underlying problem. Something undiagnosed and the chest infection triggered it.'

'Do you think he'll be okay?'

'I don't know, Faith.'

'He's a link to Kelly and he knows all of her history, the good and bad, not just the airbrushed version. It's good to be able to talk about her. We've been hanging out. He seems to understand the way I am now.' She groaned and covered her eyes. 'I feel like I'm such a drag, to myself and other people. Maybe it'd have been better if the hammer had finished me off.'

'You've had a bad shock. Have you felt like that before tonight?'

'Now and again. There are times when I don't want to wake up. Don't see any point in going on, not like this.'

'Have you told your doctor or therapist?'

She shrugged and looked away, digging her nails into her palms. His phone rang and he saw Ruth's name on the caller display. 'Sorry, I have to get this,' he said.

Ruth sounded relaxed. 'Hello, Ty. I just wanted to say night-night to Branna. Is everything okay?'

'Branna's fine. We had a good day, lots of activity and Louis came to play.'

'Great. Let me just have a chat with her.'

'Well, the thing is . . .'

'She's not asleep yet, is she? I thought I'd timed it okay.'

'The thing is, I'm not at home at the moment.'

'What do you mean? Are you out with Branna somewhere? It's a bit late.'

'No, I was called out. Branna's at home. Chand's minding her for an hour or so.'

'Chand? The guy upstairs?'

'Yes. Chand Malla. You know, he moved in a while back.'

A cold silence. Then her voice rose. 'You've left Branna on her own with your tenant? She hardly knows him.'

'She's met him a couple of times. She was fine with him. I'm not going to be long, and she was ready for bed. He's giving her some supper.'

'I can't believe this. Where are you?'

'I'm at a hospital with Faith Black. I'm working with her at the moment and she found her close friend collapsed in his flat, so I—'

'For God's sake, Ty! What is it with you? Hold on.'

There was another voice. Bloody Vaudin poking his nose in. Ruth related what was happening to him.

'Ruth, there's nothing to worry about. Chand's fine. I wouldn't have left him with Branna if I didn't think so. You know that my work sometimes means I have to deal with the unexpected and this is complex.'

'Oh well, I suppose I have to be grateful that at least this collapsed person wasn't in your house for Branna to stumble across when she was playing. Don't you think that when she's with you, she should be your priority? Oh, we've had this conversation before. It's like Groundhog Day. Don't bother answering. I don't want to listen to your excuses. Give me Chand's number. I want to speak to my daughter and make sure she's okay. I warn you, Ty, at this rate you'll be lucky if I let Branna stay with you ever again.'

'Ruth, there's no need to—'

'Shut up and give me the number.'

He gave it to her and she rang off immediately. He put the phone down and rubbed his temples.

'Was that Branna's mum?'

'Yes.' He sighed. 'I'd better get you home.'

'I'm so sorry. I'm causing yet more trouble and you've been so kind. Just drop me at a tube station or I'll call a cab.'

He looked at her sunken eyes and heard the weariness in her voice. She was depressed and ready to drop. He couldn't let her wander around the city in this state. 'No, it's okay. I'll ring Chand as soon as I've seen you home.'

He drove as quickly as he could. He felt sweat between his shoulder blades. He didn't believe that Ruth would stop Branna visiting him. She knew how much he doted on his daughter. He wouldn't be so worried if he was dealing with just Ruth. But since she'd met Vaudin, she'd become more critical of him and quicker to judge. He could only hope that Chand had stuck to the instruction about biscuits and that Branna didn't tell her mother she'd eaten a packet.

He saw Faith through her door. 'You're sure you'll be okay on your own?'

'Yes, thanks. I just need my bed. Thanks, Ty. You're doing so much and I can't even pay you.'

He checked that the door was closed before he dashed to the car and headed home. The pavements were busy with carefree people strolling and making the most of the warm, embracing night. Heavy-hearted, he drove past, resenting their contentment.

* * *

The house was a handsome detached property, poised at the end of a steep driveway and situated on the outskirts of Guildford. The roof was covered in solar panels. Ellis Greeve was outside pruning a copper beech hedge when Swift arrived. He nodded and took off his gardening gloves, but didn't offer to shake hands.

He led Swift around the side of the house, past the open garage. It was orderly and shelved from floor to ceiling. Labelled Perspex boxes stood on shelves next to sets of drawers. Electrical equipment hung in neat rows with tidy, coiled flexes. It was a space owned by a man who would know exactly where to find things. Swift followed him past a water butt and a rose-covered trellis to the back of the house and into a wide, sunny kitchen decorated in yellow and cream with lime green curtains at the windows. There was a delicious smell of roasting pork. Swift could see it gleaming through the glass door of the oven. A dozen or so birthday cards were lined up on the window ledges.

'Take a seat. Can I offer you a tea or coffee?'

'No, thanks. Thanks for seeing me.'

Greeve poured himself a glass of water and pulled a chair out. He was a stout man with thinning, greyish hair, a sagging double chin and large, soft eyes.

'Someone's birthday?' Swift asked.

'My son's, last weekend. I took him to Paris. Lucy — my wife — and I always said that's what we'd do for his twenty-first. It means I'm fifty, which I find hard to believe.'

He looked older than fifty, but grief scored lines on faces.

'Mr Greeve, I've spoken to Chantelle Lowick who used to be the manager at the charity where Kelly Dwyer worked. I know that you were angry with Kelly over your wife's death and that Ms Lowick met with you.'

'She was a nice woman — Ms Lowick, that is. Very understanding. I didn't get to meet Kelly, which was probably just as well. Has Kelly asked you to contact me? A bit late for apologies now, even if I wanted them from her.'

Swift hadn't told Greeve about Kelly's death on the phone. He wanted to see his reaction.

'Kelly's dead, Mr Greeve. She was attacked and drowned. She was with her sister, Faith Black, on board a ferry from Ireland. Faith was also attacked with a hammer and has memory loss. I'm investigating what happened and I'm trying to help Faith recover her memory.'

Greeve looked nonplussed. He unzipped his gilet and opened the top button of his shirt. 'Well, that's a terrible thing to have happened to Kelly's sister. I'm sorry to hear it. But why would she want to remember what Kelly did to my wife? I don't see how that would help her.'

It might help me as it could give you a motive. 'The memory might come back anyway. Faith knows that something happened at Whiteleaf regarding her sister, but not the details.'

Greeve examined the nails on his right hand and picked at the skin on his thumb. 'I have a splinter in here that I can't get at. I put this sticky ointment on that's supposed to draw it out but I'm not sure it's working.' He stared at Swift, as if weighing up his words. 'Give me one reason why I should help you or Faith Black. I can't say I'm saddened that Kelly Dwyer died. I'd be lying if I did. I've recovered now from what happened, but I can't forgive Kelly. I'm sorry for her sister's troubles but they're nothing to do with me.'

'I thought you might say that. I think that you're a reasonable man, from what Ms Lowick said. Faith's been through a terrible experience, and she's in a bad way. Whatever happened to your wife was nothing to do with her, either.'

Greeve folded his arms and turned to look at the roasting pork. He sounded resigned. 'What is it you want to know?'

'Tell me about what happened at Whiteleaf.'

'Whiteleaf. That name's burned on my heart. The worst of it is, I persuaded Lucy to go there. She'd had a heart scare, and the consultant told her that if she didn't stop drinking, she'd make herself very ill. She wanted to stop, but she was going to try doing it at home with the help of her doctor and medication. I'd seen a leaflet about the clinic, and I thought she'd be better if she went in there. No temptation and constant support from trained staff, a good diet. All of that. I took her for a visit and it was superb. Like a comfortable hotel, with a gym and swimming pool and lovely woodland around it. We could afford it, and I wanted the best for her. So did Robin.'

'Robin?'

'Our son. He pleaded with Lucy to agree to go there. He was sixteen at the time and worried sick about his mum. Embarrassed, too, of course. Lucy'd fallen flat on her face at a parents' evening at his school. Down on the floor in front of everyone. Drunk as a skunk. Some kid had taken a photo of her and put it on social media and then it did the rounds, like a bloody contagion. I think his generation call it faceplanting. You can imagine how that made Robin feel.'

'That's hard. Very public shame.'

'Indeed. You expect your teenager to embarrass his parents in public, not the other way round. He showed Lucy the photo. I came home one evening, and they were both in here in tears. She was doing that thing drinkers do, saying that it wasn't as bad as it looked, she'd tripped and it could have happened to anyone. But Robin's misery finally cut through all the bluster. The next day, she agreed to book a place at the clinic. It's only a couple of miles from here, so I visited her every evening.'

'Did Robin visit her there?'

'Just the once. She was struggling with the withdrawal and tearful a lot of the time. She could see it made him uncomfortable, so she told him not to come back. Told him he'd get a newly minted mum at the end of it. She said . . .' He swallowed, waited a moment. 'She said she'd go to his next parents' evening and be a mum he could be proud of. For four weeks, I'd started to believe that. Until Kelly Dwyer got to her. Lucy talked about Kelly, said how much she liked her and that she was good company, made her laugh. I was glad that she'd met someone she got on with so well and who was cheering her up during a difficult time.' He shook his head.

'But then it all went wrong.'

'Oh, yes. Kelly Dwyer had got hold of some alcohol and had had a party with Lucy in her room. There was some man involved, too. They were all blotto. Lucy knew she'd fallen off the wagon and discharged herself shortly after. I couldn't persuade her to stay, nor could anyone at Whiteleaf. They didn't blame her for the incident and were willing to give her a second chance after all the progress she'd made. She was remorseful and apologetic when she came home, but she was back on the drink, big time. Robin had huge rows with her. You know what teenagers can be like. He was savage to her, took no prisoners. He felt so let down. Then, one Sunday morning, three weeks after she came back home, she had a stroke. She was sitting there, where you are. She looked like death warmed up, but then she often looked like that in the mornings. Grey and worn. She got up to put the kettle on, and halfway across the floor she fell down dead in front of me and Robin.'

'I'm so sorry.'

'Yes. Excuse me a moment.' He rose and opened the oven door. He lifted the roasting tray on top of the hob, turned the vegetables tucked around the joint, and then pressed the top of the pork with a fingertip. He made an effort to sound brighter. 'Robin's home tonight and he loves crackling. Thought I'd treat him.'

'Does he still live with you?'

'Not full time. His job's in Morden so he rents a room there, but he stays a couple of nights a week with me. I'm glad of the company. We don't get in each other's space and I know he gets some square meals.'

'What does Robin do?'

'He sells ceramic floors, doing very well at it. Is that it, Mr Swift? I need to get the gravy on.'

'You've been very helpful. I just want to ask you about after your wife died. I suppose you thought about what Kelly had done and you wanted to tell her how you felt?'

'I was furious. So was Robin. He felt guilty, too, because of the things he'd said to his mum. We were both in a very strange place, to be honest. Mad with grief. We'd had our hopes raised, and then we were left so alone. Robin browsed some websites and found out where Kelly Dwyer worked. He wanted to go there with me, but I persuaded him to let me see her on my own. That wasn't something a young lad should do. I wanted to make her face up to what she'd caused, hear her admit responsibility. Robin was — ah, here he is now!'

A tall young man with a shock of thick, brown hair came through the kitchen door, slung his rucksack on the floor and went straight to the fridge for a can of fizzy orange. 'Train was heaving as per. Don't know how they can charge those prices when you can't even get a seat. Smells good, Pops.'

Greeve smiled fondly at his son. 'This is Mr Swift. I mentioned that he was calling in.'

'Did you?'

'I did. You know, about Kelly Dwyer. Mr Swift is a family member.'

He raised his eyebrows. Swift thought it was a warning to his son to be careful.

'Right.' Robin pulled the can open and aimed the ring pull into a waste bin. He stood against the wall, one arm behind his back, and downed half of the orange. He had sleepy, heavy-lidded eyes, a wide, loose mouth and a sullen expression. He looked as if he was still growing into his face. 'Hope your relative has a guilty conscience, knowing what she did to my mum.'

'Let's not start on that,' his father said. 'We've put that behind us. Our dinner's almost ready. Why don't you go and have a wash?'

'In a min. What brings you here, anyway, raking it all up?'

'I'm sorry about your mother. Kelly died. I'm investigating her death.'

Robin frowned. 'How did she die? Liver failure?'

'She was attacked and thrown from a ferry. She drowned.'

'Can't offer any sympathy. Not after what she did.'

'That's okay. I wasn't looking for sympathy.'

'Oh? What are you looking for, then? My pops doesn't need any more grief from anyone. I don't know why he's giving you the time of day.'

He was gruff, but there was a baffled look in his eyes, one that Swift was familiar with. He still couldn't believe he'd never see his mother again.

His father gave him an anxious glance and placed a hand on his arm. 'It's okay, Robin. We're nearly done here. I was about to finish telling Mr Swift what happened. I went to visit Ms Dwyer at her workplace, but Ms Lowick saw me. I'm glad she did and that I didn't confront Kelly. Talking to Ms Lowick helped, and I saw a bereavement counsellor. I still think that Kelly Dwyer played a part in Lucy's death, but I know that she might have died anyway, and we can't directly attribute her stroke to what happened at Whiteleaf. Lucy had been an alcoholic for a long time, and she was responsible for the damage to her health. We've accepted that. Now, this food will spoil if we don't eat soon.'

Swift had been watching Robin while his father talked. He had a curiously blank expression, as if he was suppressing emotion. Swift wasn't convinced that he shared his father's acceptance that Lucy Greeve had accelerated her own demise.

'It's hard, losing your mother when you're young,' he said to Robin. 'I lost my mum when I was fifteen and Kelly's mother died when she was a teenager. So she'd had her own grief to deal with.'

Robin smirked. 'You don't need to bother with the false empathy. It's so patronising. I don't give a toss about Kelly or her mother.'

'Have you ever travelled from Ireland by ferry?'

The young man backed away like a wary dog, his eyes watchful. Greeve was turned away from them, busy at the hob. Robin glanced at his father and then mouthed *'Fuck you'* at Swift. He gulped the rest of his drink, burped and wiped his mouth with the back of his hand.

Greeve was dropping a stock cube into the roasting tray. 'Manners, Rob! Why are you asking my son that, Mr Swift?'

'No particular reason. I just wondered.'

Robin resumed his blank look, flipped his can into the bin and shouldered through the kitchen door, saying he was going to grab a quick shower.

'Can I ask you the same question — have you travelled on a ferry from Ireland?'

Greeve was adding cornflour to the pork juices. 'No, I haven't, and Rob's never been to Ireland, either. Now, I really need to finish the dinner.'

Swift left him and walked back down the drive. At the bottom, he turned and looked up at the house. Robin was standing in the front bedroom window, staring down. He raised two fingers and kept them there. Swift shrugged and walked to his car. An angry man. Angry enough to nurse his resentment and plan Kelly's murder?

CHAPTER 13

'I can see Ruth's point of view,' Bella said. 'She doesn't know Chand and although we appreciate that he's lovely, she's not been in his company.'

'Yes, okay. Sorry I dropped you in it, Chand.'

'No worries. As soon as Ruth rang, I put Branna on to her and then I spoke to her. In the end, she seemed to find it amusing that I'd taught Branna the chorus of "Return to Sender" — she sang it to her mum.'

'So you see, Branna *was* being tormented by her minder, but in the nicest possible way.' Bella laughed. 'So did Ruth give you an ear-bending, Ty?'

'To start with. We spoke when I took Branna home and she was more conciliatory.' It had been a cool conversation, with Swift having to promise that he would never leave Branna with anyone else again without first discussing it with her mother. Events in Rossdown were revisited and picked over. He'd felt as if he was a defendant asking for previous convictions not to be taken into account, while Ruth was the judge, handing down a sentence with conditions attached. He'd been aware, too, of Vaudin lurking in the background like an invisible jury member.

They were sitting around Chand's table, eating his mother's spicy battered fish with mixed pickles. Bella had been Swift's girlfriend at university. They'd met up again after many years and he'd introduced her to Chand. They were now a devoted couple, always touching each other lightly and exchanging fond glances. Swift was just thinking how well-suited they were when Chand tapped his glass with his fork.

'Ty, we've asked you to dinner to give you some news.'

'Go on.' He reckoned he might know what it was.

'We're getting married!' Bella said.

'Congratulations! I'm very happy for you. When's the big day?'

'To be decided, but next year. You're the first person we've told, after our families. After all, you brought us together. You and Nora will come to the wedding, won't you?'

'Of course.' Two thoughts struck him. The first was whether he and Nora would still be together by then. Then, 'Does that mean you'll be moving out, Chand?'

'I will, yes. Not for a while, though. I'll be moving in with Bella to start with. Then we're going to look for a house.'

'We want a big family, so we'll have to get on with it,' Bella told him. 'I don't think you'll have any trouble finding a new tenant.'

'I'm sure I'll manage. But I'll miss the King singing to me regularly, and what will I do without Mrs Malla's food?'

'Oh, no worries. My mother will still provide me with meals, even after I'm married, so I can keep you supplied. She doesn't believe that any other woman can cook properly. She's already given Bella the third degree about her culinary skills.'

'Yes,' Bella said. 'Chand's mum was horrified that I don't grind all my own spices. I tried to explain that I work and have limited time in the kitchen, but I could see from the look in her eyes that I didn't come up to snuff. When I suggested that she could teach Chand how to cook, I might as well have asked her to send him to the moon.'

'Will it be an Elvis-themed wedding?' Swift asked with a grin.

Bella held up a warning finger. 'No. There's strict rationing. One Elvis song will be allowed at the reception.'

'How about you and Nora — any plans to move in together or maybe even marry?' Chand passed more fish around.

'We like things the way they are for now,' Swift said. Bella gave him a knowing glance. She'd encountered Nora's short fuse in the past and seen her crackle with temper. He couldn't begin to imagine being under the same roof as Nora and quickly pushed the prospect away. He asked where they were planning to marry, happy to sit back, listen to their ideas and bask in their contentment.

Nora phoned him as Chand was making coffee. They were taking up Fitz Blackmore's offer to go rowing with him the following weekend, and she'd been checking that she could get the time off. He was replete with good food and wine and happy for his friends, so her chilly tone was a shock.

'Can you talk?'

'Hi, I'm just having dinner at Chand's. His mum's amazing homemade pickles. Chand and Bella are getting married, they've just told me.'

'How lovely.'

He wondered if she was being curt because she was still at work and could be overheard. 'Are you still grafting? How are you?'

'Pissed off, to be honest.' Her voice was tight and angry.

'Problems at work? Can't you get the weekend off?'

'No. That's the easy bit. The problem's with you.'

'Me? What do you mean?'

'I hear you've been gossiping to Fitz about me. Apparently, I'm hard work.'

'What? I don't understand. Who told you that?'

'A guy who's just joined my team. He used to work with Fitz in Cornford and still keeps in touch with him. He came to the pub this evening and enjoyed telling me that I'm short-tempered and difficult. He asked if I was like that at work and if he'd need a riot shield handy. He said Fitz told him you let him know how impossible I am.'

His heart sank to his toes. The perils of too much drink and a loose tongue last winter. He'd thought he could rely on Blackmore to keep those confidences to himself.

'You've gone quiet, Ty. Suppose that tells me what I need to know.'

'Nora, I'm really sorry that's happened. I did talk to Fitz once, when I first met him. It was in the middle of that Roscoe case and we were chatting at his place late at night. I stayed over, remember? Because of heavy snowfall. I'd had a bit to drink and I was . . . unguarded.'

'Unguarded? So you meant it — you just wish that Fitz hadn't leaked it and it's got back to me?'

He could see Bella pretending to read a magazine but glancing at him. 'Can I ring you back? I'm upstairs, and—'

'No, you bloody well can't. We need to sort this out now.'

'Hang on, then.' He asked Bella to tell Chand he'd have to skip coffee and headed downstairs to his flat, where he went into the garden. What was he hoping — that the cool evening air would filter through to Nora and calm her temper? 'Still there, Nora?'

'Yes. Just. So, explain this crap to me. If you can.'

Honesty was the only way. 'We do have our ups and downs. As I told you, I was talking to Fitz. I can't even remember a lot about what I said. I was quite a few beers in. I'm sorry. I didn't mean it to be gossip for other people.'

'That was kind of you, talking about our relationship to a guy you hardly knew at the time. And a cop, too. You know how this stuff works, you were in the Met. Some blokes love undermining women with little labels.'

'I can only say I'm sorry. Fitz should have kept his mouth shut.'

'No, *you* should have kept your mouth shut!'

'All right, Nora. I've apologized. Is it such a big deal that this new colleague has swapped some gossip? You're big enough to ignore it, and you have a strong reputation.'

'Oh, here we go! Now you're placing the responsibility on me, making this my problem!'

'That's not what I meant—'

'Yes, it is. You know it's still hard for women to get taken seriously in the force. Some men love to point an arrow saying "difficult and cranky" at you. Handy phrases that cover so many prejudices. I thought better of you. I thought you were different. I thought you had my back!'

He tore off a sycamore leaf. Might as well go for broke when your own back was to the wall. 'You do know that you can be bad-tempered and tricky, don't you?'

'So what? I'm only human. And not at work, I'm not.'

'Thanks for saving it for me, then. You know I find it hard going, I've told you. And you've been bad-tempered with Branna, which is a whole other issue. You've ducked that when I've tried to discuss it. And by the way, that "only human" riff is a cop out. Ruth nearly stopped you from seeing Branna again after our holiday because of how you behaved. You don't see how you upset people, and when I try to talk to you about it, you won't engage. I'm fed up of being on tenterhooks around you, especially where Branna's concerned. I apologize that this has crossed over into your professional life, and I didn't intend it to, but there are a lot of things we never seem to sort out.'

There was a long, cold silence. 'Well, I'm glad that's all out in the open. I wouldn't want to get on the wrong side of Ruth. She's always the most important woman in your life, after all. Ruth comes first, every time. She's where the power lies.'

'Don't start on that. You know that's not true.'

'Oh, yes it is. I think the real problem here is that you can't see the truth of it.'

'We've had this conversation before.'

'Yes, and it never resolves anything. You're tied to her and Branna in a way that's just not healthy. I don't see how you'll ever commit to anyone else while that's the case. Even if she marries Vaudin, you'll be hanging around in case he gets run over or falls off a cliff.'

'Now you're being ridiculous.'

'No, Ty. You're the one who's ridiculous, dancing to Ruth's tune. I'm not the only one who thinks so.'

He hated this but if she wanted to fight dirty, she could bring it on. 'Who else thinks so?'

'I can think of a few. Mary does, that's for certain.'

'No, that won't wash. Mary is concerned about your temper, though, and the example it sets for Branna. And the more I think about that, the more I think that you're not a good influence on my daughter.'

Silence. He thought she'd gone, but then she said with quiet anger, 'Maybe we're just not suited.'

'Maybe you're right.'

'Yeah. Well, at least we agree on something. Fine. Think I'll pass on the weekend trip. Doesn't appeal much and I can't see how I'd fit in. You and Fitz can have a boys' outing and moan about how awful women are. Fitz will be up for that. You can tell him I'm not going. I don't want to have anything more to do with that gossiping lothario. Maybe the two of you can pull a couple of those women who like blokes using them as doormats. You can start a new rowing club — The Floating Misogynists. Enjoy.'

She'd gone. He paced the small garden and then leaned against the wall, looking up at a jet's vapour trail in the clear sky. Nigel leaped up behind him and rubbed his face against Swift's neck, pushing against his skin. His nose was cold, his breath warm and fishy. His owners were away and he was lonely. He issued a plaintive meow. Swift stroked his head. 'You and me both,' he said. He saw that he had a missed call from Faith, took a breath and phoned her.

She sounded faint. 'I'm at the hospital. Been here most of the day. Sol's a tiny bit better. Squeezed my hand earlier. It made me cry. Not that that's difficult.'

'Are you holding up okay?'

'Yeah. At least if I collapse I'm in the right place. His mum's coming tomorrow, so I'll stay away, get some sleep. Did I get you into a lot of trouble about Branna?'

'I'm fine. Just take care of yourself. Stay in touch.'

* * *

Hey there Swift,

I expect this finds you meddling in someone's life. Probably causing them more grief than joy, knowing you.

I'm continuing to enjoy my studies. I've seen Oliver again. He brought me some lovely biscuits. I find him caring and friendly. Nothing like the nasty person you and your solicitor tried to paint him as in court, but of course, you've got your own agenda there. You spent so much time and energy weaselling your way into Cedric's good books, you have to bad-mouth his son to make yourself feel better.

Just thought I'd pass on this gem that I read about a successfully contested will recently. The barrister commented that the case highlighted that 'although people can decide to disinherit their children, they will have to have good reasons for doing so. It would be advisable to document those reasons carefully and in detail.' Oh dear, Cedric forgot to do that latter bit. Shame. For you, anyway.

I'd also draw your attention, M'lud, to the case of JW in the High Court, 1972. The court held that the father had not made proper provision for his son. It awarded him half of his father's estate.

Hope your solicitor's up to the job. NOT!

Thinking about you,

CF

He was sitting in his car near Bridesmaid Dreams, on the edge of West Hampstead. He was early, so was eating a croissant and checking emails. He looked up the case that Camilla had referred to. Her facts were correct, as he'd known they would be. He rang his solicitor. She'd heard nothing further about a hearing and there was no action she could take to speed it up. She told him to try and not worry. They had a strong case and if the last court hearing was anything to go by, Oliver would shoot himself in the foot anyway. '*Yes, but he didn't have Camilla Finley onside then*,' Swift wanted to say, but there didn't seem to be much point.

Next, he rang Fitz Blackmore to tell him that Nora wouldn't be able to make it this weekend and left a message, lying that she couldn't get time off work. The last thing he needed was Blackmore giving him heavy-handed relationship advice, which was likely to be of the '*Just move on and find some fresh totty*' variety. He flicked pastry flakes from his shirt and saw a woman turn the corner. She let herself into the house he was aiming for. She was in her fifties, well-built and blonde, and he recognized her from the photo on her company website.

He waited a couple of minutes and then followed a sign inside the gate, asking him to ring a bell and directing him to the side of the house for Bridesmaid Dreams. He walked down a hedged, paved path and then saw that the business was housed in a wide, timber-framed garden office at the end of a lawn. Amber Oxendon was waiting with the door open. She wore a smart, cream dress with a matching jacket.

'I've just put the kettle on if you want a tea or coffee, Mr Swift.'

'Coffee would be good, thanks.' He looked around at the light-drenched office. One wall was covered with wedding photos, focusing on beaming brides and their paid bridesmaids. He recognized Faith in one of them, dressed in pale apricot muslin and looking like a character from Jane Austen. He knew the style of her dress was empire line from his time with Kris Jelen. She'd been a talented seamstress and had taught him facts about clothing that he retained, to his great surprise. 'This is a lovely space.'

'Thanks. It actually started life as my dad's annexe when he moved to live with us. He liked being at arm's length. After he died and I decided to start the business, it seemed a good idea to use it as my office.' She waved to a wicker chair.

'What made you think of supplying bridesmaids?'

She smiled, speaking in a light, crisp tone. 'My own daughter's wedding. She was stressed to high doh, and her two bridesmaids fell out with each other over losing weight and the accessories they should wear. It's amazing, how competitive this has all become. I suppose reality TV plays its part. Then their mothers got involved, and there were emails flying. One of them reneged on the day, pretending sickness, but I know it was just sour grapes because she'd discovered the other bridesmaid had had a spray tan done. That was naughty, because they'd agreed not to. I watched it all and saw my daughter getting paler by the minute. I thought there had to be a better way of organizing things. I didn't come up with the original idea, but there's certainly a market for having professional, disinterested help on your big day.'

'How did you recruit Faith?'

'She answered an online ad and as soon as I interviewed her, I knew she was right for the job. She was pretty, very fit — you need lots of energy — intelligent and even-tempered. How is she, these days? I asked her to keep in touch but I've not heard from her.' Amber had a square, hard-looking face and no-nonsense manner, but her eyes were lively and warm.

'She's working hard at her recovery, but it's slow going. She doesn't socialize much. She finds it difficult and tiring.'

'That was so dreadful, what happened. Makes me shiver. And you're investigating what happened to her and her sister?'

'That's right. I wanted to talk to you because Faith's memory has been quite badly affected, and she's lost track of details about her life. I need to build up the picture.'

'Okay. I don't know what I can tell you.'

'Had Faith got into any problems at work or got on the wrong side of anyone? As you said, weddings can be stressful occasions.'

Amber puffed her cheeks out and tapped the arm of her chair with a deep red fingernail. 'What has Faith told you about her work?'

'General stuff. Her role as a bridesmaid, the duties it entailed. She said it was a combination of being a best friend, therapist, PA and peacekeeper.'

Amber smiled. 'That's the description I give people. Most of the time, Faith did really well and I had lovely feedback about her. She was popular, good at anticipating problems and responding quickly when they came up. She had a natural flair for blending in, as well, which is so important in this line of work.'

'Can I hear a "but" hovering?'

She nodded. 'I did have to have words with Faith about a situation. I think it happened because she's young and misjudged things — and, well, it was her sister's fault as much as hers.' She paused. 'Faith hasn't told you this herself, about the complications over the stag night?'

'She hasn't mentioned a stag night. She probably doesn't remember. Sounds like the kind of information I need to know.' *Especially if it involved Kelly.*

'Yes, I see. Well, it was last summer — July, I think. We had a bride who was suspicious about her husband-to-be. They were getting married in August and she wasn't sure about his commitment, thought he might use his stag weekend in Amsterdam to play away. So she wanted Faith to stay in the same hotel for the weekend and observe him, report back on what he got up to.' She laughed. 'Doing your kind of job, really, being a private eye. It was all expenses paid, so Faith agreed to do it.'

'Wasn't that a bit outside of the bridesmaid remit?'

She shook her head. 'You'd be surprised at some of the requests we get. If it's legal and decent, we always consider it.'

'And did the groom behave?'

'Oh, yes. He wasn't the problem. The first glitch was that at the last minute, Kelly decided to go with Faith and booked a room in the same hotel. I wasn't aware of that, and I wouldn't have approved of it. Faith was working and she needed to focus.'

'And the second problem?'

'One of the groom's friends saw Kelly hanging around with Faith. I suspect that Faith wasn't much good at being undercover, could have done with some tips from you, and of course, two pretty young women would attract attention. This chap — his name was Higham — started chatting to Kelly and ended up exchanging numbers with her. Faith told me she knew nothing about that. She was too busy keeping an eye on the groom. I believed her. Higham rang Kelly when they got back to London and she met up with him. She didn't tell Faith, maybe because she knew it might not go down so well. Then the proverbial hit the fan.'

'Why did it cause problems?'

'For the very good reason that Higham was married to the groom's sister, who got suspicious about her husband and checked his phone. She found Kelly's details, grilled Higham about it and then all hell was let loose when she discovered the link to Faith. This all happened the day before the wedding. I had the bride in tears, her parents threatening me with legal action and the angry wife burning my ears on the phone. The bride refused to have Faith anywhere near her, and I was in no position to argue the case. I had to agree to send a replacement bridesmaid, refund the Amsterdam costs and reduce the fee.'

Kelly and Faith had had quite a few things in common, and one of them seemed to be that they both liked to sabotage themselves at work and annoy their managers.

'Did you sack Faith?'

'I considered it, but no. She was deeply apologetic, and I could see that Kelly had persuaded her to let her go to Amsterdam. I have a forceful older sister myself, so I know what that's like. I remember she said that Kelly had always been a bit of a trouble magnet, but she'd settled down more in recent years. Faith had been so skilled and reliable up to then, I gave her another chance. She agreed to work her next wedding for half-pay to compensate me. I could see that she was really kicking herself over what had happened. And — well, I was young and a bit daft once myself. Faith was doing fine and was due to attend another wedding the week after she came back from Ireland.'

'How did she take what Kelly had done — hooking up with this Higham behind her back and sabotaging her work?'

'She seemed to put it down to experience, once she knew she still had her job. She said Kelly hadn't realized that Higham was married, that it would cause so much trouble.'

The phone had been ringing constantly and taking messages while they were talking. Amber glanced at the winking light on the answerphone. Swift was about to wind up the interview when she picked up a pen and rolled it between her fingers.

'Faith once mentioned that she was a bit concerned about her sister. Something about a friend of hers and problems she was having.'

'When was this?'

'I can't remember exactly. Not long after Faith started with me, which would have been over two years ago. I was busy, so I didn't pay it too much attention. Faith asked me about — what was it — oh, some friend of her sister's who'd had marriage troubles. This friend had cut her sister off, hadn't spoken to her for a good while. Something of that nature. I think I said that maybe it was best to just let it go.'

'Did Faith mention the friend's name?'

'I don't think so. If she did, I don't recall it.'

He asked her to contact him if she remembered anything else. She sent a quick text, picked up a bag and camera and said she'd walk him out.

'I'm taking some fresh photos to put online. My daughters are modelling our latest dresses. Sometimes the brides want to choose them, but we also have a bespoke selection.'

The back door opened as they neared the house and two young women came out, one blonde and one with the shade of raven black hair that used to be Swift's colour before the silver streaks had crept in. Both were lightly made up and wearing flimsy, strappy shoes. The blonde one wore a short, high-waisted dress, deep blue with ivory lace bodice panels and a layered skirt. The dark-haired one was in a long, dusky pink dress with a dropped waist and sequinned bodice, and she was running her fingers around her hairline.

'I hate this wig, mum. It's scratchy.'

'Bear with it. It won't be for long, and I need the contrast.'

Swift followed them out as they crossed the road towards his car and a small park called Mapesbury Dell. They made an odd group on a bright weekday afternoon, as if they were stray guests who'd mislaid the wedding party.

'Isn't this park lovely?' Amber asked him. 'It used to be a wasteland when we first moved here and now it's a haven for people and wildlife. Do you want to stay while we do our photo session? It'd be good for the girls to have an audience, make them up their game.'

He was aware of the smart-looking trio and his own faded black jeans and T-shirt. Mary claimed his look was shabby chic, which he thought was her polite way of saying 'scruffy'.

'No, thanks. I'll head off.'

'Don't forget about our service. Are you married?'

'No.'

'Well, maybe one day — and then we can help make it special.'

He couldn't imagine it, but nodded. Amber's daughters were taking props from the bag their mother had been carrying — small flower posies, garlands, parasols and champagne flutes. They took position by a small pond surrounded by rose bushes. The grumpy one who hated her wig switched on a practised, radiant smile and turned slightly sideways, one arm behind her back as her mother raised the camera.

CHAPTER 14

Swift sat in the peaceful pub garden under a cherry tree while Blackmore fetched beers and gave their food order. The garden stretched down to the river and he could see their boat rocking gently at its mooring. He was on a rower's high, his skin glowing with energy, his lungs pumped with oxygen. They'd rowed for two hours on the Lea under a misty sun, on quiet waters with an almost imperceptible current. When they had picked up speed, they had been doing twenty oar strokes to the minute. Most of the time they'd travelled in companionable, rhythmic silence, focusing on the glide of the boat and the feathering of their oars in the calm waters. Blackmore seemed in an unusually contemplative mood. None of his usual cockiness and provocative remarks. Swift thought maybe this was the effect the river had on him and why he sought it out on his time off, just as Swift did himself. Whatever the reason, it made Blackmore easy company for a change.

While he waited, he examined an email he'd had from Dermot Dwyer.

I was looking through some stuff and found a letter from my gran that she sent me after Neil died. Thought it might be of interest, so I've scanned it to you. I can't remember receiving it, but looking at the date, I was in hospital at the time and drugged up, so that's not surprising. I don't know what Gran is talking about. Maybe it will make sense to you.

The attached letter was in an elegant hand on lined paper and dated August 2017.

My dear Dermot,

I hope you're being well-looked-after in hospital. I wish I could come and see you, but my own health isn't so good. I pray for you every day.

The neighbours are very kind, but it's strange to be on my own and I miss Neil. He always made me laugh. God forgive me, but I'll never forgive Kelly for what happened. I worry about the night Neil died. Maybe if I'd stepped in between them, he'd be alive now. I heard some of the terrible row they had that night. Neil was very upset and saying that Kelly was responsible for what had happened to someone called Mia. I heard him shout something about Kelly taking responsibility instead of letting this Mia person shoulder the blame. She was yelling back that he wasn't lily-white himself and should mind his own business.

I suppose there's no point dwelling on it now, but I can't help going over it in my mind.

Take care of yourself now, Dermot, and I hope and pray that you'll be better soon.

Gran xx

It sounded as if the row that Mrs Dwyer had overheard referred to more than Kelly helping Mia Wilson to leave her husband. What was 'shouldering the blame' about? Neil must have seen or heard something. That could have happened when he'd visited Willesden. This resonated with the comment that Amber Oxendon had made regarding Faith's concern about Kelly and a friend falling out.

He ran through the information he had on this case. Kelly had seen someone she knew on the ferry. According to DC Keane, Orla and Faith hadn't recognized any names on the passenger manifest, but Kelly might have, if she'd been alive to read it. He thought that Emilia Sheppard had the strongest motive for wanting her out of the way and she was the only suspect who he knew had been on board. He thought of her father's comment, '*What Emmy wants Emmy gets.*' Chantelle Lowick certainly had reasons to hold a grudge and had been away from work when the sisters were attacked. Then there was Robin Greeve, who was still nursing resentment over his mother's death. Of course, Ellis Greeve might have been pretending that he'd forgiven and moved on. They could all be described as dark-haired, fitting Faith's description — if that memory could be trusted. He pictured Sarah Ennis's scar. Orla had checked with Sarah's family in Ireland and had confirmation that she'd been visiting them on the night of 2 October. Then there was the fiasco over Bridesmaid Dreams and the wedding, which had ultimately been Kelly's fault. But surely Faith would have known those family members if they'd been on board the ferry and anyway, Amber Oxendon had compensated them generously for the trouble caused.

He decided that, for now, he'd focus on Emilia and her brother and contact Mia Wilson. Something had gone on with Mia and it appeared to be another complicated situation that Kelly had got herself involved in. Now that he understood more about Kelly's life, he decided that she'd been a meddler with a nose for trouble and without the sense to keep out of it. He shook his head as he contemplated her disasters. Her busy fingers had been in so many pies. Unfortunately for Faith, she'd got caught up in her sister's chaotic slipstream.

He put his head back to feel the sun on his face and eavesdropped on two couples at the next table, talking about the fees at a local private school.

'They're putting them up next year, but we think it's worth it.'

'Oh, definitely. There's so much on offer!'

'I think Chloe would refuse to talk to us if we even considered removing her. She loves it so much.'

Ruth had mentioned the possibility of Branna attending a private school. Swift could tell she was keen on the idea. She'd said there would be much smaller classes, which would benefit Branna, and the social opportunities would be good. Vaudin had been quoted, of course. Swift wanted the best for his daughter, but he wasn't convinced that a private education was the way to achieve it. That would be a battle for another day.

Blackmore returned carrying two pints of a local brew called Brock Bitter.

'This was recommended as "no-nonsense", so I thought we'd try it.'

Swift tasted the light golden, bittersweet ale. 'Just right, thanks. Hits the spot.' It was wonderful and reviving after the strenuous exercise. He drank half of it down.

Blackmore stretched in his chair with his legs out. When he was in languorous mode, he looked like a big, lazy cat. The kind that could deceive you and suddenly pounce. 'I heard yesterday that Camilla Finley's trial date has been set for next month. Have you heard from her again?'

'Oh yes. She's studying law now. She sends me examples of court cases where the judge has found in favour of the person challenging a will. Work has slowed down and I worry that the bad press has put people off.'

'Cow. It's all frustration and spite. Have you ever considered re-joining the Met? I'm sure they'd have you like a shot.'

'Not for me, not now. I'm too fond of my liberty, even if it's uncertain.' Although he did sometimes miss the camaraderie and he'd have had no trouble accessing a passenger manifest in the Met.

Blackmore gazed into his drink and then glanced up from under his thick, sooty eyelashes. His skin was the same warm, glowing tone as his ale. 'Ahm . . . Ron, mate . . . I think I might have dobbed you in with Nora.'

Swift looked him in the eye. He didn't want to discuss this, but it was probably best to get it out of the way. 'She did hear gossip from someone you worked with.'

'Ah, right. Sorry. That'd be Mac Camley. He's moved to her office. We were in the pub and he asked me about her after he'd been for interview. Scoping the territory. I was pretty pissed. Opened my gob when I shouldn't have. Is she mad at you?'

'Yes. And at me, rather than you. I'm not sure that's fair, but that's how she is. It's all icy at present.'

'That's the real reason she hasn't come today?'

'That's right. I wish you had kept your gob shut.'

'Okay, but come on, it wasn't that bad. Nora's overreacting. She can ride out a bit of tittle-tattle. God knows what people say about me and most of it's probably true. Is that the problem for Nora — it hit home?'

'I don't know, Fitz. But Nora didn't take kindly to being talked about. I could have done without the grief. The stuff I told you was in confidence, not to be spread around.'

Blackmore could go from languid to abrasive in seconds. 'Oh, come on, you're sounding all girly. You know us blokes aren't the best at fireside chats. Are you telling me things were hot between you and Nora before they got icy? 'Cos it didn't look like that to me at my party.'

Swift didn't like his tone. 'That's none of your business, so wind your neck in,' he snapped. 'Let's leave the subject. The damage is done. Enough said.'

Blackmore raised a hand in acknowledgement, his manner mild again. 'Okay, okay. Touchy topic.' He looked down at the river. 'Did you know there was a battle on the River Lea in the ninth century?'

'I didn't. Tell me.'

'The English squared up to the Danes. They'd rowed up the Thames and made a fortress on the Lea — about twenty miles from here. King Alfred was involved and the Danes were routed. They found a Viking sword around Lockwood reservoir. Some warrior must have dropped it in a hurry when he was legging it.'

Their food arrived and silence fell as they tucked in. As Swift cut into his chicken pie, he wondered how Blackmore had known that Nora was angry about the gossip that had been passed on.

'Have you spoken to Mac Camley recently?' he asked.

'Mac? No, not since he left us. Hey — thought we'd dropped that topic?'

'We have. How's your roast?'

'Great. Smashing spuds. They told me they cook them in goose fat.'

Swift watched him stab a crisp potato. Blackmore had suddenly sounded shifty. He'd think about the question that had been left hanging another time.

* * *

He'd found an address, email and phone number for Mia Wilson in Kelly's contacts. She hadn't responded to an email, so he tried ringing her when he got home that night. His limbs were aching in a good way and he felt optimistic after the day's exercise. A woman answered, confirming that she was Mia Wilson. He explained who he was and his connection to Kelly. There was a silence.

'I did email you, but I didn't hear back. That's why I'm ringing.'

'I don't always check my email.'

'I don't know if you're aware, but Kelly Dwyer drowned last October.'

'No. I didn't know that,' she said slowly. 'I haven't been in touch with Kelly for a long time.'

Her tone told him the friendship hadn't ended well. He was losing count of the people Kelly had upset or got on the wrong side of. But ever onwards.

'Kelly was attacked and thrown from a ferry. Her sister was travelling with her and she was attacked, too, but she survived.'

'I'm sorry. That's dreadful. When did you say this was?'

'The incident took place on the second of October, last year, on the Dublin to Liverpool ferry.'

'Well . . . that's so sad.'

'I know you were friendly with Kelly at one time. I'd like to meet up with you if possible, ask you more about it.'

Mia sounded as if she was choosing her words carefully. 'I was friends with Kelly. But we'd drifted apart. I really can't tell you anything about her.'

'Do you still live in Willesden?' He'd looked her up and knew she did.

'Why are you asking?'

'I heard that Kelly helped you find a place to live there and that maybe her husband had visited her at your flat, so it would be useful to—'

The line went dead. He rang the number again and it went to voicemail. He didn't bother leaving one but phoned Faith, who was at Sol's flat.

'He came out of hospital today, so I'm staying here for a while until he's back on his feet properly.' She sounded tired but cheerful.

Swift wondered if Sol ever managed to get on his feet properly. 'Are you okay to talk? I need to check something with you.'

'Sure. Is it grim? Hope not.'

'Not that bad. I visited Amber Oxendon.' He decided not to mention the trip to Amsterdam and the subsequent fallout. He repeated what Amber had told him about Faith's concern regarding Kelly's friend. 'Does that mean anything to you? Do you think that you might have been referring to Mia Wilson?'

'Ahm . . . I'm sorry, I can't remember talking about that to Amber. I know that Kelly was great friends with Mia at one time, but that's all. Can you ask Mia Wilson?'

'I haven't got anywhere so far with trying to talk to her. I'd like to come over and chat to Sol again and see you. D'you think he'd be well enough?'

'Sure. Just leave it a couple of days.'

He poured a glass of wine and ate a hunk of cheese. The glow of the river still with him, he phoned Nora. He had no idea what he'd say but he hated unpleasant, tension-filled silences. Always had. If the relationship was over, he'd rather end it on a kinder note. He didn't have to say anything, as she didn't pick up either. He left a brief message, saying he hoped she was well and it would be good to talk. *Would it, though?* A little voice posed the question in his head as he switched on the TV.

* * *

A cold call on Mia Wilson might work. He caught an early train to Willesden junction the following morning and found her address, a ground-floor flat in an end of terrace house. Well-kept, in a pleasant street. It was quarter to eight, and he decided to wait and see if she came out to go to work. There was nowhere to hide in the street, no door to slam. He'd looked her up on Facebook and seen her photo. She had distinctive red hair.

He loitered in a supermarket across the road, drinking coffee from a machine and looking at racks of international newspapers by the front window. He was scanning front pages when he saw the door of the house open and a slim woman with russet hair step out. An older man waved her down the path and then closed the door. Swift was exiting the supermarket and about to cross the road when a car pulled up and Mia Wilson climbed in. The car joined the stream of traffic.

Damn. Swift hesitated for a minute. He was here. He might as well try his luck. When he rang Mia's bell, the older man opened the door. He was wearing a paint-spattered T-shirt and jeans and holding a roll of masking tape.

'I was hoping to see Mia Wilson.'

'You've just missed her. Can I help?'

Swift explained why he was calling and showed his ID. He had to raise his voice over the noise of a truck that had arrived next door and was unloading a heap of sand into the small front garden. The man looked as if he was about to refuse to talk and then nodded.

'You'd better come in a minute, I can't hear myself think.'

The man led him to the back of the flat, into a kitchen with a table pushed against the wall. Chairs, a rubbish bin and a vegetable rack had been stacked on the table. A box of light fittings and other electrical equipment lay open on the floor. He turned off a chattering radio.

'I'm Ken Drover, Mia's dad. I came early to do this lighting today. There's nowhere to sit and I don't want to go in the living room in this gear.'

They both propped themselves against worktops. Drover was a solid man with a round, freckly face like his daughter's, and huge jug ears.

'I tried contacting Mia by email, but she didn't get back to me. It might be an out-of-date address,' Swift said, massaging the truth.

Drover didn't react. 'That's the trouble with emails. People change them and they don't let you know. Fat lot of use that is.'

'I know that Kelly Dwyer and Mia were friends at one time. I think they met when they were both working at a charity. I'm looking at Kelly's background. Did you know her?'

'Barely. I met her once, when she tried to visit Mia in hospital and I refused. But I heard plenty about her and she gave me sleepless nights, I can tell you. I asked you in because I don't want you talking to Mia. It would only upset her. Anyway, I don't reckon she'd give you the time of day.'

'I gather the friendship ended? Someone told me that Mia had had marriage problems and Kelly had helped her find this place to live.'

'Oh yes, the friendship ended.' He picked up a large screwdriver and hefted it from hand to hand. He seemed to be calculating how to proceed. 'Look, if I tell you about what happened, I need your word that you won't bother Mia. I don't want her getting anxious, and talking about Kelly doesn't do her any favours. She's put all that behind her and I want it to stay that way.'

'If you can tell me about what happened with her and Kelly, I don't see why I should need to contact Mia.' A white lie. He told lots of those in his line of business.

Drover nodded his head and looked out of the window. It had rained overnight and the small garden was steaming in the sun. Raindrops trembled on the leaves of a towering honeysuckle. A sparrow pecked greedily at a bird feeder attached to the windowpane.

'You got children?' Drover asked.

'A daughter. Just little but a handful.'

That made Drover smile. 'You'll know, then, that you'd do anything to keep her safe and how much it hurts if anything goes wrong for her.'

'I'm discovering that. It takes my breath away sometimes.'

Drover tapped a finger to his lips. Then he swung two chairs down from the table, leaning on one for a moment to catch his breath. 'Here. This'll take more than a few minutes.'

They sat on the narrow chairs. Swift sat up straight to give his long legs room. Drover cleared his throat and picked at a splash of paint on his T-shirt.

'Mia was having marriage problems when she met Kelly at work. Her husband, Freddie, had been made redundant and there were rows. I knew there was trouble from things Mia mentioned. Then Kelly came on the scene and she gave Mia a load of chat about how she'd escaped her marriage and set herself up on her own. How you could do it if you wanted. Lots of rubbish about being a free spirit. I suppose Mia was at a low ebb and Kelly was persuasive.'

'I never met Kelly either, but I get the impression she was a meddler. And at that point an alcoholic.'

'Hmm. To cut a long story short, Mia told Freddie she was leaving him. Kelly had helped her find this place to rent. Made it easier for Mia, I suppose. Helped the tipping point.' He reached a hand behind him and rubbed his back, wincing.

Swift could see that. You might be hesitating, but if someone cleared the way and nudged you, the decision became simpler.

'Mia could only just afford this flat,' Drover continued. 'It was shabby when she moved in, but Kelly helped her give it a lick of paint. I think Kelly made it all seem like an adventure and Mia got caught up in it. I didn't know anything about it until she'd moved in here.'

'How did Freddie react?'

'He was in bits. Cried on the phone to me. I didn't know what to say. I was cross with Mia. You don't just give up on a marriage when it gets tricky. See, the other thing was that Mia was two months pregnant when she left Freddie. That's what I really couldn't credit. Freddie might not be Mr Wonderful but he was a well-meaning bloke having a temporary blip, and yet Mia was thinking about trying to bring a child up on her own. Madness! And I mean that — I think Mia was out of her senses for a while. Not thinking straight. Then when I heard more about it all, I realized Kelly had been steering her.'

'Is that why the friendship ended — because Kelly had interfered?'

Drover suddenly looked tired and distracted. 'It was a terrible time. Mia had a fall and lost the baby. She was reaching to fix a shelf in the living room and missed her footing. She was in a bad way for a while. Freddie was by her side all the way through it. They got back together and Freddie moved in here. So — you know, something good came out of it. Kelly wanted to visit Mia in hospital, but Mia wouldn't have it. Freddie wouldn't either and put his foot down over it. Mia said she never wanted to see Kelly again and wished she'd never listened to her. She told Kelly to back off in no uncertain terms.'

'It was a strong reaction from Mia. Kelly wasn't responsible for the accident and miscarriage.'

'I suppose the shock was part of it. And of course, she'd had time to think about how Kelly had influenced her. In the end, she valued her marriage more than her friendship with a boozer. I'm sure you can understand that.'

Swift mulled this over. He supposed it made sense, especially if Mia's husband and father had put a lot of pressure on her to abandon the friendship. Yet he felt as if he was being bought off in some way that he couldn't put his finger on.

'Kelly's husband, Neil Dwyer, visited her in London. I believe that he came here once and there was an argument, or something happened. Certainly, he was very upset after he'd been here. Do you know anything about that — has Mia ever mentioned it?'

Dover's answer came quickly. Too quickly. 'I never heard of that. I think you must have that wrong.'

'I don't think so. Neil's brother told me.'

A shake of the head. 'Well — I can ask Mia if you like, but I think I'm right.'

'Maybe I could check that out with Mia myself. Just to clarify.'

A flash of anger, immediately masked. 'No. Please don't. My daughter went through a terrible experience and it took her a long time to get over the loss of the baby. We don't mention Kelly Dwyer. That name brings back bad memories. Mia's happy now with Freddie and their marriage is stronger than ever. I'm not having her upset.' He stood and opened the kitchen door. 'I've got to get on now, or these lights will never be finished.'

Swift pointed at a photo of Mia with a blond man on a pinboard by the door. 'Is that Freddie?'

'Yes, that's him.' He cleared his throat. 'I've been helpful and answered your questions, so leave Mia alone to get on with her life. I mean it. I'm not having old sorrows dragged up for her.'

Swift left and crossed the road to the supermarket. He'd noticed they had irons on special offer, and his had died a month ago. He browsed the boxes, looking for the cheapest.

Ken Drover had an honest face, but he hadn't been honest. Or he'd lied by omission. But what part of his story had been false?

Swift was baffled by the varieties of iron on offer. Did he want vertical steam vents, anti-calcium function or self-cleaning? Maybe he should emulate Blackmore and send his clothes to a laundry service, but he wasn't sure they could cope with his loose buttons and threadbare seams.

He gave up, and bought one because he liked the sleek lines and dark blue colour.

Blackmore. There was another man who hadn't been telling the truth.

CHAPTER 15

It was a quietish morning in Morden. Swift looked through the window of the shop called Floored. It was an upmarket place. You wouldn't come here for bargains. He saw Robin Greeve talking to a couple. They stood in front of a stand of floor tiles, with Greeve gesturing at the different layers. He was wearing a grey suit, open-necked pink shirt and lime socks. Swift walked around for a few minutes, then headed back. The shop was empty and Greeve sat at a desk, staring at a computer screen.

'Morning,' Swift said. 'Can I have a word? We met at your dad's house.'

Greeve stood up, wearing his wary dog expression again. 'Do you want to talk about flooring?'

'No. It all looks lovely, especially the Persian blue, but I'm not sure I can afford it. It's about your mum and Kelly Dwyer.'

He rubbed his drooping bottom lip. 'Got nothing to say on that subject.'

Swift touched the cool, striated surface of a deep yellow tile. 'I gathered that you didn't take to me.'

'Too right. I don't know why you've bothered to come here.'

He had a lost look, as if there was a map in front of him that he couldn't read. When his mum was alive and sober, she'd have cheered him up with food and hugs. Offering comfort might be a way in.

'Are you due a break? It's mid-morning.'

'Why?'

'I'll buy you a coffee. We won't be long. If I find out who murdered Kelly, you can send them thank you flowers.'

Greeve looked interested, despite himself. He slouched to the door and called through that he was taking a quick break. A woman came out, glanced at Swift and parked herself at the computer.

In the café over the road, Greeve asked for a caramel macchiato. Swift winced, ordered an Americano for himself, and bought two chocolate chip biscuits. Greeve slumped at a table, tearing little strips from a paper napkin.

'Here, have a sugar rush.'

Greeve took a biscuit, but pulled a mulish face. 'Don't pretend you like me, it won't get you anywhere.'

'I don't know you, so I don't know if I like you. It's okay to just say thanks when someone gives you something.'

He had the grace to look uncomfortable. 'What do you want?'

'Did you attack Faith Black and kill Kelly Dwyer?'

'No. Why would you even ask that?' The biscuits were brittle and he sprayed crumbs.

Swift dunked his in his coffee to avoid the same fate. 'I'd guess you felt guilty about your mum, because you'd said awful things to her, and then she died and you couldn't take the cruel words back. You could have been flailing around, looking for someone to punish.'

Greeve flinched and stared at the table.

'You hated Kelly,' Swift went on, 'so you had motive. If you were on the ferry, you had opportunity. If you carried something like a hammer, you had means.'

Greeve ran his tongue across his teeth and lifted foam from his coffee with a spoon. 'You're right, I did hate Kelly

Dwyer — or I thought I did. I reckoned my dad was a wimp for letting that Lowick woman fob him off and send him for counselling. I wanted him to front up to Kelly and make her realize what she'd done. So I saw her and told her myself.'

'You saw Kelly?'

'Yeah. You're not the only one who can doorstep people. I waited for her outside work one night. She was heading for the pub so I followed her there and stopped her outside. I told her about my mum's death and what she'd done to Dad and me. Told her exactly what I thought of her. It didn't make me feel as good as I expected it to.'

'Why was that?'

'For a start, she was beautiful and I hadn't expected that. So I was sort of unnerved. Confused.' He looked startled, remembering it.

'What did Kelly say?'

'Lots of stuff about being sorry . . . never meant to cause trouble . . . I suppose at least she didn't try to deny what she'd done or blame it on my mum. She said something like, "*I'm like a contagious illness, I cause problems wherever I go.*" She started crying and I could see they were real tears. I could smell booze on her. I thought she was drop-dead gorgeous and pathetic. When I'd said my piece, I ran from her. At least I'd looked her in the eye. I never told Dad.'

'Where were you last October second?'

He took his phone out and checked. 'At work. I'd used up all my holidays by then. Feel free to ask my manager. I've nothing to hide. And I don't own a hammer. Dad does, but I had dinner with him that night and stayed over, so we were both at home together.' Greeve held his hands out. 'Has any of that helped you?'

'Probably. Sometimes it's hard to know what's helping until I can see things fall into place. Why were you so antsy when I came to see your father?'

'Just thought you were stirring up miserable memories. My dad doesn't need that. I didn't mean some of the things I said. I have a love–hate relationship when I go home now. I want to be there, but sometimes when I walk in, it all hits me again. I remember shouting at Mum and calling her names. I just couldn't cope with how she was. I thought she was weak, drinking like she did, choosing to show me up. I took it out on her. Since she died, I've read stuff about alcoholism being a disease and I've felt bad that I didn't understand that at the time.'

'It's hard enough trying to understand yourself when you're a teenager, let alone anyone else. It's a selfish time of life, when the world's supposed to be all about you.'

'Maybe. But I should have made more effort. Whenever I walk into the kitchen at home, I see Mum lying on the floor. I've asked Dad to change some of the furnishings, redecorate, just so not everything reminds me of her. In fact, I wish he'd sell that house, have a new start.' He looked away. 'Sometimes I think I'm a rotten son.'

'Your dad doesn't seem to think so.'

Greeve stirred the frothy top of his drink and took a couple of sips. 'I don't even like this much. Mum did. The smell of coffee and caramel reminds me of her.'

Swift tilted his cup. 'Here's to your mum.'

Greeve managed a tight smile. 'She'd have preferred being toasted with brandy.'

* * *

The Tower of London fascinated Branna. Swift had no idea where this interest had come from. She told him that she'd been helping to make a model of it at nursery. She was particularly keen on the bloodier aspects of its history, knew about Anne Boleyn — or Anne Boiling as she pronounced the doomed queen's name — and signed '*dungeon*' with relish.

He stood with his daughter perched on his shoulders downriver from the Tower, watching the pageant of the annual Tudor Pull as it completed its journey from Hampton Court. She clapped with delight and drummed her feet against his chest as the flotilla of richly decorated barges came into sight. Flags and pennants rippled in the breeze, and the sun flickered on the bright reds and golds of the livery. The crews of the watermen's cutters rowed steadily while the crowds cheered. Swift lifted Branna down to settle on his hip and took a selfie. She pulled a face. In almost every photo he had of his daughter, she was gurning, sticking her tongue out or crossing her eyes. He thought with satisfaction that a posh school probably wouldn't let her through the doors. She was more of a St Trinian's candidate.

She was flushed with the excitement of the occasion. Her one disappointment was that she wouldn't be able to go into the Tower for the Stela ceremony.

'What's thing they bringing?' she asked for the umpteenth time.

'It's called a Stela. It's a bit of wooden water pipe and it's about the power of the Thames. The pipe stays here for a year and then it goes back to Hampton Court palace for the next Tudor Pull.'

'Why can't we go see?'

'Because we're the public and we're not allowed in. Only officials and the governor of the Tower.'

'Don't want be public.'

'It has its disadvantages.'

'When I grow up, I be guvnor.'

'You might well be. Then you can boss everyone around. You'd be good at that.'

She pointed across the river. 'That where Anne Boiling had head chopped off!'

'It was somewhere around there.'

She clasped her hands around her neck and made a gasping noise. 'Did it hurt?'

'It was done with a sharp sword, very fast, so probably not. Have you heard the song about Anne Boleyn's ghost?' He made his voice gruff and rolled his eyes: '*With her head tucked underneath her arm, she walks the bloody tower. With her head tucked underneath her arm, at the midnight hour.*'

Branna squealed with delight and made him sing it again. She reached up and twisted his lips together with hot little fingers. 'Lots lovely blood!'

He looked down into her big grin and dancing eyes and thought that she might make a good detective. Or maybe a pathologist. He bought ice creams and they sat by the river, watching the boats go up and down.

'We going Guernsey for summer,' Branna said, dipping her nose into a chocolate swirl.

He looked down. This was the first he'd heard of it. 'To Marcel's?'

'Yep. Play beach all day. Weeks an' weeks! You come too?'

He caught a drip of ice cream before it landed on her knee. 'I've got to work.'

'Oh. Nice if you come.'

'I know. We'll do something, you and me.'

'Hmm. Not Nora. Don't want her come.'

'Okay.'

Branna rubbed her lips with the back of her hand. 'Anne Boiling's ghost in tower. She go woooooooooooo!'

'You crack me up, you do.' He stroked her hair back. Were Ruth and Marcel being negative about Nora? Perhaps it didn't matter, given that he hadn't heard from her. It did matter that plans had been made for the summer without any consultation with him. If Branna had it right, and she was going to Fermain Bay for the whole of the holidays, he'd go weeks without seeing her.

Time to fight his corner.

* * *

He had his head under the kitchen sink, trying to trace where a tiny leak was coming from, when his phone rang. He banged his forehead hard as he reached for it and sat on the floor to take the call from Ruth.

'Hi, you left me a message.' She sounded chirpy.

'Yeah. Branna told me you're going to Guernsey for the summer. Is that right?'

'We're going for August, yes.'

'The whole month?' He rubbed his throbbing temples.

'Pretty much. Marcel's niece Anna, who's five, is going to join us for ten days of it, so Branna will have someone to play with.'

'What happened to negotiation? I thought we'd agreed to discuss holidays. I'd rather not find out about a done deal from Branna.'

'She must have overheard us talking about it. We've only just firmed things up. I've checked that I have the month free from lectures. I was going to tell you about it this week.'

'Tell — not discuss. I don't like the idea of going a month without seeing her.'

'Did you have plans?' Ruth's voice had cooled.

'That's not the point. It's a long time. You should have talked to me.'

'It's not that long and it's a lovely opportunity for her. The beach is just below the house and she can swim in the sea. She loves that. Better for her than spending the summer in North London's traffic fumes and noise. Surely you want that for her, especially when she's got surgery to face later this year?'

Outflanked. When did Ruth get so manipulative? She and Marcel were always cornering him, leaving him no wriggle room.

'Can we agree to discuss these things in future?'

'Yes, okay, but that means that you need to consult me about what you're doing with Branna and, more importantly, who you're leaving her with. Anyway, it will give you a month free to devote to your case with the troubled sister. How's that going?'

Nowhere fast. 'Okay.'

'By the way, Branna had a great time at the Tower. She wants to spend a night there with you to see if she can spot Anne Boleyn's ghost. Good luck with that. She's always happiest when she's been just with you, the two of you on your own.'

'Uh-huh. I have to go. I'm mending a leak.'

'Bye, then. I know a good plumber if you need one. Marcel found him when I couldn't turn the tap off.'

Bully for Marcel. He stuck his head back under the sink and spent a frustrating fifteen minutes failing to find the source of the leak. He gave up in a foul mood and put a bowl under the pipes to catch the drips. He'd revisit the YouTube tutorial later. As he backed out, he banged his head again, on the back of his skull this time, just to even things out. He sat on the floor, staring out of the window. It was a dank day, with a threatening, pewter sky, sharp bursts of rain and gusting winds. He felt restless and scratchy. He wanted to take his boat out, but not in these awful conditions. He'd make a coffee and some calls. When he put the kettle on, a fuse blew. He cursed loudly and while he was unplugging it, the doorbell rang. With the kind of luck he was having, it would be someone wanting to sell him something, or convert him.

A man with narrow shoulders, a chubby face and choppy brown hair stood on the doorstep. The wind hurled dust around his head and he shielded his eyes.

'Are you Mr Swift?'

'That's right.'

'My name's Cameron Sheppard, Emmy's brother.'

'Hello. I've met your sister.'

'I know. Can we talk? I suppose I should have made an appointment, but this is important. Have you got time now?'

'Sure. Let's go down to my office.'

Swift led him quickly down the steps as another burst of rain pelted them and unlocked the office door.

'Would you like a coffee?'

'Please, if it's no trouble. Milk, one sugar.'

Swift started the machine, thinking that Cameron seemed meeker than his father or sister. The young man sat in silence, rubbing his neck while the coffee brewed. His creamy, dense skin reminded Swift of the evaporated milk that Lily used to pour over fruit salad. He switched a lamp on to offset the basement gloom and gave Sheppard a mug.

'You've talked to my father as well as my sister,' he said in his light, timid voice. His jaw lacked definition and he'd have a double chin there before too long.

'That's right. Your dad came here — sat where you are now, and I met Emilia in a grotty café. I'm glad you've turned up. I was going to phone you today.'

'Really? Why?' He looked up nervously.

'I've still got some questions about Kelly Dwyer and her sister. You know what happened to them?'

Sheppard nodded. 'Dad told me about it. Terrible.' He was tense, taking rapid sips of coffee and then blowing on it to cool it down. 'I was hoping you can help me, or explain what's happening now. I feel so confused and I'm not sure what's going on.' His hair fell over his brow. He pushed it back impatiently.

Swift had expected defensiveness and anger when he met Cameron Sheppard, not a plea for help. There was something undefined and puny about him. 'I don't know what you mean. How do you think I can help you?'

'Emmy's chucked me out of our flat and I don't understand why. She's stopped talking to me, confiding in me. We used to chat about everything. But she's been weird and temperamental since she met you, so I reckon it must be something to do with that.'

'What reason has Emmy given you?'

'None, really. Just that she needs space and she's got a lot on her plate with campaigns and her surgery. Something about wanting to use professional staff rather than family. That doesn't make sense. I always help her with all of that stuff, try to ease the burden as much as possible.'

'What does your father say?'

'Dad can't understand it either and she won't talk to him about it. He's been abroad a lot recently so he hasn't really got his head around it. I've had to move back in with him, got nowhere else to go. It's all so peculiar.' He was whining now, sounding as if he might wail '*It's not fair!*'

Swift thought he'd have to pick his way through this carefully. Sheppard had a dark forest of nasal hairs with one longer strand curling from his right nostril. Swift couldn't help but think of Faith's report of his hairy bum.

'Can Emmy ask you to move out? From what he said, I thought your father had bought your flat in Fulham for both of you.'

'It's in both our names. But what can I do if she says she won't have me there? I got back from a work trip and she'd packed up my stuff. She got really stroppy when I tried to talk to her about it.' He sniffed sulkily and now he did say it. 'It's not fair. I've done loads to help her with her career — leafleting, going to meetings, canvassing, talking tactics. Now it feels like she's dropped me, but I just don't get why she'd do that.' He sounded like the spurned lover that he was.

It wouldn't do much for Emmy's close family image if word got round that she'd thrown her sibling out. She must have weighed the situation up and decided that dumping Cameron posed the least threat. Rain cracked against the windows and a blind flapped in the breeze. Swift got up to secure it.

'It does seem strange, given that your sister has waxed lyrical about family support and strength in her publicity,' he said.

'Exactly. That's why what she's done doesn't make sense. I've been going over it. Dad said he saw her the evening of the day she'd met you and she was in a crap mood, but didn't want to talk about it. I thought you might be able to throw some light on what's going on with her.'

'I might. You might not like what I have to say.'

Sheppard crossed his arms, giving himself comforting taps on the elbows with his fingers. 'It has to be better than not knowing.'

Swift drank some coffee. 'Did you know that Emmy was travelling on the same ferry that Kelly Dwyer and her sister were on, the night they were attacked?'

Sheppard shook his head. 'No. What — you mean she'd been in Ireland?'

'Yes, to a friend's engagement party. The police spoke to her after the incident. You weren't with her on the ferry?'

Sheppard frowned. 'No, of course not. When was this?'

'Last October, the second.'

'Oh, right. I was away in Glasgow, on a course. I remember she said something about an engagement do, but I didn't know it was in Ireland.'

'She took her car, spent a few days there.'

'Okay. So what?'

'She was on the passenger list, so the police contacted her about the incident on board. She didn't tell them that she had known Kelly previously, when you'd had a gas boiler fitted.'

'Oh, that fiasco. I was all for reporting Kelly about that, but Emmy wouldn't wear it. She had a soft spot for Kelly.' He raised a finger. 'What are you saying — that the police might have thought Emmy was a suspect?'

'Well, it would be a possible line of enquiry. Kelly was murdered and someone who'd previously had a grievance with her was on board at the time.'

'But the point is that Emmy didn't have a grievance. She was all touchy-feely towards Kelly about the boiler. Tried Dad's patience, I can tell you. We were both puzzled by it, because Emmy's usually a tough cookie about anything like that. Doesn't suffer fools gladly. But she insisted, so we gave in to her over it.'

'Yes, that's what your father told me. But as far as Emmy was concerned, there was another, more significant problem with Kelly.'

'How d'you mean?'

'Kelly saw something that shocked her one day, when she was working at your flat. You and your sister were together in a certain situation. Emmy knew what Kelly had witnessed.'

A peachy bloom was creeping along Sheppard's cheeks. 'I don't know what you're talking about.'

'I'm referring to an intimate situation.'

'I don't get it. What situation?'

If he wanted it spelled out, that was fine. 'Your sister didn't tell you about that day, about how Kelly almost walked in on you when you were having sex in the living room?'

A shake of the head. His cheeks were blazing now, bright scarlet, and he was gaping at Swift.

'Mr Sheppard, I don't know when your incestuous relationship with your sister started, and it's none of my business, but Kelly saw you having sex and she told someone else about it. That person informed me and I discussed it with your sister the day we met. It's my understanding that Emmy was uncharacteristically forgiving about the error with the boiler because she thought it would mean that Kelly would keep her mouth shut about what she'd seen. And it did — Kelly told just one other person. Given that Emmy was on the ferry, it's reasonable to consider her a suspect. She'd gone into public life and Kelly's knowledge could have been very damaging had she ever revealed it. I'll ask you again. Did you know that Kelly had seen you together?'

He thought that might provoke anger and denial but unlike his sister, Cameron crumpled immediately. Tears spurted down his cheeks. 'For God's sake! No, I didn't know!'

His anguish made Swift believe him. He'd folded into himself and sat doubled over in the chair, his face almost on his lap. He was crying and whimpering, '*OhGodohGodohGod*.' Swift poured more coffee and placed it in front of him with a box of tissues.

'I think that your sister has told you to move out because she can't afford to have you living with her now. She's too worried about gossip and potential scandal blighting her career, so she's got rid of you. Sorry if that sounds harsh, but at least it's an explanation of her behaviour.'

Sheppard's chest heaved and he fought to regain control. He took a handful of tissues, pressed them against his eyes and dabbed at his mouth. He fingered the coffee mug but didn't pick it up. His face was rigid with misery. When he spoke, his breath was ragged. 'Why didn't Emmy tell me that Kelly had seen us? We could have dealt with it together, talked to her. I can't believe she kept that from me and now there's this fucking mess. I love her so much. Miss her so much. I can't function, haven't been going to work. Nothing's right without Emmy.'

'I can imagine. It must be very hard for you.' Yet his sister had disposed of him like a pet who'd become too much bother to keep. Sheppard put his head back in the chair and took deep, shuddering gulps of air. He was murmuring something over and over. It sounded like '*always*.' Swift reckoned he'd want to spill it all now, get it out of his system. It would be a relief, after years of hiding and camouflage. 'You must have been under intense strain for a long time,' he said.

'Strain! More like agony. More like slow torture. Loving someone but not being able to tell anyone. Having to keep secrets and always worrying that someone would find out. I've got a gay friend and when he told me about the nightmare of coming out to his family, I wanted to say "*I know all about it*", but the difference for me is that I can never, ever come out of the closet.'

'Have you and Emmy been lovers for a long time?'

'We've been . . . together . . . together like that since I was twelve and Emmy was fourteen. We even made sure we went to the same college, couldn't bear to be parted. I talked to her about emigrating once, going somewhere in the world where our love wouldn't be taboo but Emmy couldn't face that upheaval. We've always been so careful. Had to be — especially after she got the politics bug. We knew it would be tricky because the press are always crawling all over politicians' lives, but we were used to hiding in plain sight. We reckoned we'd manage it. Emmy's been the only one for me. I can't cope without her. Feels like half of me is missing. Just one bloody slip-up and now all this is happening . . .'

Swift couldn't think of anything to say. He wondered if it had worked that way for Emmy, or if she'd had other lovers. It was fascinating, but he didn't want to rub salt in Sheppard's wounds by asking.

'I guess your father doesn't know,' he said after a long pause.

Sheppard shook his head. 'No way!'

'Handy, though, that he could buy you a flat together.'

Sheppard rubbed his face. 'That was easy. Dad offered and it seemed like we'd be free. I don't know what to think now. I feel so confused. Why didn't Emmy tell me that she'd been on that ferry? I don't get it. I can't believe that she'd hurt anyone, let alone attack two people.'

Swift wasn't sure about that, but the more he thought about it, the more unlikely it seemed that Emilia would have sent an apologetic note to Faith. It just wouldn't be her style. She was a 'Never apologize, never explain' type.

Sheppard looked at him. 'Are you going to tell anyone about me and Emmy?'

'I've no reason to — unless I discover that your sister is responsible for what happened to Kelly and Faith and that what Kelly witnessed in your flat was a motive for murder.'

'I have to see Emmy and talk to her, try and sort things out. There must be a way to do that, a way to stay together. I can't manage without her. Once she knows you've told me everything, we'll be able to find a way through.' Sheppard shot up, looked around blindly as if he couldn't remember where the door was, and then almost ran out of the room and up the steps.

Swift could only wish him luck with that.

He made a fresh coffee, rested his legs on the desk and reflected on the case. What did he have about that wild October night on the Irish Sea? Not that much. Faith thought she remembered someone with dark hair wearing a blue anorak, the person who Kelly had wanted to avoid. But that might not have been the perpetrator. There might have been someone else on board who Kelly would have avoided if she'd known of their presence. He went through his notes, winnowing, summarizing and narrowing down suspects and motives.

He stared at the list and underlined *Mia Wilson*. There was something there, he was sure, something more to the story of the falling out with Kelly.

CHAPTER 16

Sol Waters was lying on the sofa under a duvet with a glass of brandy and a packet of medication on the coffee table beside him. It also held a carton of apple juice, a bottle of water, some oranges and a Scrabble board. He wore a sleeveless vest that exposed his rake-thin shoulders. His hair had been washed, with little curls sprouting at the front.

It was a warm day, but the windows were closed. The sun struggled in through the half-drawn curtains. The room smelled of sweat, stale breath and spirits, but the place was a bit cleaner than it had been on Swift's last visit. He guessed that Faith had vacuumed. When he'd arrived, she and Sol had been playing Scrabble and arguing if there was such a word as '*vela*'. Faith had appealed to Swift, who'd said he had no idea. Sol maintained that it meant a glass screen.

Swift sat and watched them play for a few minutes. Sol coughed frequently and pressed his hand to his chest. It was good to hear Faith chuckle and see some colour in her cheeks.

'Have you told Ty about the break-in?' Sol gave Faith a nudge.

She was sitting on the floor by the sofa. 'Not yet.' She glanced at Swift. 'I don't want to run to you with everything, Ty. It's not fair.'

'What break-in?'

She sighed. 'At my place. I went back yesterday lunchtime to fetch some clean clothes and stuff. The front door had been forced.'

There it was, that cadence in her speech that reminded him of his mother. If he closed his eyes and listened, it could almost be her in the room. 'Did you call the police?'

'Yep. Well — I rang Sol first and he told me to. They arrived an hour later. By that time, I could see that nothing had been taken. In fact, as far as I could tell, nothing had been touched or moved. It was weird, almost as if no one had actually come in. They checked for fingerprints, but once I said nothing had been stolen, they didn't seem that interested. They gave me a crime number and said they'd be in touch.'

She seemed to have dealt with it with remarkable composure. 'Did you ask your neighbours if they'd seen or heard anything?'

'I asked the people either side. They hadn't. There's CCTV at the corner of the building, but it's broken. Whoever did it had pulled the door to on the way out, so it wasn't obvious. I'd been away for three nights so I don't even know when it happened. The maintenance guy was really helpful, he came and fixed another lock so I could leave the place secure. I don't fancy going back there again just yet.'

'You can stay here as long as you want,' Sol wheezed. 'Plenty of room for my nurse companion. And I enjoy beating you at Scrabble.' He flashed his yellow teeth at Swift. 'Maybe between us we just about make one working brain.'

'Thanks, Sol.' She smiled up at him and tucked the duvet around his feet.

'You seem remarkably calm about the break-in,' Swift said.

'Yeah. I surprised myself. It was horrible, thinking that someone had been in there and I'm sure I would have been terrified if I'd been at home. But I wasn't and I knew I'd be coming back here, to a safe place. I might look for another flat, something more secure. Although given that I haven't got anything worth nicking, I don't think whoever did it will be back.'

Swift wasn't so sure. 'Have there been any other break-ins around you?'

Faith yawned and stretched. 'Not recently, I don't think. But, you know – it's London, it happens.'

'You should have phoned me. I'd have come over and helped you.'

'I have to stand on my own two feet sometimes and I've been causing you enough bother. Like I said, nothing was touched. It was probably kids after drug money, looking for cash or portable gadgets. I'm short on both.' She sounded testy, the way she had when he'd first met her.

Swift thought that those types of kids would probably have trashed the place while they were looking. Burglars didn't glide through rooms without causing disturbance. Something didn't smell good and it wasn't just Sol's living room.

Sol patted her head. 'You were lucky it wasn't a camogie thief. They'd have been in seventh heaven.'

She gave one of her jittery laughs. 'Shut up, idiot!'

Sol had a fit of coughing and Swift thought he'd better press on before the man tired and the stuffiness of the room rendered them all half asleep.

'I want to ask you both again about Mia Wilson, Kelly's friend. I talked about her before.'

Sol looked vague, shivering despite the warmth and pulling the duvet up to his chin. Faith nodded, gathering up the Scrabble tiles. Swift thought he'd better do a quick summary, given that both of them had patchy memories.

'Kelly worked with Mia at a charity. She helped Mia to find a flat in Willesden when she left her marriage. Something went badly wrong with the friendship. I've seen a letter from Neil's grandmother to his brother, Dermot Dwyer, in which she alluded to a row that Neil had with Kelly on the night he died. She heard Neil say that Kelly was letting Mia take responsibility for something. I believe that Neil visited Mia's flat once when he was visiting London. I've spoken to Mia's father because she wouldn't talk to me. He said that Mia was pregnant when she moved in to the flat in Willesden and that she lost the baby when she had a fall there. She got back together with her husband and decided to cut Kelly out of her life. There's something about the story that bothers me. Do either of you remember anything else about Mia, or the flat she moved to, or anything that Kelly said about it?'

Sol had closed his eyes, but shook his head. 'Kelly never said much about her after Mia moved to the flat. All I knew was that it was in Willesden.'

Faith made a tiny noise like a gasp. 'A blue front door.' She put a hand to her mouth. 'The flat had a blue door and Mia had reddish hair. How do I know that?' She gave Swift a startled look.

'Did you visit the flat? Can you remember being there?'

'I don't know.'

'You visited Kelly before you moved to London, didn't you?'

Faith nodded. 'That's right. A couple of times.'

'So you might have been to this flat in Willesden. It's on the ground floor of a terraced house, opposite a supermarket. It does have a blue front door. Dark blue. And Mia has red hair.'

Faith put her hands on the crown of her head and squeezed, as if she might press information out. 'I must have been there. I don't remember. Sorry, Ty.'

'Will you drive there with me? If you see it, it might jog your memory. It needn't take long.'

She glanced at Sol. 'Will you be okay?'

'Sure. I'm a sleepyhead now anyway. I'm going to crash for a while. You do your thing.'

She fussed around before they left, making sure that Sol had everything he needed, fetching him a glass of water — Swift didn't think there was much danger of him drinking that, unless it was to splash in the brandy — and telling him he needed to take his antibiotic in an hour. Swift watched, seeing that being in charge of Sol's welfare reassured her and gave her a role, a much-needed stability. It reassured him, too. Thinking about Sol would take her mind away from any notions of self-harm.

* * *

There was a barbecue in the garden of the Silver Mermaid. Swift bought a hot chicken sandwich and settled in a quiet corner with a pint of London Pride. The visit to Willesden had been fruitless. He'd sat with Faith in the car while she stared at the house and front door and shook her head.

'Sorry, Ty. I'm sure I've been in that house, but I can't remember when or anything that happened.' She banged the dashboard. 'It's so frustrating.'

'Okay, maybe try your visualization technique later and see if anything comes of it.'

She'd looked at him with tired, grave eyes. 'Do you think you're anywhere near finding out who attacked us?'

'I'm not sure. Possibly.' *But how will I ever prove it?*

'And it would help if my brain wasn't so rotten and soggy.'

He'd grown fond of this injured woman who was doing her utmost to reestablish her life. He thought of all the negative things he'd found out about her sister — the trail of mischief and damage she'd woven. It would be better for Faith if she never knew just how much damage. 'Don't worry about it. Let's get you home. Have you told anyone else you're staying at Sol's?'

'No. Why?'

'Don't tell anyone and ask him not to. Just a precaution while I'm still investigating.'

She frowned and bit a nail. 'But that note the attacker sent me said sorry. You don't think they'd come after me again?'

'The note indicated that they wouldn't. Best to be careful, though. So don't reveal your Lewisham address. As you said, it's a safe place, so keep it that way.'

When he'd dropped her back at Sol's, he checked that she had no plans to return alone to her flat, and said that he'd accompany her if she needed to fetch anything. He waited while she let herself in, a slight figure with her hair rippling down her back. He was thinking about the unusual intruder who hadn't bothered to search, move or take anything from her flat. Possibly because they'd come for her and she wasn't there.

He tucked into his sandwich and took a deep draught of ale. Bliss. He checked his phone. Nothing from Nora. He had an olive branch email from Ruth.

I wondered if you'd like to have Branna for a week before we go to Guernsey. She's up for it. I know it's a way off, but best to get it sorted, so let me know.

He didn't want to commit to anything while he was working on this case so sent a vague reply.

Sounds good. Let me check work schedule and get back to you.

He finished his sandwich and scrutinized Mia Wilson's Facebook page. He scrolled through, seeing lots of inspirational quotes of the '*When life gives you lemons, make lemonade*' variety, and photos of sunsets and rainbows. He stopped at a post from April with a photo of a large group of young, smiling people. They were standing outside a building, below a bright red sign: Roundstone Youth Centre. The caption below stated that fundraising was now up to £5,600. He scanned the comments: *Well done, so much hard work! Way to go! When's the fun run?* Mia had replied to that comment: *Hi, it's in July. I'm here Weds nights if you want to come and train.* He googled Roundstone Youth Centre and found it on the Willesden/Harlesden borders. It was open every evening and at weekends.

He was contemplating another pint when Jon Sheppard phoned, sounding choleric.

'Swift, what the fuck have you done to my son? He's in a terrible state. I've just got back today after a long business trip and found him in tears, ranting on about seeing you and stuff about Emmy and Kelly Dwyer. I can't get any sense out of him. I need this like a hole in the head after just flying long haul. What the hell's going on?'

'Cameron contacted me, came to see me unannounced. He wanted to ask me questions.'

'What questions? Listen, I gave you my time and so did Emmy, told you what you needed to know. Now you've been messing with Cameron's head.'

'Sounds like his sister's already done that.'

'Now you listen to me, Swift, I'm fucking exhausted and I've a full on day tomorrow so—'

'No, you listen to me, Sheppard, and stop yelling. My ear's hurting. Your son came to me for help.'

'Help? What kind of help?'

'He was trying to understand why Emmy had chucked him out of their flat.'

Some heavy breaths. 'Oh that — that'll blow over. Emmy gets wound up and she's very pressured right now. Best to leave her alone when she's like this.'

'I think there's more to it than that.'

'Like what?'

'For starters, did you know that Emmy was travelling on the same ferry from Ireland that Kelly Dwyer and her sister were on?'

Sheppard was quieter, more cautious. 'No, I didn't know. And what do you mean, "for starters"?'

Swift reached for his jacket. He wanted to check out Jon Sheppard, find out where he'd been early last October. He sounded on the back foot right now, jet-lagged, surprised. This was a useful, if tricky, way in. 'I'm in a public place. It's difficult to discuss. I could call round now and see you. If that's convenient.'

'Ahm . . . well . . . yes, okay. I could do with some clarity, I must say.'

* * *

The Georgian house stood on the curve of a road overlooking Kensington Square and was exactly as Swift had expected it to be: vast and elegant, with a front porch flanked by Doric columns and a cast iron balcony on the first floor. A woman in her fifties with upswept hair answered the door, checked his ID and asked him to follow her up to the drawing room. The stairs were illuminated with rainbow-coloured neon lights. There was nothing Georgian about the interior of the house, which looked as if someone had gutted it and started again. The drawing room was a symphony in dazzling white with pale grey leather furniture and glass tables. There were acres of parquet flooring on which an occasional white rug sat like an ice floe. The tall, beautiful sculpture of a polar bear by the back window seemed entirely fitting.

Cameron was there with swollen eyes, sipping a glass of red wine. He flicked a worried glance at Swift and looked at the ceiling. His father was calm again and in control. He wore a tight, cream vest that emphasized his barrel chest, and tracksuit bottoms. They sat on a sofa each on three sides of a massive smoked glass table. It was empty except for a small bowl of potpourri and a tray with glasses and bottles of drink. Sheppard asked Swift what he'd like. He'd spotted a bottle of Glenlivet and opted for a whisky. He needed fortification for this discussion and a single malt would help.

Sheppard topped up his own whisky and sat opposite him. 'I didn't know Cameron had been to see you. We talked about that while we were waiting for you. Cam told me that you'd found out that Emmy was on that Irish ferry. I can't understand why she didn't tell me. I've tried ringing her but can't raise her. I just want to get all of this nonsense sorted out and put to bed.'

Swift thought that was an unfortunate phrase, given his children's relationship. He took a sip of the smooth, creamy drink. Comfort in a glass. He wanted to get his question in before things got too tricky. 'Where were you on October the second last year, Mr Sheppard?' The man seemed so far away across the vast table, he felt as if he needed to raise his voice. This wasn't a house for intimacy.

Sheppard drew his head back in surprise and then laughed. 'Oh, okay, I get it. You think that I plotted murder on the high seas with my daughter. Because of a fucking gas boiler? You think I have time in my life to worry about that kind of detail? No wonder you get some crap reviews if that's your standard of detection.'

'It would help if you could answer my question. This is great whisky.'

Sheppard shook his head in disgust, but lifted an iPad on the sofa beside him. He scrolled while Cameron watched him and poured himself another glass of wine, leaving the bottle within reach. His movements were slow and he looked dazed.

'I was in our offices in Zurich and Madrid the first six days of October last. Here, you can see for yourself.'

He stood and held the iPad in front of Swift. The days were blocked out, as he'd said.

'Satisfied that I wasn't on a ferry with ill intent?' He snorted and sat back down.

'Emmy was on the ferry, though,' Cameron muttered. 'She was there, wasn't she?'

Sheppard looked at his son, his face expressionless. 'He speaks, but to what purpose!' he said. 'From what I understand, Emmy was on the ferry with good reason. There's no crime in attending a friend's engagement party.'

'No, but she didn't tell the police she was on board,' Swift said.

'Just a detail,' Sheppard replied. 'Have you told them?'

'No. Not yet.'

'Are you planning to?'

'If and when I think it's necessary.'

'Look,' Sheppard said, 'I don't know why Emmy's got in a snit with Cameron. I expect she's had too much on her plate and siblings do fall out. I'll sort that out when I can. Knock their heads together. But she wouldn't have attacked Kelly Dwyer or her sister. She had no reason to. The gas boiler business was done and dusted. Her being on the ferry was just a coincidence.'

His newly warm, conciliatory tone reminded Swift of his daughter's, when she'd wanted to mend fences. Swift looked at Cameron, who was sitting with his head ducked. Trying to avoid the anticipated bullets.

'I agree with you about the gas boiler. That wouldn't have been a motive for killing Kelly.' He could taste toffee notes in the whisky now.

'Good. Same hymn sheet, at last.' Sheppard smiled. 'I'm glad we've resolved that. Hear that, Cam? Sorted.' His son didn't look up. 'Oh, do get a grip,' his father said. 'I'm bushed now, need to get my head down. Mrs Magee will see you out, Mr Swift.'

'Hold on,' Swift said. 'It's not about the gas boiler. It's never really been about that, just about the circumstances surrounding it.'

Sheppard sank back down. 'This is like fucking riddle-me-ree. What are you talking about now?'

'Emmy could have had another, stronger motive for wanting Kelly out of the way. Kelly knew something that could have caused her a lot of damage.'

Sheppard threw back his drink. 'What the fuck are you on about now, Swift? I can't stand all this fannying around. Just spit it out, man.'

Swift looked at Cameron, who flinched. Sheppard's phone rang.

'Fuck it, I've got to take this.'

He walked to the back window and started talking with quick bursts of questions. Swift edged across yards of soft sofa to Cameron and clicked his fingers in front of his down-turned face. He looked up, blinking.

'Tell me the truth now, or I'll tell your father about you and Emmy. Did you break into Faith Black's flat in Cricklewood?'

Cameron licked his dry lips. 'Faith Black?'

'Yes. Kelly's sister. Did you break into her flat? I'm warning you, you'd better be truthful.'

He gave a wild shake of his head, sending his thick fringe tumbling. 'I don't know what you're talking about. I don't even know where she lives. Honestly! I haven't been able to move from here. I've been calling in sick to work, too done in.'

Swift believed him. The man looked as if he had just enough energy to raise his wine glass. He looked into Cameron's tormented eyes and felt sorry for him. His only crime was having fallen in love with the wrong person. He moved back to his seat as Sheppard finished the call.

'Look, Swift, I've got to deal with an urgent matter. So much for getting some shut-eye. Be quick — what were you on about, saying that Kelly Dwyer knew something?'

Swift had what he'd come for. He stood and walked over to the bear sculpture, touched its head. He recalled a trip to the dentist where he'd read a *National Geographic* article about incest and interbreeding among polar bears.

Sheppard was standing, hand on hips, looking expectant. 'Well? If you've something to say, say it.'

He wasn't a family therapist and he didn't think that Emmy had attacked the two women. Coincidences were sometimes just that. These people could sort out their own problems. 'That's for your children to discuss with you. Maybe they'll get a chance when you meet up so that you can knock their heads together.'

CHAPTER 17

It was drizzling and misty on Wednesday evening, with a chill in the air. More like autumn than early summer. The streets looked forlorn and smelled damp and dusty. Swift arrived at the Roundstone Youth Centre at six thirty. It was built of brick and breezeblocks with windows painted a utilitarian green that reminded him of the codebreaking huts at Bletchley Park. A group of about twenty young people were waiting outside while a hefty man with a huge bunch of keys opened up. Swift zipped up his leather jacket and headed to the door.

'I'm here to see Mia Wilson,' Swift told him. 'It's about fundraising.'

'Okay, sure. She'll be here any minute. Hey, guys, give me a chance to get the doors open!'

A couple of the bigger boys jostled their way in and Swift slipped through with them. Inside, the building was dingy and smelled stale but the walls were covered with posters and news about summer camps, drama clubs, five-a-side competitions, snooker, assertiveness training, literacy mentoring, ping-pong and DJ nights. There was an amateurish mural depicting the history of the youth centre since it opened in 1952, encompassing the passing trends through the decades: Teddy boys, mods, rockers, hippies, skinheads, punks, ska, Rastas, glam rockers, New Romantics, goths and rude boys. Although Swift was too young to have been one of the original tribe, Mary often accused him of being an aspiring hippie. For his last birthday present, she'd sourced a pair of flared jeans covered in flower patches. A fundraising chart showed a target of fifty thousand pounds with the current amount raised at seventeen thousand. Above it, there was a quote from Martin Luther King: '*Love is the only force capable of transforming an enemy into a friend.*'

Two girls stood near him. One was crying on the other's shoulder while her friend patted her back, saying, 'You're better off without him, he's not worth it.' The friend glanced over at Swift. She raised her eyebrows and mouthed, '*She's a bit emotional.*' Swift nodded and moved away. He recalled the thrilling complexity and torment of teenage hormones. His thoughts wandered to Cameron and Emilia. It was hard enough, dealing with average adolescent turmoil, never mind falling in love with your sibling.

He saw Mia Wilson dart through the door, folding an umbrella. Her hair glowed under the hood of her raincoat. He waited while she spoke to a couple of girls about a drama class, slipping her coat off and wiping raindrops from her forehead.

He approached her as she opened the door to an office and switched the lights on. 'Ms Wilson? Can I have a quick word?'

She smiled at him. She had little gaps between her front teeth. Close up, her hair was a glowing bronze, her eyes flecked with gold. 'Hi. Are you a parent?'

'Yes, but not of anyone here. My name's Tyrone Swift. I phoned you recently.'

Her smile froze, her lips a thin, hard line. 'How did you know where to find me?'

'Social media. Give me five minutes. That's all I ask.'

She looked around. 'I told you I didn't want to talk to you.'

'I know.' He stepped closer. 'Kelly was my family. She was brutally murdered. She was your close friend once. Five minutes, please?'

A group of girls fell through the front door in a tangle of shoves and giggles. The air was filled with a burst of energy, hair products and cheap perfume. They called to Mia and waved. She waved back, saying that she'd be with them in a minute.

She waited until they'd vanished, then made a little gesture, as if she was swatting a fly. 'Five minutes, then.'

They sat in the office at a round, wicker table with worn edges. It was a dilapidated room, full of plastic crates and ring binders. There was a smell of gym sweat and pine cleaner. Mia was wearing jeans and a red sweatshirt with the Roundstone Youth Centre logo. She was slim and looked as if she worked out. Her dark freckles blended at the corners of her eyes like dirty smudges.

'What is it you want?' She slipped her hands under her cuffs. Her mouth was tight and sullen.

There was no space for his long legs under the table, so he twisted sideways, pulling his lower back. Sometimes he wished he had a more compact frame so that he wasn't always having to shift around on furniture and struggle for legroom. 'What I want is the truth. It's not always easy to come by.'

'I'll do my best,' she said.

'I've been asking questions about you and Kelly. There are some things I know. You like, or used to like, cashew nuts.'

The attempt at humour fell flat. She looked at him with narrowed eyes. 'Who have you been questioning?'

'Various people. I know that Kelly helped you find your flat in Willesden when you left your husband. You were pregnant. At some point, Neil Dwyer visited Kelly while she was staying there with you and something happened that upset him. Am I right so far?'

Her eyes blazed for a moment and then she dropped her gaze. She thought it over, took her time. He sensed a quick intelligence. 'Neil did come to the flat once. He'd turned up in London unexpectedly. Kelly didn't want him to come to my place because we were busy decorating, but he was so keen on seeing her, we gave in. I suppose he was upset because Kelly told him again that she was never going back to him.'

Neil would have been used to hearing that. Expecting it. Why would he have been shaking and sobbing at his brother's flat afterwards? Why would he have said the visit had been a nightmare? And Mia had looked down and fiddled with her cuff. Lying didn't come easily to her. He took out his phone and scrolled through his emails.

'Neil's grandmother sent a letter to a family member after he died. In it, she said that on the night he was killed, Neil and Kelly had a blazing row. Let me quote the letter. According to his gran, Neil said that "Kelly was responsible for what had happened to someone called Mia. I heard him shout something about Kelly taking responsibility instead of letting this Mia shoulder the blame." What was Neil talking about, Mia?'

Music was vibrating through the wall and floor, pounding rhythms. Some boys yelled outside and there was a shout of manic laughter.

'I don't know what Neil meant.' There was a tremor in her voice. 'Those two were always arguing and trading insults. He was probably just winding Kelly up. Or maybe . . . maybe he was talking about Kelly's part in persuading me to leave Freddie. Yes — that must have been it. Neil knew the story and I could see that he didn't approve of what I'd done, or Kelly's actions.' She faltered and he saw that she was struggling with overwhelming emotion.

There was an undercurrent, a murky wash of history that he couldn't see through. 'I'm sorry about your miscarriage. I understand you ended your friendship with Kelly after that.'

She sat up, took a breath. 'I miscarried because I had a stupid accident. It's a difficult memory. I don't want to talk about that.'

'It's just that I find it hard to understand why you cut Kelly out of your life afterwards. You'd been so close.'

She made eye contact now. On surer ground. 'We were close. But I wanted my husband back and I felt that Kelly had been completely negative about my marriage and had a bad influence on me. She was so . . . persuasive. She took all my little niggles about Freddie and blew them up into major faults. She kept telling me I'd be better off without him and I came to agree with her. I'd always been wary of her drinking and I had time to reflect after I lost the baby. Freddie — my husband — never left my side when I was in hospital. It was a terrible time for both of us and I realised what was really important to me. I began to think that because her marriage had failed, Kelly had wanted mine to. Not consciously, maybe, but she had this thing about marriage being a trap. Freddie said that Kelly was like one of those teasels that stick to you when you pass them. Sometimes you have to let go of friends who aren't good for you. I'm sorry about what happened to Kelly, but my life was better once I'd removed her from it.'

He could see that she was juggling inner conflict. 'Some of that makes sense. I've learned that Kelly could be trouble and I've met other people who had let their friendships with her lapse. But I think you've given me half-truths. I think something happened when Neil came to your flat. Did he row with Kelly? Those two were a volatile mix. Did you try to intervene?'

'I've told you what I can. You have to go now. I have people waiting for me.'

He sensed a stubbornness in her. She'd grown less pliable since the days when she'd known Kelly. Life crushed some people and toughened others. Time to notch up the pressure. 'I spoke to your dad, at your flat. I don't suppose he told you.'

'No, he didn't.' Her voice trembled. 'Why did you do that?'

'Because you hung up on me. Your dad warned me off talking to you.'

'You had no right to do that.'

'If we're talking about rights, that's fine with me. Faith, Kelly's sister, had every right not to be attacked and left brain-damaged, and she has every right now to know who did it and killed her sister. Did Faith visit your flat with Kelly? She believes that she did.'

'I've no idea why she thinks that. I've never met Faith.'

'Okay. Where were you, last year, October second?'

'Oh, just go away,' she said wearily. 'Kelly was gone from my life long before then, and to be honest, I didn't miss her.' She glanced at a wall clock. 'There's going to be a fire alarm test any minute. Please leave the building.'

He thought it had been a ploy to get rid of him, but the alarm did sound as he left and scores of annoyed teenagers poured through the doors behind him.

'No way, that's mental!'

'It's just a practice, right?'

'How long we gonna be out here?'

'And in the rain!'

'Come on, this is way too much!'

'I was winning, man!'

'I don't see no flames!'

He pulled up his jacket collar and walked to his car through the kind of drifting mizzle that was a Connemara specialty. As he opened it, he saw a van slow down and park outside the centre. He recognized the grey-haired man driving it: Mia's father, Ken Drover. The company logo on the side of the van read Carnegie Sport Distribution. He watched as Drover walked slowly to the door and spoke to Mia, who was checking a list. She called to the man who'd opened up the building. He and Drover went to the van and started to unload boxes with Drover stopping to ease his lower back with the heels of his hands. Mia glanced up, saw Swift across the road, frowned and turned away.

She was a worried woman.

* * *

‘I don’t know who you think you are, prying into people’s private business.’ Chantelle Lowick was so enraged, Swift thought he’d see steam issuing from his phone.

‘Murder makes privacy irrelevant.’

‘Oh, very high-handed. I don’t appreciate you sneaking around and contacting my admin to ask about my whereabouts last year. It would have been more polite to ask me!’

He was standing by his boat on the slipway below Tamesas, ready to launch. There was a brisk breeze interfering with the phone signal. He turned away from the river. ‘I found you a bit high-handed when we met. Aloof and not that keen to share information. Would you have told me if I’d asked?’

‘That’s not the point. Ronan was anxious about your call afterwards. It was playing on his mind. I knew something was wrong and he finally told me this morning.’

‘Tell Ronan I’m sorry about that. So — where were you at the beginning of last October?’

‘You really are an intrusive man.’

‘That’s me.’

‘If I tell you — not that it’s any of your business — will you leave me and my staff alone?’

‘Definitely, if it’s the truth. Hold on, this signal’s weak.’ He walked up to Tamesas and stood inside the doorway. ‘Okay.’

‘On the first of October last year, I booked into a private hospital in Brighton for a small operation. I left the hospital on October the fourth. I’m not telling you anything about the surgery. That’s certainly none of your business. I have given the hospital permission to confirm that basic information with you. I don’t want to hear from you again.’

‘You won’t.’

‘Good. Have you found out anything about who committed that awful crime?’

‘I’m trying. It helps if people give me information.’

She told him the name of the hospital and he rang. The woman on reception confirmed Chantelle’s account. Another suspect struck off the list.

He donned his waterproof jacket — rain was forecast — slid the boat into the water and set off towards Chiswick Pier. The river was in a sluggish mood and an iron-grey colour, with small splashes of silver where the oars parted the surface. He'd worked up to a steady speed when the rain started in an immediate downpour. He decided to pull in by a bank of trees. The overarching leaves would offer some shelter.

He drank some water and looked out at the cascading rain patterning the river, making little whirlpools. He thought about Nora. If she were here, she'd be handing him fruit from her rucksack and saying it was '*fierce wild*.' He missed her but it was never going to work. The thought of trying to talk to her about Branna or the future dismayed him. He kept going back to what she'd told him about her childhood — the arguments, the trading of punches, the mercurial mother. He understood more about her, but the knowledge distanced him from her. He didn't want a life of slamming doors, uncertain moods and sudden outbursts.

The rain stopped as suddenly as it had started, the clouds drew apart like curtains, and the sun slid out in a burst of gold. He looked up into the canopy of plane trees, seeing Mia Wilson's wary, moist eyes. He felt as if he was pressing on a door handle that wouldn't give. The sun flitted through the leathery leaves, casting tiny spotlights. He watched the dancing light, following the interplay of umber and green shades until he was in a kind of trance and thinking back to London Harps. His thoughts shifted to the Wilsons and the gaps underlying their words. He sensed the door handle shift a little while he played through a possible scene at the flat in Willesden, one that would make sense of Neil Dwyer's angry accusation. What if something had happened involving Kelly during Neil's visit to the flat, something that resulted in Mia's miscarriage? It would explain Mia's rejection of her friend. But why would Mia have lied about it and say that she'd lost the baby because of fixing a shelf?

He reached for his phone and rang Mia's number.

'Don't hang up on me,' he said. 'I think that your miscarriage was something to do with Kelly. Something happened on the day Neil Dwyer was at your flat.'

'You can think what you like. You're wrong and way out of line. My miscarriage was nothing to do with Kelly. What you're doing now is really cruel and you have to stop. If you contact me again, I'm going to call the police and report you for harassment.'

'Why was your father at the youth centre the other night?'

But she'd rung off. He removed his jacket and rowed on, sifting through what he knew about Mia's family. He needed to talk to Una Bassek again and take a look at her year planner for last autumn.

* * *

Faith alerted him to the story. He found her text when he stepped out of the shower.

Have you seen the news? Sol's just told me. Cameron Sheppard's outed himself and Emilia.

Swift sat on the sofa wrapped in a towel and searched online. It was on the front page of the *Evening Standard* and featured on all the major news channels. He saw that the story had originated in the *Daily Mail*, where the banner headline screamed, *My Sister, My Lover!*

Cameron Sheppard, 26, has announced that he has been having a long-term incestuous relationship with his sister, Emilia Sheppard. Ms Sheppard, 29, is a local councillor in Hammersmith and Fulham. Tipped as a rising star, destined for government, she has been campaigning about knife crime in the capital and has often talked about promoting family values.

Mr Sheppard told us that his sister was worried that their relationship would become public knowledge and that she had sacrificed him for her political career, having recently thrown him out of their shared flat in Fulham. A tearful Cameron said, "I've tried to reach out to Emmy. I've phoned her and emailed her. I've gone and knocked on the door but she won't talk to me. She's had the locks changed. I love her and she's cut me out of her life. I've got no home. I'm in pieces. I've been feeling suicidal and I even rang the Samaritans. It's not fair. I didn't want to go public like this, but if it's the only way of getting Emmy to talk to me, so be it. I know lots of people will disapprove of us but I don't see what's wrong with loving Emmy. You don't get to choose who you fall in love with. It doesn't make us bad people. I'm fed up with living a lie. We'd always planned a future together and now I feel as if Emmy's snatched that away from me for her own selfish reasons."

Mr Sheppard appealed for his sister to contact him.

Ms Sheppard and her local office have not responded to requests for comment.

Swift leaned back, resting his damp hair on a cushion. Cameron's utter misery had made him destructive. He didn't think Emmy's political aspirations stood much chance now. He was on his way to the Silver Mermaid when Jon Sheppard rang, sounding shocked and bellicose.

'I suppose you've seen the news about Cameron and Emmy?'

'Just saw it tonight.'

'Did you know about their relationship? Is it true, what he's saying?'

'You'll have to ask Cameron and Emmy if it's true. I thought you were going to talk to them about their rift?'

'Haven't had time. Now she won't answer my calls and he's gone off somewhere. Just told the housekeeper he'd be at a friend's. God almighty, this is unbelievable!'

'I'm sorry you've had a shock. I believe it is true. Kelly knew because she saw them being intimate. She told someone who informed me. That was why Emmy let her off so lightly over the boiler. When I broached it with Emmy, she denied it, but I thought she was lying. Cameron told me about it when he came to see me.'

'Christ's sake, Swift! Why didn't you tell me?'

'Not my place to, unless it was a secret that led to murder. I did suspect Emmy because it gave her a motive and she was on the ferry. But I don't think she attacked the sisters.'

'Is that supposed to make me feel better?'

'I don't think anything would do that at the moment.'

'It's all gone to pot. Emmy's always led Cam by the nose, but I'd no idea she was leading him by another part of his anatomy as well! What sort of career can she have now? They'll both be social pariahs.'

'Not necessarily. And maybe not having to keep a secret any longer will be a relief, given time. These things blow over. It's probably best if they both lie low for a while.'

Sheppard snapped back at him. 'Blow over! That's not bloody likely! This is all your fault, rooting around in our lives and raking up crap. And for what? It hasn't got you anywhere. No wonder people put negative stuff out there about you. I've a mind to do that myself, tell people you're a vicious, sad bastard.'

Swift had stopped across from the pub and looked down at the river. There was a full tide and the water glowed under the red evening sun. A twelve-woman crew rowed upriver, powering past while their cox leaned forward, urging them on.

'Don't threaten me,' he said. 'I'd remind you that I could have told the police that Emmy omitted to inform them that she'd been on the ferry when they contacted her. She withheld information, which she could be prosecuted for. I could still tell the police. Then the press would have more fuel to add to the fire.'

'People like you snooping around, causing all this grief. I bet you wound Cam up with your questions and made him feel sorry for himself. He's had a spiteful streak ever since he was little, and you tapped into it. You appal me.'

'Oh, I suspect you're more appalled with yourself, for not knowing about your children's activities and because you bought them a home together, which was exactly what they needed to carry on in secret.'

That caused a shocked silence and he used it to end the call. It had given him no pleasure to goad Sheppard, but this particular crap didn't belong at his door.

He watched the rowers' oars dipping and rising, slicing the water cleanly. The boat grew smaller and smaller, dwindling until it vanished into the blueish evening haze. He crossed to the pub.

CHAPTER 18

When Swift was in his boat, he could smell rain on the wind — that sharp, metallic scent. Now he could sniff an end to this case and he reckoned that it was nothing to do with angry or grieving relatives, or two siblings and their incestuous relationship.

He'd been to London Harps, spoken to Una Bassek about the running of the club and had a cup of tea and too many custard creams. She'd found last year's wall chart in a cupboard and rolled it out on her desk for him. He'd checked October, confirming what he'd thought.

'Did you find what you were looking for?' Una asked.

'I think so. You've been a great help.'

'It's so good that Faith is back in the fold,' Una said. 'She comes twice a week now, and I'd say she's feeling the benefit of being around people and feeling useful. I worry for her, but at least now I can keep an eye on her. I've told her that when she's up to doing a bit more, I've plenty for her here. I was worried that she might feel frustrated because she can't play, but she seems happy enough for now with coaching and planning.'

'I think any activity that takes Faith out of herself is beneficial and she loves this club. It's better than any medication.

When I first met her, she was completely isolated and that's never going to help her recovery.'

'Yes, I like to think we're part of her therapy — her family, even.'

He thanked Una and headed for his car, where he made a call and then found the number for the next person he needed. Now for a touch of blackmail of the kind he thought Branna might have a worrying talent for. He rang DC Keane in Liverpool.

'Got any news about our sisters?' Keane asked breezily.

'I might have soon. In the meantime, I'm looking for your help.'

'Oh yeah?' He sounded cagey.

'You remember the first time we spoke, you were a bit insensitive in the way you talked about my relatives?'

'Hmm.'

'And I was generous. I didn't take that any further.'

'Yeah. So?'

'So, I've run up against data protection regarding the ship's manifest for last October. Fair enough, but I like to find a way around the bureaucracy. I want to ask you something, but I think it'll be better if you ring me from your own phone.'

'Off the record, like?'

'Exactly. It would help if you have a copy of the ship's manifest with you.'

'I don't know . . .'

'I did let you off the hook before. I really wouldn't want to complain and cause any problems for you. I'm sure a young man like you is looking for promotion and I wouldn't want anything to hold you back.'

'Okay, okay. Gimme ten mins.'

He waited in the car, watching a camogie game on the field between teams with blue and yellow shirts. It was so fast, it was hard to keep track of the ball and he felt his breath catch with excitement. When Keane rang back, Swift told him that he was going to say a name and if that name featured on the manifest, Keane only had to say yes.

'That's it, like? That's all you want?'

'That's all I want.'

He said the name and after a few moments received the reply. '*Yes.*' He ended the call and checked the time. It was late afternoon and he had a while before the person he needed to see would be home from work. He continued to watch the game. There was a woman with Faith's build who was a demon on the pitch, darting, twirling, fast and light. Poetry in motion. How Faith must be missing this! Yet the last couple of times he'd seen her, he'd sensed a growing acceptance of having to adapt to her injuries. The blue team were on the offensive throughout, and he cheered silently as the yellow side's goalie deflected yet another goal with her stick. The game ended with an overwhelming victory for the blues. He started the engine.

* * *

The semi-detached in Brondesbury Park was pebble-dashed with a deep front garden filled with blowsy, pale mauve hydrangeas. The van stood in the drive and when Swift got to the front door, he could smell cooking. He was about to spoil dinner. He rang the bell twice before he heard footsteps.

'What do you want now?' Ken Drover had changed into shorts, T-shirt and slippers. He'd washed the grit of the working day off and had just shaved, judging by the tiny nick on his chin.

'Can I come in? I want to talk to you.'

'It's not convenient. I said what I had to say last time.' He looked paler and thinner and his hair had been cropped to a shadowy stubble.

'There's a lot more to be said. I know you were on the same ferry as Kelly and Faith last year.'

He licked his bottom lip. 'You can't prove that.'

'No, but the passenger manifest does. You were booked on with your van. I rang your firm and they confirmed that you sometimes make deliveries in Ireland. Just as you've done regularly at London Harps camogie club.'

Drover stood in the doorway, scanning the street. He tucked a wayward strand of climbing clematis into its frame and then moved back. 'Come in.'

Swift followed him into a living room at the rear of the house. The TV was on, showing the news. A picture of Emilia Sheppard flashed up on screen and Swift saw the rolling headline below: *Local councillor resigns amid incest scandal.* Drover switched it off and sat in an armchair, gesturing at another for Swift. There was a tray on the table beside Drover, with a half-eaten corned beef hash and a glass of beer. He took a sip of the beer and ran a finger around the rim of the glass, making a faint musical sound.

'Go on, then. Say whatever you've come to say.'

'I believe that you attacked Faith Black and Kelly Dwyer on board the ferry and you threw Kelly overboard.'

'Why would I have done that?'

'Because Kelly was the cause of your daughter's miscarriage and you hated her for it and for encouraging Mia to leave her marriage.'

A faint smile played around Drover's lips. 'That's what you think, is it?'

'Yes. Kelly was arguing with her husband, Neil, when he visited Mia's flat. Something happened to Mia that caused her to lose the baby. I don't know why she said it was to do with fixing a shelf. I asked her but she wouldn't tell me.'

'You spoke to Mia? I told you not to do that.' He sounded weary, resigned.

Swift found it hard to judge the man's mood. It was almost as if he didn't much care about this visit. 'I don't take orders from people. I had to speak to her because I knew you hadn't told me the truth. I visited her at the youth club and I saw you arrive in your work van. That's how I knew you deliver sports equipment and I recalled seeing your company logo in the office at London Harps. You'd made a delivery in the office there last September and you could have read the year planner on the wall, recording when Kelly and Faith were on holiday.'

'Clever old you,' he said.

'Thanks.'

Drover sipped some more beer. He had a faraway look. A little absent. Swift had expected surprise, anger or defensiveness, not this odd calm. His meal was congealing, the melted butter solidifying into a yellowy lump around the plate.

'Are you recording this?' Drover asked.

'No. Do you want me to?'

'Give me your phone. Hand it over or you can go now. I'll give it back when you leave.'

Swift hesitated, then passed it over. Drover checked it and put it on the tray. He lifted his glass, stretched his legs out and crossed them at the ankles. He had purplish, rigid varicose veins furrowing down the back of his left calf. He tapped the glass absentmindedly. He seemed to have forgotten that Swift was there until he ran a hand over his prickles of hair and looked across at him.

'You seem a decent enough bloke. You've got a job to do and this one involves your family.'

Swift nodded. 'Yesterday I remembered what you said to me about my daughter when we first met. *"You'll know then that you'd do anything to keep her safe and how much it hurts if anything goes wrong for her."* You were talking about yourself as well, Mr Drover.'

He nodded. 'I was. Imagine how I felt when I heard that Mia had had the miscarriage. It's hard, seeing your child's misery.'

'Yes. When did you find out what really happened — that Kelly played a part in that, too?'

Drover tapped another musical tattoo on his almost empty glass. 'You've got the wrong sister.'

'What do you mean?' For a mad moment, he thought Drover was about to name Orla.

'It was Faith's actions that led to the miscarriage, not Kelly's.'

Swift stared. 'Faith? I don't get it.'

Swift's phone rang. They watched it vibrate until it switched to answerphone.

'Mia finally told me what really happened last August. She and Freddie were trying for another baby at the time with no success. She was feeling down and terribly guilty about losing her first. Kelly had phoned her the previous day, asking how she was, saying she missed her and it would be good to meet up. Trying to snake back into her life. Mia said no, but it threw her. She was round here and she told me that the miscarriage was nothing to do with a shelf. She unburdened herself. I'm glad she did. That's what parents are for, isn't it? No matter how old your child, you help pick up the pieces, put a plaster on the wound.'

'Some parents do that.'

'Well, this one does. That time when Kelly's husband was at Mia's flat, Faith was there, too, visiting from Ireland. They were all in the living room. Neil was sober, but Kelly had been drinking. They started arguing and it got heated. Neil was criticizing Kelly for meddling in Mia's life. Kelly threw a mug at Neil and went to pick up a plate. Faith was trying to calm things down, asking Kelly to stop shouting. Kelly ignored her, so Faith got up to go to her, but she tripped on a loose dust cover, lost her balance and crashed into Mia. Mia fell heavily on the floor, but she picked herself up and thought everything was okay at first. Then she started bleeding and had to call an ambulance.'

'It was an accident, then. Faith didn't intend to harm Mia and the baby.'

'Maybe so, but she did and all in the cause of protecting her drunken, meddling waster of a sister.' Harsh words, but Drover remained composed.

Swift collected his thoughts. 'Why did Mia lie about the cause of the miscarriage?'

'To protect Freddie. She worried that if she told us the truth, Freddie might go after Faith and Kelly. He had a conviction in his teens for common assault. He got into a fight outside a pub and spent four months in jail. He's never been in trouble since and most of the time he's a pussycat, but he can see the old red mist very quickly when he's upset. Mia already felt guilty about leaving him. She didn't want to risk any more trouble.'

'But then she told you the truth.'

'She did and I made her swear never to tell Freddie. I said all the right things to her, just like you have — it was an accident, no one's fault. But that's not what I thought when she left here and I sat and went over it all. I was mad at those two women. Kelly had encouraged Mia to make the biggest mistake of her life and then she'd brought her sister to Mia's home. Between them, they damaged her and killed her baby.' For the first time, there was a flicker of antagonism. He drained his beer and reached for a cool pack on the sideboard, taking out two bottles of Leffe. 'Want one of these?'

Swift's father had had a saying for when a story was long. '*It's a thirsty tale.*'

'Sure.' He waited while Drover flipped the top and handed him a bottle.

'Want a glass with that?'

'No, this will do.' He lifted the bottle to his lips. 'When did you decide to take revenge for your daughter?'

Drover poured his beer slowly. There was a heavy silence as it bubbled into the glass. 'I sat up all night after Mia told me the truth about what had happened. I thought about Kelly contacting Mia again and I worried what might happen if she persisted, the trouble she could cause again in Mia's marriage. What if she provoked Freddie and he did something that got him jailed? She was like a weed that keeps coming back in your garden, no matter what you do. That clinched it for me. If she'd never got back in touch with Mia, she'd be alive now and her sister wouldn't be the way she is.

It was her own fault for not being able to learn when enough is enough.'

'You could have talked to Kelly, explained your worries about Freddie and warned her to back off.'

'You think that would have worked? Women like her never go away. And I wasn't prepared to chance that when my Mia's happiness was at stake. I decided I had to act. You were right about London Harps. I knew Kelly played there because there's an information board with photos and names of the players. I'd seen a picture of her and Faith on there. So when I made a delivery last September, I looked on the year planner and saw that they'd be on holiday in October. I had a chat with a groundsman and found out that Kelly was a gas fitter. She'd told him that she and Faith were off to Ireland on the boat. I came home and thought about what I could do. It seemed a bit of a gift, the sea journey. I reckoned I could make my move more easily on a ferry and stand a good chance of getting home undiscovered.'

Swift's phone rang again.

'You're popular,' Drover said.

'It's okay, leave it.'

'Up to you. You're wondering how I knew which ferry they'd be coming back on. That was easy. I rang Kelly, asking about a gas installation. Gave a false name, put on a brogue. Did the "I'm from the old country, too" bit, got her chatting about the journey and when she'd be coming back, so that we could talk again about my new heating system. I arranged to make a Dublin delivery on the morning of the second of October and booked the ferry back that evening. I watched Kelly and Faith when they got on, saw which cabin they were in and then followed them around.'

'Were you planning to kill them both?'

'Yes. The miscarriage was Faith's fault but she'd never have been there if her sister hadn't stuck her nose into Mia's life.'

'Did you know that Kelly recognized you in the café on the ferry?'

'I wondered if she had. I saw her glance over at me. I wasn't sure she'd clocked who I was, because she'd only seen me the once. To be honest, I only had a rough plan. I'd brought a hammer from the van and I was just going to take whatever chance I got — break into the cabin if needed. I lost sight of them for a couple of minutes and then I saw Faith going up to the top deck, so I followed her. I didn't realize that Kelly was already up there. Bloody hell — there was a howling gale up top and I nearly slipped over when I stepped on deck. It was hard to see properly in the dark and spray, but then I spotted that Faith was right in front of me and I hit her fast with the hammer. I thought I'd killed her. Then I saw Kelly standing by the rail with her back to me. She hadn't heard a thing because of the storm. The ship was pitching like mad and I almost lost my bottle and scarpered. But then I thought that if Kelly had recognized me in the café, the police would come after me. She turned her head just as I went for her. I hit her and threw her over. It happened fast. When we'd spoken on the phone, she'd told me how much she loved the sea, so I reckoned she could have her fill of it.' He took a drink. His hand was steady on the glass.

'Why didn't you throw Faith over the side?'

'I was going to, but I felt seasick. I didn't want to hang around, push my luck. Like I said, I thought she was dead, so I dragged her over by the ventilation shaft. I went down to my cabin. I got violently sick and I didn't sleep. I was back in my van as soon as the tannoy notice came on about docking.' Drover tilted his glass. 'This doesn't seem to taste as good as it used to.'

'Maybe that's because you're a murderer and everything's tainted now.'

'Maybe.'

The next door neighbour started to mow their lawn. Drover got up and closed the window. He pressed a fist against his back and stood looking out. Swift sipped his beer, glad of the fresh taste in his mouth. It was a vicious story for a calm, suburban summer evening.

'Why did you write to Faith?'

Drover sat down again. He looked grey. 'I read that she was alive but brain-damaged. That was a shock. I was worried that she might remember that Kelly had seen me. Then I thought that I could use the fact that she'd survived to confuse the investigation. It seemed a good idea to say that Kelly had been the only target, that Faith had just been in the way. And I genuinely regretted that I'd left Faith in that state. That probably sounds twisted to you, but I'd thought she was a goner. I wouldn't wish a life of brain damage on anyone.'

'It all sounds twisted to me. Never ceases to amaze me, how killers measure and apportion types of justice.'

'I crossed a line. Once you're on the other side, everything changes. I'd do it again if I had to for my Mia.'

'And you were going to, weren't you, when you broke into Faith's flat?'

He nodded. 'You'd turned up, asking questions. I could see you were nobody's fool. I worried that Faith might remember things, so it would be best to finish it. But she wasn't there and I couldn't find out where she'd gone.'

Thank goodness for Sol and his crumbling health. A wasp had found the half-eaten food and was cruising around the plate. Drover took a newspaper, folded it and smashed it down. The plate rattled and the wasp fell into the waxy butter, twitched and died.

'That food tasted like sawdust anyway,' Drover said. 'I suppose you'll contact the police now.' He sounded disinterested.

'That's the general idea.'

'Before you do, let me show you something,' Drover took a white envelope from the sideboard and passed it over.

Swift saw '*Central Middlesex Hospital*' stamped on the front of the envelope. He took the letter out and read:

Dear Mr Drover,

I am writing to you following your last appointment and the discussion we held.

I am sorry that I had to advise you that we can offer no more intervention and that palliative treatment is now the best option. One of our nursing team will be in touch with you this week to talk about these options more fully and to ensure that you have support with however you decide to proceed.

I have sent updated information to your GP and to our cancer care team.

Kind Regards,
Ms L Gallagher
Consultant, Oncology

'Pancreatic cancer,' Drover said. 'One of the fastest. The nice consultant gave me the news earlier this week. They don't talk timescales but I've probably got a couple of months, max. I'm leaving work tomorrow, can't manage it any longer.'

It explained his weight loss, pallid look and general air of not caring much. Swift handed him the letter. 'I'm sorry.'

'That's okay. I've accepted it.'

'Are you asking me not to contact the police because of this?'

'Yes, but not for me. What's it to me? I'll be dead before a trial. Mia told me a couple of weeks ago that she's pregnant. Almost four months gone now. I haven't told her about the cancer yet and I don't want to until I've no option. I just want as much time with her now as I can get.'

'What about Faith Black? How do I know you won't try to harm her again?'

'I've enough to cope with now without going after her. She's safe from me. I give you my word. I've no right to ask you not to tell the police and I don't expect it will make any difference to you. I can only ask you to leave me be, to see my short days out and spend time with Mia. That's all I'm interested in now. Think it over. I'm not going anywhere except the morgue. Here.' He handed back the phone. 'You can see yourself out. I'm too tired to move now.'

Outside, Swift saw that he'd had two missed calls from Faith. He got in the car and rang her.

'Hi. I just wanted to check in with you like you asked, because I'll be moving back to my place.' She sounded flat.

'Is Sol much better?'

‘A bit. That’s not why, though. His family’s taken him off to . . . where is it again . . . yeah, Somerset. His mum was here with one of his sisters, eyeing the place up and saying it was squalid. They packed his stuff and they were gone within an hour.’

‘Did he want to go?’

‘I’m not sure. I think he was too weak to protest. He just said to me that it was probably for the best. So, I’m going to pack my things now.’

‘Hold on, Faith. Can you stay at Sol’s for now?’

‘Suppose. I don’t really want to. It’s funny without him. Lonely. I’d rather be back at mine.’

Drover wasn’t dead yet. Despite his assurances, he might decide on a last hurrah. ‘I don’t think that’s a good idea. Whoever broke into your flat might have been looking to harm you. If you’d rather not be at Sol’s, come and stay with me for now.’

‘You haven’t got a spare room.’

‘I’ve a bed I can put in the basement. I can sleep down there. I’ve done it before.’

‘But why do you think someone would still want to harm me?’

‘I just have a feeling about it. Don’t risk it, please. Let me look out for you.’

‘Okay,’ she said. ‘I’ll stay here tonight. I can clear up a bit, put the rubbish out. I’ll come to yours tomorrow.’

‘Fine. But I can pick you up. I’ll be there mid-morning.’

He drove home under an uneasy sky. The fat clouds were dishwater dull. He thought of the defeated look in Drover’s eyes. He felt tired and troubled.

CHAPTER 19

Swift couldn't sleep. He tossed and turned. Three a.m. found him in the garden, pacing. The grass was soft and damp under his bare feet. The air smelled earthy, slightly bitter.

It was simple. He should inform the police about Ken Drover.

It was far more complicated than that.

If he turned Drover in, Faith would find out that she had caused Mia's miscarriage and that he'd intended to kill her, too. She'd learn all the grim details of her sister's tortuous path in life. That wouldn't do much for her already fragile mental state. She'd spoken about feeling worthless and any more shocks might make her act on those feelings. She'd started to reintegrate at the camogie club and find purpose there. It was her lifeline, but if all of this came out, London Harps might no longer be such a welcoming place for her. Freddie Wilson would know that his wife had lied to him about her miscarriage because she hadn't trusted him. The marriage might fragment. Pregnant Mia would be traumatized. She had yet to learn about Drover's cancer and she'd lose her father for the last months of his life. The shock could cause another miscarriage. Drover would die with police guards watching him and his loved ones.

Faith had a right to know who had injured her and killed her sister. Orla had a right to know, too. But would the knowledge do them any good? It would reveal hurtful information about both of the sisters and they would never see justice administered through a trial.

He thought about Kelly. Difficult, interfering Kelly. She'd led Faith a dance, intruded in her work and got her involved in her trail of troubles. Faith was permanently injured because she'd tried to stop her sister causing hurt. Kelly was beyond any of this fallout.

He crouched down by Cedric's tea rose and stroked a petal. He knew that his old friend would always err on the side of compassion.

Drover would have his death sentence soon enough.

* * *

Swift spoke to his cousin Mary first thing. She talked to her partner Simone and phoned him back. He sorted out beds and fetched Faith from Sol's flat. They had soup for lunch. Faith managed half a bowl before she put her spoon down. She was fidgety and dejected.

'I wonder if Sol will stay in Somerset now.' She crumbled a slice of bread.

'You were getting on well with him.'

'Surprisingly well. We sort of propped each other up. He made me laugh. We were talking about the plan he and Kelly had had, to buy a camper van. He showed me the toy one she bought him. We reckoned we might get one, head off for . . . where was it . . . Cornwall, like he'd always wanted. Don't suppose that will happen now.'

Swift thought it sounded a crazy scheme. Faith couldn't drive and would forget the route and Sol would hardly be reliable at the wheel. 'How would you have coped with Sol's drinking?'

'Hmm. Not sure. It just sounded such a lovely idea. Away from everyone and everything, just coasting the days.'

She smiled at him. 'I can see you're doubtful. I suppose it was a pipe dream.'

'It's good to have those but not always best to act on them.'

'You sound like Orla. Sensible.'

'I'll take that as a compliment. I do think you're better off staying in London, sticking with your camogie club, rebuilding your life here.'

She pulled out the clip that was holding her hair up and repositioned it. 'I was thinking about Mia Wilson's flat last night.'

He tensed. 'Oh yes?'

'Mm. I remembered a striped wallpaper like candy floss.'

He finished his soup and looked at her. 'Anything else?'

She shook her head. 'No, sorry.'

'It doesn't matter. I don't think Mia's relevant after all. I reckon I've come to the end of what I can do with my investigation, Faith. I've asked a lot of questions, but I don't think I'm going to find out what happened on the ferry. It was always going to be a long shot.'

She nodded. 'That's okay. I'm relieved, to be honest. I was going to ask you to stop investigating. Some of the stuff you found out worried me. It began to feel like yet another burden. Maybe it's best to try and put it behind me now.'

'I think you might be right. I hope you don't regret me getting involved.'

'You're joking! You've got me in touch with people again and I've found family I didn't know I had. You're like a kind of big brother to me now — is it okay to say that?'

'Of course.' Family lost, family gained. *There you are, long lost Tyrone. Account settled.*

'Thanks, Ty. You know, I don't think about that shadow at my back so often now. So . . . you know . . . I'm inching forwards.'

'Can I make a suggestion?'

'Go on.'

'Longer term, I don't think you should be on your own. Being with Sol has lifted your mood, done you good. Stay here for a while, until we see if Sol comes back. If he doesn't, my cousin Mary has a spare room in Clerkenwell — very posh with en suite et cetera — and she's said you'd be welcome to stay with them at mate's rates and in return for a bit of babysitting with Louis.'

Her face lit up with relief. 'I was dreading being on my own again. Being alone with my thoughts. They drag me down.'

'You don't need to be. Just a warning. Branna's coming for the weekend so it will be non-stop mayhem. You can talk camogie. And another thing. Will you email or phone Orla and let her know what's happening?'

'Yeah, okay. I suppose it's only fair.'

'I'd say so. After all, she put me in touch with you.'

He left her dozing on the sofa after they'd cleared up. In the garden, he texted Ken Drover.

If you do nothing further, I'll do nothing further.

He had no idea if he'd made the right decision, but it seemed the decent thing to do.

* * *

Brilliant sun was forecast for the weekend. Swift was looking forward to relaxing with Branna and Faith. He planned to take Branna out in the boat on Sunday morning and show her the Tower from the river. She'd be thrilled to see where Anne Boleyn had passed through Traitor's Gate.

But now he needed to clear the slate with Nora.

He got off the train at Herne Hill on Friday evening and headed for her flat. He'd sent her an email, saying he'd call by around eight, but had had no reply. If she wasn't in, he'd leave the note he'd written. Although the relationship seemed dead in the water, he'd rather end it in person and hopefully in a conciliatory way.

He walked through the warm, fume-filled streets, brushing past an overgrown privet hedge that released a pungent smell of animal fur. When he turned into Nora's road, he saw a cab pull up outside her block. Nora got out, followed by Fitz Blackmore. He slid his arm around her as she searched for her keys and she reached up to kiss him. Swift felt a chill, but no surprise. The clues had been there. It added up. They hadn't seen him and he had no desire to speak to them.

He waited until they'd gone into the building and then took the envelope and a pen from his pocket. He rested the envelope on top of a wall, thought for a few moments, and wrote on the back.

I was about to ring your bell but saw you and Fitz arrive, so I didn't want to disturb you. I wanted to speak in person but the note inside says what I came to say. Be happy, Ty.

Suddenly, he was ravenous and strangely light-hearted. There was a takeaway curry place on the corner, one that Nora frequented. He ordered a chicken biryani. While he waited, he drank a beer and stood looking out of the window, thinking about nothing in particular.

He tucked into the biryani as he walked back to the station. It wasn't a patch on Mrs Malla's food but it was just what he needed on this bittersweet evening.

THE END

OTHER BOOKS BY GRETTA MULROONEY

THE TYRONE SWIFT SERIES
Book 1: THE LADY VANISHED
Book 2: BLOOD SECRETS
Book 3: TWO LOVERS, SIX DEATHS
Book 4: WATCHING YOU
Book 5: LOW LAKE
Book 6: YOUR LAST LIE
Book 7: HER LOST SISTER

DETECTIVE SIV DRUMMOND SERIES
Book 1: THESE LITTLE LIES

Join the Joffe Books mailing list to be the first to hear about the new books in these series:

www.joffebooks.co

FREE KINDLE BOOKS

Please join our mailing list for free Kindle crime thriller, detective, mystery, romance books and new releases! www.joffebooks.com

Follow us on Facebook, Twitter and Instagram @joffebooks

Thank you for reading this book. If you enjoyed it please leave feedback on Amazon, and if there is anything we missed or you have a question about then please get in touch. The author and publishing team appreciate your feedback and time reading this book.

We're very grateful to eagle-eyed readers who take the time to contact us. Please send any errors you find to corrections@joffebooks.com

Printed in Great Britain
by Amazon

83985348R00150